PRAISE FOR
NO SPECIAL HURRY

"A well-crafted detective story. Conroy is a talented storyteller; the narrative is well paced, includes engaging, fully dimensional characters, and feels like an episode of one's favorite crime drama. . . . Seamus's struggle with alcoholism is portrayed with both incredible detail and potency. . . . [The] plot entails multiple twists that are sure to keep even the most avid murder mystery fans on their toes."

—**KIRKUS REVIEWS**

"Smart, tense San Francisco mystery. . . . With fleet, conversational prose befitting its columnist sleuth, Conroy's debut is a gripping thriller, steeped in local flavor, that deftly builds on the suspense it establishes on the first page—with just the right amount of leads, red herrings, and nail-biting action. However, the novel also shines in the fleeting yet firm glimpses of Seamus's life—his inner turmoil and the personal journey he inadvertently takes. Conroy infuses his hero with witty self-awareness, street smarts, and fierce loyalty."

—**BOOKLIFE REVIEW FROM** *PUBLISHERS WEEKLY*, Editor's Pick

"When his best friend is accused of murdering a young girl, an alcoholic ex-journalist finds the weight of the world on his shoulders as he attempts to prove his friend innocent. *No Special Hurry* will have readers cheering on its imperfect protagonist, Seamus Shea, as he battles his inner demons and takes on corrupt individuals in his San Francisco neighborhood. Well written with a solid plot and colorful characters, this book is perfect for James Patterson and David Baldacci fans."

—**SAN FRANCISCO BOOK REVIEW**

"Colman Conroy's Seamus Shea will take you on a tour of a San Francisco that is not yet quite forgotten and still intermingles within what San Francisco is and is becoming. As Seamus seeks to uncover a mystery that threatens a close friend, he must also find and open his own broken heart. *No Special Hurry* unfolds in the type of hurry that keeps a reader locked in place with the book open. It features heroes and villains aplenty, some of whom seem somehow familiar yet are their own unique and timely representations of good and evil."

—**JOHN KRALIK**, author of *A Simple Act of Gratitude* and *Three Bodies by the River*

"*No Special Hurry* stars Seamus the Shamus as he tries to free his jailed friend for a murder he, presumedly, did not commit. The former columnist has been warned to 'Let It Be' and not get involved in the investigation while he battles alcoholism, guilt, and grief from a death in the family, along with various beatings and altercations. Colman Conroy takes the reader on a ride around San Francisco using his creative and descriptive prose, allowing the reader to almost solve the case. This action-thriller is beautifully crafted storytelling that will keep the reader on the edge of their seat and unable to lay the book down. A solid offering from this author, with hopes of more to come."

—**BILL SHEEHAN**, author of *A Tail Among Tales*

"*No Special Hurry* is a gripping crime thriller that brings San Francisco to vivid life. With an unforgettable protagonist in Seamus Shea and a twisting mystery that will keep readers guessing until the end, Colman Conroy has crafted a stellar debut. Crime fiction at its best. Fans of gritty detective stories and complex characters will find much to love in this atmospheric page-turner."

—**JEFFREY K. SCHMOLL**, award-winning author of *The Treasure of Tundavala Gap*

"With a smooth, personal voice, this gripping thriller will have you turning pages late into the night. Colman Conroy brings Seamus Shea to life—a lovable but deeply flawed character navigating the shadowed streets of San Francisco. When his friend confesses to murder, Seamus plunges into a relentless race to uncover the truth. As we follow him, layer after layer of his own troubled past unfolds, including the impact of his destructive drinking. Conroy sets a fast, tension-filled pace in this must-read novel, pulling readers along without ever losing momentum. Don't miss this opportunity to add *No Special Hurry* to your list of favorites!"

—**KIMBERLEY LA FARGE BERLIN**, author of *Rise in Recovery: The Spiritual Path for Healing Addiction*

"If you like San Francisco or mysteries, you'll love this modern homage to classic detective fiction set in the City by the Bay. Seamus, the reluctant hometown hero, heads a diverse, well-drawn group of characters that will leave you wanting more."

—**DEBORAH DOYLE**, president ALA United for Libraries

"*No Special Hurry* is an edge-of-your-seat whodunnit that will keep you guessing. An eclectic cast of characters, led by Seamus Shea, take you on a wild ride through the streets of San Francisco. With humor and heartbreak, Seamus joins a renowned list of San Francisco investigators determined to find the truth."

—**ROBERT MOSER**, assistant chief SFPD, retired

No Special Hurry

by Colman Conroy

© Copyright 2024 Colman Conroy

ISBN 979-8-88824-509-5

All rights reserved. No part of this publication may be reproduced, stored in a retrieval system, or transmitted in any form or by any means—electronic, mechanical, photocopy, recording, or any other—except for brief quotations in printed reviews, without the prior written permission of the author.

This is a work of fiction. All the characters in this book are fictitious, and any resemblance to actual persons, living or dead, is purely coincidental. The names, incidents, dialogue, and opinions expressed are products of the author's imagination and are not to be construed as real.

Published by

köehlerbooks™

3705 Shore Drive
Virginia Beach, VA 23455
800-435-4811
www.koehlerbooks.com

NO SPECIAL HURRY

A SEAMUS SHEA NOVEL

COLMAN CONROY

VIRGINIA BEACH
CAPE CHARLES

For Colum and AMCB

The world breaks everyone and afterward many are strong at the broken places. But those that will not break it kills. It kills the very good and the very gentle and the very brave impartially. If you are none of these you can be sure it will kill you too but there will be no special hurry.

—Ernest Hemingway, *A Farewell to Arms*

PROLOGUE

HE FIRST NOTICED THE BLOOD, a small pool crawling across gray vinyl.

The classroom was silent save the faint chatter of early arriving students gathering in the yard three floors below. The janitor thought of running, but he didn't move. He could smell the blood—a metallic, honeyed scent.

The girl lay crumpled in the far corner of the classroom. Face up, body contorted. The blood gathering and growing next to her. A young girl, a student, dressed in ripped blue jeans, a gray hoodie, and white sneakers.

A trim man crouched over her, his back to the janitor. The man touched her dark cheek with his left hand, a chef's knife in his right hand, an eight-inch blade splattered red.

The janitor had known this man for five and a half years: a teacher, a coach. The man stood and opened his right hand. The knife fell, piercing the room's silence as it clattered on the vinyl floor.

The janitor wanted to move toward the girl, to examine her, to check on her, to help her. He stayed frozen. It was not so much fear as confusion that kept him still. He could not process what was happening.

The man turned slowly, aware of the janitor for the first time. Generous tears filled his large brown eyes. The man stumbled to his desk and collapsed in his chair. He did not look at the janitor.

An old radiator, jailed for safety, sprang to life and rattled in the corner.

The janitor flinched. He could not process the scene. His senses *slowed to a crawl. The man sat slumped in his chair. The girl, the student, lay motionless in the far corner, blood surrounding her.*

The janitor blessed himself: Father, Son, and Holy Ghost. He did not know what else to do.

The man dropped his head into the palms of his hands.

"She's gone," he said, "she's gone."

FRIDAY

CHAPTER ONE

I WAS SOBER.
Maybe.
I was sure as shit hungover.
The faint light from my double-hung window taunted me. I've wanted to get blackout drapes, but what's the use? On my bed, lying on my back, I counted the imperfections on my stuccoed bedroom ceiling. I spent hours counting. Half a morning of efficiency lost to said hangover. I could've been writing checks for overdue bills, job hunting, washing my whites, clipping nails, composting. Instead, I counted the flaws: small bubbles, long strips, random discolorations. Most impressively, I saw an inverted face in the far-right corner—a water stain that looked like the face of Jesus. Imagine: Jesus, our Lord and Savior, with his well-conditioned, chestnut hair; his neatly trimmed beard; those dreamy, fair eyes; the whitest Middle Eastern you'd ever see gracing my ceiling. The feel-good story of the Christmas season: Jesus appeared on an unemployed journalist's bedroom ceiling.

Yes, unemployed. I had been fired from my dream job writing a slice-of-life column three days a week for the *San Francisco Chronicle*. You might have seen me: front page of the metro section, above the fold, "City Views" by Seamus Shea in bold just below my head shot with a Giants cap, multiple chins, expressive eyes, and Mona Lisa smile.

And yes, *Seamus Shea*. Like all Irish names, it sounds nothing like it looks: Shaymus Shay. Not as bad as Oisin (O-sheen) or Niamh

(Neave), but you get a little tired being called See-Moose-She-Uh. That was me: a thirty-nine-year-old, oddly named, divorced, plump, pale, unemployed, selfish, handsome, fearful Irish-American. I had failed as a husband. I had failed as a brother. I was husky. I never flossed. I couldn't finish a crossword puzzle. I was magnesium deficient. I was a success at failing.

Love had been my biggest failure. I didn't know how to love, and I came up short over and over and over. My ex and I had been separated for eight months and she was already dating. And not just anyone, but J. J. Johnson, former All-Pro running back for the 49ers, known for his pounding running style and popularity with the ladies. Less than a year apart, and she was having sex without me. Worse, she *loathed* football.

Perhaps ceiling Jesus was a sign. I could've built a shrine, charged a nominal entrance fee. Used the proceeds to feed the poor, cure lepers, take orphans to space camp. I could've had quite the "City Views" column on such a miracle. This could've been my comeback. Think of the headlines: *Look Up for Jesus, Ceiling Savior Summoned, Seamus Shea Sees Savior.* He's appeared on toast, potato chips, hillsides, socks, half-eaten Kit Kats, and pancakes.

Why not my ceiling?

But Jesus looked tired. Too much water to wine? Maybe we were both hungover. I closed my eyes and took a deep breath. I was ready to fall back asleep, but my cell phone started dancing on the nightstand.

"Oh, Seamus, you are home. You must help. *Por favor!*"

"Mamá, what's wrong?" Her voice was quivering.

"You must help. You must help Pedro."

"Of course, I will. Tell me what's wrong."

She took a deep breath, and I heard what sounded like her hand slamming on a table.

"Pedro. My Pedro. He has been arrested. Taken to jails. My Pedro."

I took my own deep breath and exhaled into the phone.

"Why was he arrested?"

"They say murder. Murder! You must see him. It must be a mistake. Help him, will you? Please!"

"Yes, of course, Mamá. I will go see him right now."

"Right now, yes. Thank you. My Pedro!" There was a deluge of sobs before she clicked off.

Mamá was Eliana Gomez, my best friend's mother: a gentle, loving woman who I had known for thirty years and who had always treated me like a son. Murder? What the hell happened to Pedro?

I scrolled through the directory of names on my phone and clicked on Donald Johnson.

"Don, it's Shame." Shame was my nickname, short for Seamus.

"I was expecting your call," he answered with his gravelly voice. Don worked SFPD Homicide. He was six-five, beefy, and serious. He had been close with my brother Danny; they had graduated from the police academy together.

"Pedro's mom just called me. She said he's been arrested?"

"Shame . . ." his tone said I should not get involved.

"Come on, Don. We've known each other too long."

He let out a deep sigh.

"Yes, Pedro," he said. "We're holding him for murder."

"Murder? Who?"

"Monique Profit, one of his students. She was stabbed to death in his classroom early this morning. A janitor came in and found Pedro holding a knife covered in blood."

"Pedro's no killer, Don."

"He confessed."

"He confessed?"

"Yes."

I dropped back on my bed and looked up at ceiling Jesus for some sign of help.

"Look. I've said too much Shame . . ."

"I need to see him, Don."

"Are you insane?" His tone shifted again.

"I need to see him, Don."

He had been expecting this. He knew me well enough; I wouldn't take no for an answer.

"I can get you five minutes—maybe. You gotta be discreet, Shame, this is going to blow up in the press. Teacher kills student? Christ!" He paused. "Can you make it to the Hall in fifteen?"

"On my way."

"I'll be honest, Shame. This doesn't look good at all for your boy."

I had first met Pedro Gomez nearly thirty years ago in the sixth grade playing pickup basketball during lunchtime. He had transferred to my school, Our Lady of Angels, and I knew nothing about him. On a breakaway layup, PG had plowed me over; his scrawny, Latin frame somehow knocking me right on my white, Irish ass. I jumped up and went after him, but he just laughed. He apologized saying he had no idea I was such a pushover. He kept laughing and all I could do was join him.

We would call him PG because of his initials, but also because he'd been an all-city point guard. We'd played together in the backcourt for three years in grammar school and another four years in high school. Our senior year, we made a run at the state title, losing by three to a tough Los Angeles team with three future Division I college players. PG went on to Stanford and graduated—summa cum laud-a really big deal-a—but had passed up making a fortune in Silicon Valley to teach English at Thomas Jefferson, a rough-hewn high school on the edge of the Bayview. He'd been there for fifteen years and had coached the varsity girls' hoop team for the past ten, seven of which ended with league titles.

And now he'd been accused of murdering one of his students? Confessing?

We'd had dinner just a few days ago. Southern comfort food in Hayes Valley. Mint juleps, spicy fried chicken, buttermilk biscuits, bacon mac and cheese. I'd done most of the talking: my ex dating, the humiliation of being fired, the lingering pain of Danny.

PG had always been a good listener.

"You're in your head too much, Shame. You always are. Thinking too much about the future or the past. Just take it one day at a time. Okay?" He'd been pretty good with advice, too.

"Easier said than done," I'd said.

"Just remember, nothing is either good or bad but thinking makes it so."

"What?"

"Nothing is good or bad but thinking makes it so," he repeated.

"That's clever."

"*Hamlet*, my man. We're reading it in my AP class," he had said. "You think you got it rough? His uncle kills his father and then marries his mother a couple months later. His dad, who was the king, comes back as a ghost. Tells him to seek revenge on his uncle. Good or bad? It's how you think about it."

"I read it in college. Or at least the Cliff Notes," I'd said.

"You should read it again. Lots of good advice for today's chaos."

After I had downed multiple mint juleps and an equal number of single malts, PG had practically carried me to a cab that night and sent me on my way.

"Nothing is good or bad, Shame," he'd said, as he tapped on the cab's roof. "But thinking makes it so."

CHAPTER TWO

FOURTEEN MINUTES AND TWENTY-THREE SECONDS AFTER I HUNG UP WITH DON, I veered off 101 onto Bryant Street and found a rock star parking spot across from the San Francisco Hall of Justice. My ride was a Ford Ranger pickup truck that I had bought six months ago. Single cab. Fire-engine red. I had no need for a truck, and I'm not exactly sure why I bought it. Mid-life crisis I suppose, and I couldn't afford a Porsche.

The parking spot was one of those new meter-less jobs in front of a worn-down storefront that had a blue awning reading "Barry's Bail Bonds." I guessed they had no affiliation with the former Home Run King, but I admired their moxie. The spot saved me significant time, and I skipped the walk to the ATM-like machine in the middle of the block where I would have had to pay for a dashboard ticket. Instead, I dodged traffic crossing the one-way street and headed up the cement steps into the San Francisco Hall of Justice.

I took my place in a long line snaking toward the metal detectors. Only one of the detectors worked, and it blared and flashed as an elderly Chinese man wearing a white "I ♥ San Francisco" sweatshirt set it off. A collective groan rose up in the long line before me. He spoke little English and threw up his hands in disgust as if surrendering, ready to chuck the whole American justice system into the nearest trash can. I recognized Jimmy, a steroid-pumped sheriff's deputy, who directed the old man to extend his arms and spread his legs. He traced the outline of the man's body with a hand-held device that erupted as it passed over his belly button. The crowd gave a muffled cheer. Jimmy motioned for him to lift his sweatshirt, which he did, uncovering a brass belt buckle shaped like the state of Texas. The old man smiled and tapped his head in a gesture of absent-mindedness.

The line moved quickly after that, and Jimmy gave me a nod as I silently passed through the detectors.

"Good to see you again, Mr. Shea."

He smiled, revealing pristine white teeth and honest, gray eyes. His face was angled, grainy, and slightly orange, thanks to a bronzer that he also used on his bulging arms, which stretched his uniform's tight sleeves.

"Thanks, Jimmy, you're looking good. Keep up the protein shakes."

"We miss you around here," he said.

Before I'd become a columnist, I had been the *Chronicle* crime reporter, and the Hall of Justice was practically my office. I would see Jimmy every day.

"Hey, what happened to 'City Views?' Haven't seen it in a while."

I went to the office shit-faced and puked in the conference room trash can in front of my editor.

"Budget cuts," I said.

I found Don waiting for me, arms crossed, face crosser.

"Five minutes, Shame. That's it," he said.

I nodded and he led me toward the elevators. Don was close with my brother Danny, and I had no reason to dislike him, although I thought he was a little over the top. He wore a fashionable gray suit and black fedora, embracing his high-profile role of San Francisco homicide detective in the spirit of Mike Stone or Harry Callahan. His last name was Johnson though, so he might have been closer to Nash Bridges. He had a wide, resolute face that made most people anxious. At six-foot-five, he was only three inches taller than me, but he probably spotted me a good sixty pounds. Danny had said he was a hell of a rugby player in his day. As we walked, I stared at his broad back and granite shoulders and had no idea how anyone could tackle him.

We rode two floors below. I stayed a few feet behind Don as he exited the elevator and headed down a narrow hallway that smelled like Pine-Sol.

The Hall of Justice felt like a suburban high school more than a site where the innocent and guilty defended themselves. Forest green floors, worn wooden benches, and glossy walls all implied English 101 or Algebra 2, not three to five or twenty-five to life.

Don stopped at the last door on the left. Two uniformed patrolmen stood guard outside. Don nodded to them, looked back at me, and pushed in. The room had a large, rectangular mirror on the left wall, a small metallic table, two folding chairs, and dust. PG sat at the table facing the entrance, his handcuffed hands resting on the tabletop as if he were praying. Maybe he was.

"Five minutes, Shame," Don repeated. He nodded toward the mirror. I couldn't tell if he meant folks were watching or he'd keep the coast clear.

I waited for him to depart and turned to PG. He just shook his head.

"I knew you'd come," he said, staring at me with large brown eyes.

"What the hell is going on?" I took a seat across from him, my back to the door, the mirror on my left. From the neck up, he looked hip and youthful like a high school English teacher should: an unruly swathe of thick, black hair; the makings of a thin mustache and stubbly goatee; wide brown eyes; tawny skin untouched by blemishes. But below the neck, he wore a wrinkled and oversized orange prison-issued jumpsuit.

"Mamá called me; she's terrified," I said.

He exhaled.

For as long as I've known him, every inch of PG's five-foot-ten-inch frame bubbled with restless energy. As a point guard, he'd bounce across the court, driving, attacking, keeping any and all defenders on their heels. I imagine he'd do the same as a teacher: boundless energy zipping around his classroom, keeping students on their toes. Yet, the man that sat across from me seemed lifeless, save for the nervous tapping of his right foot. I hated myself for thinking it, but part of me thought he looked—guilty.

"Tell me what happened."

"There was a student of mine, a young girl, she's dead."

"Okay, how did she die?"

"I stabbed her."

I rubbed my eyes with the palms of each hand. I looked at my reflection in the mirror looming on my left. No doubt, Don stood behind it. His nod to me had to be that he'd be watching. As close as we were, both of us knew that I couldn't be left completely alone with a murder suspect. PG knew that too.

"You stabbed her? What are you talking about?"

He dropped his head and ran his right hand through his hair while the handcuffs kept his left hand flailing on top.

"It's over, Shame, let it go."

"This is absurd, PG. Absurd."

A sharp memory of Danny's death came over me. The surrealness of it all; the feeling that time had stopped. The same feeling overwhelmed me. I could not process what was happening: a student killed gruesomely in PG's classroom—by PG.

"I need you to do a couple things for me. Can you do that?" he asked.

I nodded.

"Can you go see Father Ryan and have him say a prayer for me?"

"Father Ryan?"

"Yes, please. Just go see him, face to face, and have him pray for me."

"Of course."

"See him in person, face to face, okay?"

"Okay. No problem."

Father Ryan was an aging priest from our grammar school days at Our Lady of Angels. Last I heard, he had Alzheimer's. Not sure what he could do for PG, but I was not going to deny him any requests.

"And can you tell Mamá I love her and I want her to go stay with Uncle Carlos? Have Tito take her. It's very important she contacts Tito and goes to see Uncle Carlos. They'll help her get through this."

Tito was PG's cousin. I'd met him once. He was younger and a bit of a black sheep. PG didn't talk about him too much. I'd never met Uncle Carlos.

"I don't remember an Uncle Carlos."

He let out a heavy sigh and commanded more than asked: "It doesn't matter. Have her go see him."

"Okay, PG. I will."

I rested my elbows on the table, interlocked my fingers, and rolled my thumbs one over the other. For all his coolness, tears formed in PG's large brown eyes. He wiped them away with the back of his hand.

"Look, stay calm, and we'll get through this."

He frowned.

"Always the hero," he said. "You are always trying to save the world, and you never stop to save yourself."

"I'm doing fine."

He looked sideways at me.

"Did you hear anything I told you on Monday?"

"Nothing is either good or bad but thinking it makes it so," I said.

PG managed a smile.

"We'll get you out of here, and then we'll worry about me."

He shook his head and waved away the thought with one of his handcuffed hands.

"What about a lawyer? Rev would probably know a good one."

"Leave Rev out of this. I'm going to get a public defender."

I blinked at him.

"PG, this is bad. Bad!"

"Nothing is either good or bad but thinking makes it so!"

We both laughed meekly. As I reached for his hand to offer some comfort, the door flung open, and Detective Rhodes entered with the officers who were stationed outside.

"What the hell are you doing here, Shea?" he asked. I got hit with a light spray of spittle coming from his mouth.

"I'm selling Girl Scout Cookies. Want to buy a couple boxes? I have Thin Mints."

I had butted heads with Rhodes a few times when I worked as the lead crime reporter. And eight months ago, I wrote a harsh but honest column on how the city botched a murder investigation that sent a twenty-one-year-old away for life. Rhodes was in charge of the case. My column and a Pit Bull of a defense attorney had led to a new hearing and eventual acquittal.

"Get Gomez out of here," Rhodes said to the two officers.

PG glanced at me gravely as he stood. "Nothing is good or bad, Shame, but thinking makes it so," he said as the cops led him out of the room.

"Who let you in here?" Rhodes asked.

"Jesus," I said.

"Still a goddamn comedian, huh?"

"I'll be here all week. Tip your waitresses."

Rhodes had this thick, dark mustache that looked like someone taped a scrub brush above his mouth. He had a black belt in some martial art and a passion for deer hunting, and I imagined he owned a workshop where each weekend, he'd cut hardwood with a top-of-the-line table saw.

"Get the hell out of here," he said.

While I considered Detective Rhodes slight in mind, he was large in stature. He was six-foot-two, two hundred and twenty-five pounds of muscle with the aforementioned background in the martial arts: karate or judo or something that would likely cause me great pain. I could see that he was one step short of Bruce Lee-ing me out into the hallway.

"I'll leave, since you asked so nicely."

I stood up and pushed back from the desk, scraping my chair against the floor in the process. A slim vein bulged at the peak of his receding hairline.

"Heard you got fired from your job at the paper. 'Bout time," he said.

I didn't have a comeback for that.

"Sorry we had to bust your friend, Shea," he said. "Easiest conviction we'll have all year."

Even with his size, I didn't do well with taunting.

"What's your motive, Sherlock?"

He crossed his arms and observed me smugly.

"I'd say he was banging his student and she got tired of his limp dick. Broke it off, he goes into his Latin rage, etcetera, etcetera."

I smiled. "Great motive. I'm sure the DA will love it."

"Something funny?"

"No, not at all."

"Get the hell out of here, Shea."

I pushed past him toward the door, relishing the puzzled look on his face as if I had just asked him to divide 329 by 43.

CHAPTER THREE

PG PREFERRED MEN. It meant little in the long run, though. Unless PG withdrew his confession and told me what the hell was going on, I had no idea how to help him.

I paused on the front steps of the Hall and squinted at the traffic floating by. The morning fog had burned off, and the sun was unusually bright for November, blinding me with its reflection off the pale sidewalk.

My anxiety was rising. I had assumed going in that it was all a misunderstanding, some tragedy that PG unwittingly fell in the middle of. But after meeting PG, I could see that this was much more complicated. PG, for whatever reason, was stuck squarely in the center of a horrible murder, while doing nothing to help himself.

I tried Rev, our high school friend and former hoops teammate who worked as an immigration lawyer. No luck, so I left a voicemail. I spent a minute gathering my thoughts and courage and called Mamá.

"Hi, it's Seamus. I just want you to know that I met with Pedro. He's doing okay. He wanted me to tell you he loves you and that he is okay."

"Oh, Seamus. Thank you." A clear image of Mamá entered my mind. She was a petite but sturdy woman with dark, wrinkled skin, shoulder-length gray hair, and a comforting smile. Her brown eyes were large and circular like her only son's and her ears stuck out some, almost daring you to share with her. She'd hug me and lose her head in my chest; she'd always hugged me.

"Mamá, he *is* charged with . . ."

Sometimes the only way was through.

"He's been charged with murder. A student of his, Monique Profit. Has he ever mentioned her?"

I waited. There was no sound. I hoped she hadn't fainted.

"I . . . I do not know her. It is murder?"

She whispered the last word. I realized I should have delivered the news in person. *Jesus, was there a playbook for such things?*

"I'm afraid so."

"A student? He loves his students!"

"Pedro also said you should get Tito and go stay with Uncle Carlos," I said.

"He said Uncle Carlos?"

"Yes, does he live near here?"

There was another long pause. A wave of traffic roared down Bryant. I turned away from the street to hear better.

"Uncle Carlos is my brother, my only brother who died a few years ago in El Salvador. I used to tell Pedro stories about him and that I would send Pedro to live with him if he was bad."

"Why do you think he'd tell you to see him? If he's dead?"

"I think he wants me to go back to El Salvador."

The line to the metal detector curled out the door and down the steps. I retreated down the street, away from the commotion.

"I am not going to El Salvador. Not with my Pedro in jail."

"Okay, but will you call Tito and tell him what has happened? And that PG wants him to stay with you?"

I'd no idea what she thought of Tito.

"Okay. I will call Tito."

"Call him right after you hang up with me, okay?"

"Okay. But I need you to help Pedro. Please, Seamus!" She'd always said my name with a "t" sound on the end: "Shaymust." You must help, Shaymust.

"What can I do?"

"Find out who killed his student. He loved his students."

"I'm not a detective."

"You are with the newspapers. You have to help him. Prove him innocent."

I could only hear desperation in her voice.

"Mamá, I wouldn't know where to start."

"You have to help him."

I thought about this wonderful woman who'd hugged the life out of me every time I'd see her, who'd feed me pupusas and tamales, who'd always ask me about my soon-to-be-ex Jennifer and why we didn't have kids. How could I say no to her?

"Will you help him? Will you help my Pedro?"

I turned to look back at the street as another wave of cars flowed by.

"Of course," I finally said.

"Thank you, Seamus. Thank you."

She hung up. I wasn't sure what, if anything, I had just committed to. A Harley roared by, setting off a car alarm down the street. My phone buzzed again.

"Shame?!"

"Hey, Rev."

"What in the world is going on?"

"I'm not sure, Rev. I'm not sure."

"I go to LA for my cousin's wedding and all hell breaks loose?"

"Seems that way."

"PG's in jail—for murder? He couldn't murder a goddamn ant."

"I know. But they have a lot of evidence that's all painting a pretty ugly picture and the asshole confessed."

"Confessed?"

"I just talked to Mamá. She's a mess. No surprise."

Rev paused. He was as close to her as I was.

"Shame, we have to get him out of there."

"I know. He says not to worry about a lawyer."

"Bullshit! I'll get him a lawyer. Can you start gathering anything that might help him?"

"I'm on it. I'll do my best to try and piece it together, but it's a 2,000-piece puzzle at this point."

"Prison isn't a good place for brown people, Seamus. Hell, a courtroom is even worse."

"I know, Rev. We'll get him through this."

"What else can I do?" Rev asked.

Malcolm Calvin Thompson, a.k.a. Rev, had played high school ball with PG and me. He was six-foot-one in high tops, the fifth tallest on our high school squad, but he had played center. Defense and rebounding were his specialties. He did all the hard work and was the emotional center of our team, too. We called him Rev because he spent most of his time preaching. Not about God necessarily, though he wasn't opposed to that, but most any subject that came to mind: most artful dunker (Vince Carter), fastest rapper (Twista), best horror flick (*The Shining*). He'd had an opinion about everything and the confident, stirring cadence of a Southern preacher to back it up. He had attended undergrad at San Francisco State and law school at USF and had been working for a downtown firm specializing in immigration law ever since. He'd been married ten years to an amazing lady and fellow lawyer and had fathered two adorable young girls.

"I'm not sure what you can do yet," I said. "PG told me to see Father Ryan."

"Father Ryan?" he asked. "Doesn't he have dementia?"

"Alzheimer's, apparently. But it's all I got."

"Christ."

"Amen, Reverend."

"Remember when we played Christian Brothers senior year? Last game of the regular season and their team sucked. They wanted to ruin it for us, took all kinds of cheap shots and were just aching to fight?"

"I do."

"And you and me were raring to go. All emotion and anger and all this crap? The mick and the brother, ready to fight the man!"

"As usual."

"But then PG pulled us all together in the huddle. Said we're going on, they're not. He was completely calm and confident. He put us all in line. No dumb mistakes. Just play and let's get out of here."

"Yeah, I remember. He did that plenty of times."

"I know, right? He was always the calm, cool, Christian one of us. Always turn the other damn cheek. Smallest guy on the floor and he's the ultimate peacemaker. And now he's a killer? No way. No way, Shame."

"You are preaching to the choir, Rev."

"You talk to any of Danny's buddies?"

"One. I'll do more. But they have to do what they have to do."

He paused. I could almost hear him thinking.

"I have to stay for my cousin's wedding, Shame."

"I know."

"It's up to you, Shame. PG needs you. Hell, I need you."

"I'm on it, Rev. I am."

"Rehearsal dinner tonight. Wedding tomorrow. I'll fly back late tomorrow. I'll call you when I land."

"Okay."

"God's got a plan, Shame. And he's put you smack dab in the middle."

"I know, Rev."

"Don't fuck it up!"

CHAPTER FOUR

REV HAD A HABIT OF CUTTING TO THE CHASE. PG was in deep trouble. He was found at the scene of the brutal murder of a young girl, holding the murder weapon, and he confessed. That's, at best, life with no parole.

Father Ryan, Uncle Carlos, Tito. PG was trying to tell me something without telling me. But who was he afraid of? The cops? Who frames a high school English teacher? I would have to find out more about Monique. I would have to visit Father Ryan and make sure Tito reached Mamá. My head pounded. The adrenaline of rushing to see PG had chased away my hangover. Now, it was replaced by a stress headache that felt like a ball-peen hammer was pounding 16-penny nails into each temple.

I'd start with Father Ryan; a prayer couldn't hurt. I checked my watch. 11:37 a.m. I would go to the rectory and ask if Father Ryan would see me. I couldn't imagine that priests who were battling Alzheimer's had busy schedules.

I was about to head to my truck when I noticed a commotion up the street. Multiple news vans were double-parked on the far-left lane of Bryant Street. A cluster of reporters and cameramen were surrounding someone on the sidewalk in the shadows of the vans.

Don had called it. This would blow up in the press. No doubt the vans were here for the murder. "Teacher Kills Student" was about as sensationalist of a headline you could muster, and San Francisco loved its sensationalist headlines. This was the town where a strip club manager was crushed to death on an elevator piano that accidently rose to the ceiling, pinning him and his companion between the ceiling and piano while they were getting busy; where a supervisor killed the mayor and the city's first gay supervisor and got off easy because he ate too many Twinkies; where a tiger escaped from its enclosure to stalk and kill a teenager in the zoo; where a jailed Aryan Brotherhood's dog mauled a lacrosse coach to death; and where a drunken fight over fajitas led to the top brass of the SFPD retiring early. What did I miss? Zodiac, Zebra, Patty Hearst, Jim Jones. Hell, O. J. was born and raised here, grew up in Potrero Hill, and went to Galileo and City College.

I made my way up the street, pushing past a couple of looky-loos. Three tall men with TV cameras resting on their shoulders stood at the back of the fanned-out group. Each had a reporter standing in front of them, mic in hand. Two were male, suited, tall, and plastic looking. The third was a small blonde I recognized from KGO. Next to them stood half a dozen other reporters, mic-less but holding notepads. Print reporters. My people.

In front of all of them, with his back to the Hall of Justice building, stood a tall, pale, White man with a salt-and-pepper goatee. His hair was also salt-and-pepper but wet and flat thanks to more than a dollop of gel. He looked to be in his early forties and moved his arms somewhat frantically as he spoke. The reporters seemed more than happy to record his animation.

"I am glad the police caught this animal and put him away," the man said. "Monique Profit was a beautiful young woman with her entire life in front of her, and then this happens. It's a tragedy. Her own teacher. Her *own* teacher!" He paused and looked off up the street. Two policemen stood behind him. "Again, I'm grateful that the police were able to apprehend him without anyone else being harmed." He turned to acknowledge the men in blue behind him.

"What is your relationship to Monique?" the blonde reporter asked into her mic. She then stuck it back out toward the man.

"I am her mother's boyfriend. She was like my daughter. I can't believe she is gone."

"Why are you here?" another reporter asked.

"I am here to help the police in their investigation. I am here to answer any questions they may have and provide them all the information they may need."

He wore black jeans and a gray sport coat over a white, button-down Oxford. No tie. No belt. White sneakers. He had a firm presence, confident in tone and body language, as if speaking to the media was no big thing. His disdain for PG was palpable and puzzling.

"When did you last see Monique?" the blonde reporter asked.

"This morning. Her mother had already left for work. I cooked her breakfast and gave her a ride to school."

One of the policemen stepped toward the man and whispered in his ear.

"Any last questions?" he asked.

"Why do you think the teacher would harm her?" the blonde reporter asked.

The man looked at her for a beat before answering.

"Harm her? *Harm her*? The man killed her. He killed Monique in cold blood. A wonderful young girl who had her whole life in front of her. I do not know why he killed her. I do know I will never forgive him. I hope this monster gets the chair. Do they still have the chair?" He looked to the reporters for an answer. None came. "And after that I hope he rots in hell."

"Can you spell your name for us?"

"First name, Holden, H-O-L-D-E-N; last name, Morris, M-O-R-R-I-S."

Both policemen stepped forward this time.

"I'm sorry," he said. "That's all the time I have for questions at this point. I need to help with the investigation. We want to make sure this devil goes away for a long time or worse."

Monster? Devil?

The two police officers led him away from the small crowd of reporters who continued to bark questions at him. He made eye contact with me as he walked by. I thought he smiled.

The television reporters turned to their cameramen and asked if they got it. The blonde reporter flirted a bit with one of her male counterparts. Or maybe he was flirting with her. Or maybe that's just how television news reporters talked. In my years in the business, I had tried to stay away from the TV folks as much as possible.

As the crews packed up and moved on, I could see a few old-fashioned print reporters scribbling in their notebooks. The hard workers, the bottom feeders of the journalism food chain. The small group included, to my surprise, Jackie.

CHAPTER FIVE

JACKIE JUNAYA JAMES, *San Francisco Chronicle* crime reporter, former coworker of one Seamus Michael Shea, sat on the edge of a sizable square wooden pot that housed a growing silver birch. She kept her head low, jotting down facts in her reporter's notebook.

"Ma'am, you can't sit there," I said with my best official voice.

"Fuck off," she said back without looking up.

Two nearby reporters offered sideways glances and shuffled away.

"Kiss your mom with that mouth?" I asked.

She stopped scribbling and looked up.

"Seamus Shea? Well, I'll be. My apologies, please fuck off."

"Always a lady," I said.

She stood up and embraced me in a tight hug, burying her head in my chest. She had started at the paper three years ago, hell-bent on uncovering the next Watergate in her first week. I had to slowly convince her that wasn't how it worked. She was a Berkeley grad, 4.0 GPA, editor-in-chief of the *Daily Californian*, diminutive, vicious. She possessed that youthful optimism for the good that was to come and her inevitable success in making it happen while also holding contempt for all the failures of the past that people like me allowed. From the first day I met her, I felt an equal measure of resentment and fondness toward her.

"How are you?" she asked, her voice a mix of concern and pity.

"Been better," I answered.

"What are you doing in these parts?" She flipped her notebook closed and tucked her ballpoint behind her left ear to give me her full attention. I remembered that she was a southpaw.

"PG, the teacher they have in custody, is a good friend of mine," I said evenly.

Her face did not change. She gracefully mixed two cultures: third generation Irish on her father's side and fourth generation Japanese on her mother's side. She joked that her favorite meal was bluefin sashimi and a jar of Guinness. Physically, the combination gave her a unique look with dark hair, fair skin, and light-brown eyes.

"He didn't do it," I said.

She nodded, but her expression still did not change. She didn't care one way or the other. Just the facts, ma'am. She returned to her seat on the wooden box and motioned for me to join her.

"Why would he confess?" she asked.

"I think," I began. I looked around, but the TV crews had already sped off, and we were alone under the birch tree. "He might have been threatened. He's close to his mom, and if someone threatened her, he'd do anything to protect her."

Her eyes jumped out at me, almond shaped and distinctive, projecting a fierce intelligence. She was an odd mix of emotion and stoicism, where the stoic side always seemed to win out. Her middle name meant "peace" in Japanese. It made her a great reporter. But every now and then, that Irish temper would bubble up and the only safe play for those around her was to take cover.

"Someone kills the girl and tells him to take the fall or they'll kill his mother?" I could hear the disbelief in her voice. Frankly, as she said it out loud, it sounded a bit unbelievable.

She flipped her notebook back open and wrote down some notes.

"Maybe. It's just a theory. I'm an hour into this. Have you heard anything?"

"Not much," she said. "A girl was stabbed at Jefferson. Dead at the scene—a student. And that a teacher was the main suspect and in custody. I haven't talked to any of my sources yet. That's next on the list."

"Same."

"Okay, well if you hear anything or learn anything, you'll let me know?" she asked.

"Of course, Jackie. And I assume you'll give me the same courtesy?"

She smiled and nodded. We sat quietly for a few minutes; traffic rumbled down Bryant Street behind us.

"I am sorry about what happened," she finally said, not needing to be specific.

"Ah, I deserved it," I answered, waving my hand as if I were swatting a fly.

Twenty years in the work world and I had never been fired. That had changed a few weeks prior when my editor, the editor-in-chief of the *Chronicle*, and a couple of lawyers pulled me into the fifth-floor conference room and told me to pack my bags. I didn't argue. I couldn't. They had given me chance after chance after chance. There was a final plea: enter their forty-five-day rehab program and we could talk after that about me returning. I balked. I was polite and cordial, as I liked my bosses, but I had no interest in or need for rehab. I wanted a change anyway. And I like to drink. Big deal. I dumped my favorite mementos in a white, corrugated box they gave me, said some quick goodbyes, and walked proudly to the elevator with Arnie, our seventy-year-old security guard, limping behind me. Jackie was out of the office, so I missed saying goodbye. Seeing her now felt like a dull knife scraping against the inside of my chest, reminding me of failure.

"I called," she said.

"I know. I got your messages. Just wasn't ready to call back."

She crossed her arms.

"I miss working with you," she said. "I learned a lot from you."

"Probably what not to do more than anything."

"It just seemed unfair," she said. "I think they could have given you another chance."

I smiled.

"You're half Irish, right?" I asked.

She nodded. I reverted back to sage mentor.

"Well, Daniel Patrick Moynihan was a New York senator who worked as some assistant to an assistant in the Kennedy administration. He said after John F. Kennedy was shot that there's no point in being Irish if you don't know that eventually, the world will break your heart."

"That's kind of dark."

"Not really. It's just being aware. It's no secret that they call it Murphy's Law, not Wong's Law or Bellini's Law or Goldberg's Law. It takes an Irishman to point out that if anything can go wrong, it will."

Two sheriff deputies walked by, mumbling something about the Warriors.

"Have you heard of the Great Famine?" I asked.

She closed her eyes and rubbed her temples.

"That's life. Simple. True. Things will go wrong. Life will disappoint. Your heart will break."

"Maybe I don't miss working with you," she said.

A plane passed above us, leaving a contrail of white in its wake. She squinted her eyes and looked up at it.

"My father . . ." she began, not looking at me.

Her father drank. They had been estranged for years, but they reunited soon after she had started at the paper. I remembered her honesty about it. He went the AA route, made amends.

"I remember," I said delicately. "This is different."

She scratched her small nose.

"Look, I have to go inside and get some quotes. Can we stay in touch?" she said.

"I'd like that," I said.

"I still have your number. You call me back this time. Deal?"

"Deal."

"It was great to see you, Seamus." She reached over and hugged me again. "You take care."

I watched as she headed toward the Hall of Justice entrance. She strode more than walked, determined and displeased like any capable crime reporter. This was the first time I had seen her since I'd been fired. I liked Jackie. I missed Jackie. At least one good thing had come from this horrible morning.

CHAPTER SIX

DON'T FUCK IT UP.

Rev's words echoed in my mind as I headed back to my truck.

For most of my life, I'd held steadfast to grandiose fantasies that set me far above the troubles of my past and the ordinariness of my present. In my youth, I'd imagined I'd be an Olympic Champion and take home the gold in the Men's 800 meters. They called me the Holy Ghost, so fast you couldn't see me, a blasphemous nod to the all-boys Catholic school I attended and to my above-average speed, but mostly to my fair complexion. Post college, I had thought Oprah would warmly pat my knee on her powder-blue, mid-century, modern sofa and ask probing but thoughtful questions about my great American novel and the plight of the disillusioned, Irish-American male. I failed at both.

Then came Danny.

There's no point in being Irish if you don't know that the world will eventually break your heart.

A year later, I was divorced, unemployed, and my best friend was facing a life sentence or worse.

My phone buzzed. I didn't recognize the number.

"Is this Seamus Shea?" a deep voice asked.

"Yes. Who's this?"

"Tito."

My muscles tensed. I didn't reply.

"Mrs. G called me. She gave me your number. She said PG is in jail."

There was a lot of background noise, like he was driving with his car window down. His voice was low and monotone, so I had to strain to hear him.

"And he wants me to take her to El Salvador?" he asked.

"That's what he said."

"Murder?" He was calm and measured, which was reassuring given the circumstances.

"He's accused of killing one of his students in his classroom. He confessed. I don't know what's going on, Tito. I really don't. But he told me to have her go see Uncle Carlos and have you take her there."

"Uncle Carlos has been dead for years."

"I heard. But it seemed like PG wanted her to go to El Salvador."

A loud horn blared in the background and I heard him yell something in Spanish.

"So, she's in trouble," he stated more than asked. There was a certain confidence in his monotone voice, like he was used to being in charge.

"I think so. I mean, if he confessed, maybe someone was threatening him. Using her. He's telling us to get her out."

"She won't leave, but I can keep her safe. I'm on my way to her house now."

PG had told me a few stories about Tito. He had emigrated from El Salvador seven years ago at age seventeen. He was the eldest son of Mamá's cousin who stayed behind in El Salvador. PG and his mom helped Tito some, but he had a strong independent streak and lived mostly on his own. His connection to MS-13 remained murky. He "knew people" was all he ever told PG.

"That woman has always been good to me," he said. "I will make sure she is safe. Do we know who might be behind this?"

"I have no clue. I will find out, though. I'm a big fan of Mrs. G too. The idea of how much this is tearing at her is hard to take."

"Mrs. G said you are a high school friend. You're a . . . ?" I couldn't make out the last word, which was jumbled by the many sounds from his drive.

"I missed that last word," I said.

"A reporter? Newspapers."

"A reporter, yeah," I said.

"She said you are going to look into all this. You have some connections?"

Most people thought that reporters had some magical ability to make things happen—that if it was in print or on TV, the world would listen and act. The reality was something different. Even with my three columns a week, I'd made little impact. There were a few successes, like the 21-year-old accused of murder I'd helped get off with a column, but those were exceedingly rare. There was too much noise out there. A tumult of conflicting views that only proved to confuse and frustrate the masses.

"I'm going to try my best to get to the bottom of it and get him out of jail," I said.

He didn't speak. I could hear the wind slapping around his car cabin and another horn.

"If you need anything, you let me know. All right?" he finally said.

"I will."

"You played basketball with PG?"

"Yeah."

"Did we ever meet?"

"Once."

A loud siren approached and whizzed by him.

"All right," he said. "You do what you have to do."

"I will."

"And Seamus?"

"Yeah?"

"Don't fuck it up."

CHAPTER SEVEN

I MADE IT TO MY TRUCK AND FOUND A SEVENTY-FIVE-DOLLAR TICKET TUCKED UNDER THE DRIVER'S SIDE WINDSHIELD WIPER. Expired meter. Should have known it was going to happen, parking across from the Hall of Justice. I looked around for a meter maid or one of San Francisco's finest. None. I crumpled up the ticket in an act of defiance and threw it in the bed of my truck. Of course, I knew they mailed you a reminder a few weeks before it was due.

"Mr. Shea?"

I turned to see a small woman in khakis and a maroon turtleneck standing on the sidewalk blinking back at me.

"I'm Daniella Walsh," she said, as if we'd known each other since childhood.

"I'm sorry, have we met?"

"I'm Daniella Walsh?"

"Oh, right," I said, clueless.

"I work with Pedro. We teach together at Jefferson High. English. Ms. Daniella?"

"Of course, how can I help you, Ms. Walsh?"

She looked oddly tan for November. Her blonde hair fell just above her shoulders and the bright sun exposed a pair of delicate blue eyes. She looked Swedish or Norwegian, one of those Nordic countries where the women are stunningly beautiful and perfectly tan despite the snow. I felt a little jealous that I had no such teacher in high school, mostly overweight priests.

"You don't know me, do you?"

"I'm sorry. Pedro didn't talk much about his school," I said.

"That's surprising. He talked plenty about you. High school buddies and all your basketball championships."

I smiled politely, but my stomach turned at the compliment. None of us, Pedro included, liked to recall our glory days with anyone but us.

"I just came down here after I heard about Pedro. I thought I might be able to get in and see him, but I guess that's impossible." She ran her right hand through her hair, tucking the blonde locks behind her ear. Her nails were well-manicured and painted cabernet red.

"Shouldn't you be at the school?"

"Oh, they shut it down. Sent the kids home. Policemen are all over the place, looking for evidence. We'll supposedly be back Monday with grief counselors."

She crossed her arms under her breasts, which were noticeably large for her small frame. She tapped her right hand nervously on her left bicep. I guess having your fellow teacher arrested for murder is likely to spike anyone's fight-or-flight response.

"Did you get a chance to see him?" she asked.

"Me? No. Couldn't get past the front door." I ran my right hand through my hair, my tell, and looked up at the Barry's Bail Bonds awning. A strong whiff of urine hit my nostrils; I hated SOMA.

"But you were a reporter. Don't you have connections? I loved your column. You're kind of famous."

My ears reddened, and I knew the blood was making a beeline for my Irish cheeks. I looked the other way toward the Hall of Justice and took in a couple of big breaths.

"Oh, not so famous." I turned back and took a closer look at Ms. Walsh. She had a certain edginess to her. Despite her beauty, there was a rough-hewn quality that seemed out of place for a schoolteacher.

"Why was 'City Views' stopped?" she asked.

Let's discuss it over tequila shots and nachos.

"Oh, I needed a break. I wanted a new challenge."

She smiled.

"Really?"

"Yes. I have a few book ideas," I lied. *Jesus, I'm desperate.*

"Wonderful. Maybe I could read them some time? I am an English teacher."

Crap.

"Well, I'm in the idea stage and, you know, that can go slow. Why did you come down again?"

"I was hoping to see Pedro. To know he's okay."

"He's fine, Ms. Walsh, I assure you that."

"Did he say anything to you? Tell you anything?"

"No. He didn't have much to say. He's shaken up."

"So you did see him?"

I winced at having been caught in a white lie, but Ms. Walsh seemed harmless.

"I did see him. He's okay. This is all a mistake."

"They said he confessed!"

"I don't know."

"I mean, he might go to jail for the rest of his life, right? The rest of his life!"

"I don't know if that would be the case."

"I just can't believe this is happening," she continued. "It's so surreal. We were just talking about *Hamlet* yesterday. I was helping him with a lesson. Now it's like we're in our own tragedy."

"Did you know the girl? Monique?"

Her face changed; sympathy gave way to anger.

"No. No, I didn't. I don't know much about her."

A homeless man shuffled by us, pushing a crowded shopping cart, mumbling to himself. We were quiet.

"I suggest you go home, Ms. Walsh," I finally said.

"Call me Danny."

Danny? Christ.

"Is that your truck?" she asked.

I looked over my shoulder even though I already knew the answer. She was starting to make me nervous.

"Yep. You a truck fan?" *Truck fan?*

"I am. I grew up on a farm in Iowa. My daddy used to drive an old Ford F-100. Two-toned: blue on top, white on the bottom. I *loved* that truck."

"Where in Iowa?" I asked, fascinated.

"Oh, a little town called Alta. A handful of people there, two stoplights, nothing like this big city."

The Iowa farm girl who looked like a Nordic queen and taught English at a big city rough-and-tumble high school? And PG never mentioned her? He knew *Field of Dreams* was my favorite movie.

"Go home, Ms. Walsh. Get some rest. I know Pedro would be happy to hear you came down here for him, but there is nothing you can do."

She blinked back at me with her soft blue eyes.

"Thanks, Mr. Shea," she said, holding out her hand.

"Seamus," I answered, shaking it.

"Seamus."

She squeezed my hand and the power of her grip surprised me. Cute, confident, no ring. Why didn't Pedro ever mention her? I watched her walk down Bryant Street; she had a certain grace, a rhythm. Her hair bouncing, her khakis fitting just right. I felt a slight tightening in my stomach, a quickening of my pulse.

I thought I remembered that feeling.

Love?

No, not love—lust. But even lust would have to wait; I had a date with a priest.

CHAPTER EIGHT

I DROVE TWO MILES TO OUR LADY OF ANGELS LISTENING TO CONFUSING AND CONFLICTING RADIO REPORTS ON THE LOCAL NEWS STATIONS. One station had a teacher also being hurt, one said it was a male student who had died, and a third just talked about the sad state of public schools in the city.

I turned the radio off and parked in front of Our Lady of Angels. The church was about five blocks from my mother's house in the center of Noe Valley. Staring at the building's faded facade, I couldn't help but feel nostalgic. Random memories still clung to me: the bell-shaped lights hanging above, the blood-red color of the carpet, the cooing of pigeons nesting outside the stained-glass windows. I must have said a thousand prayers in that building; not sure if any were answered. This church, this school, had shaped me. It'd shaped PG, too. And Danny. All of us, for better or for worse.

Bless me father for I have sinned; it has been ten, fifteen, twenty years since my last confession; I hope you have a while.

I popped a couple of Altoids and made my way up the six rectory steps that led to a wide mahogany door. I knocked firmly to the right of a plaque hanging just under the peephole that read:

For with God, nothing will be impossible.

Luke 1:37

I sure as shit hoped so.

An older, heavyset woman with pale, abrasive skin answered.

She wore a beige apron and used it to clean her thick hands, which stirred up a thin mist of white powder.

"Yes, yes. How can I help ya?" she asked. I recognized a clear Irish brogue.

"I was hoping to see Father Ryan."

She looked at me sideways and took a half step back as if expecting me to rush the door. She used the back of her right hand to wipe her forehead.

"Is he expecting ya now?"

"No. I'd like to talk to him about Pedro Gomez. He's been arrested. I just need a minute of his time."

Her eyebrows jumped.

"You're a friend, are ya now?"

"Yes. A friend of Pedro's. Seamus Shea."

The woman leaned forward and nodded.

"I'm very sorry. Pedro is a nice man; he visits often. Just one moment."

She left me standing alone on the stoop, the rectory door half-open. I could feel the heat escaping and the sounds of a television game show blaring. For an art project in the fourth grade, they'd asked us to draw a picture of Father Ryan. I drew him as a giant human tree, roots stuck firmly in the ground, thick branches for arms, and a trunk covered in tough bark. He had been assigned as pastor to Our Lady of Angels in 1949, coming straight from County Kilkenny in the south of Ireland. I once asked him who Kenny was and why people wanted to kill him. He tousled my hair and told my mother I was a bright boy.

A few minutes passed, and she returned, smiling.

"Okay, he'll see ya." She opened the door wide and gestured for me to come in. "He is, ah . . ." she began and crinkled her face. "He has his moments now and then, do ya understand? Gotta be patient with him."

She stretched out the a: "paaaaytient." I nodded and offered a sympathetic scowl.

She led me through a short hallway. I had been inside once before, some thirty years ago. My mother, my brother Danny, and I had visited Father Ryan for reasons we don't talk about.

Except for feeling smaller, the rectory looked much like it did back then: stuffy and humid with bare colors and borrowed furniture. The heat gauge must have been pushing ninety degrees. My apron-clad friend introduced herself as Mara. She walked briskly and I tried to keep up. She led me to a rec room with a worn couch, a La-Z-Boy recliner, and a prehistoric console television that actually had knobs to change channels. Father Ryan sat stretched out in the La-Z-Boy wearing a navy blue bathrobe over plaid pajamas and fawn-colored slippers. The TV screamed.

"Father, Father," she said in a sing-song voice, "Sure here is Seamus Shea. He wants to talk to ya now."

He sat up slowly and looked me up and down. He was far from the tree I once drew. His large frame had withered to the point that he seemed mostly just bones and folds of pale skin. His face was still wide and rugged but also had a sallow hue with most of its color drained.

"Do I know you?" he asked gruffly.

"Yes, sir. Seamus Shea. Mary Shea's son. I went to school here a long time ago."

"Mary Shea? Oh, yes, you've grown. You are a man now."

"I suppose I am," I smiled awkwardly. Mara, the caretaker, impressed that he remembered me, retreated to the kitchen.

"How can I help you, my son?"

"Pedro Gomez has been arrested."

"Pedro? What for?"

"Murder."

The old priest's face registered a certain shock. He took a break from our conversation and returned his focus to the television where *The Price Is Right* boomed at volume that made me think Drew Carey was in the room with us.

"Higher!" he screamed at the television.

The room felt even warmer than the hallway. The stench of cigarette smoke made my eyes water. I noticed a full ashtray and an open pack on the TV tray table propped up next to his La-Z-Boy. The table also housed a small pharmacy with at least five different pill bottles. A faded black leather couch sagged against the far wall near a dented gray filing cabinet. The walls might once have been white but seemed relegated to a gray hue from the smoke.

The wall behind his La-Z-Boy was adorned with a hodgepodge of pictures tacked up randomly with push pins. I could make out children's drawings, a Giants team picture circa 1982, faded newspaper clippings, pictures of parishioners and the good Father, and a 49ers poster from 1989. It seemed to be a disjointed wall of fame, with fifty years of memories sporadically displayed. There were no windows in the room, and the only light came from the glow of the screaming television, which flickered off the gray walls bringing sporadic light to his wall of fame.

I watched the television with him.

"Great show," I said.

He turned and looked me over again. His once-dark hair had thinned and turned completely white. It rose above his head haphazardly as if some invisible current of static electricity willed it higher. The white hairs of his eyebrows, ears, and even nose had grown long and unruly. It looked like he nicked himself shaving a couple times, as dried blood blotted his chin and cheek.

"Do I know you?" he asked.

"Yes, sir. I'm Seamus Shea. Mary Shea's son." I raised my voice to overcome the din of a Tide commercial.

He scratched the top of his head with his left hand and made a cross face.

"Yes, Seamus. You're the one with the brother," he said coldly.

I nodded. The smells of the room made me feel woozy: an odd combination of Lysol, Vicks Vapor Rub, and cigarette smoke.

"That was a sad day. I remember it well. Thanksgiving."

He returned his gaze to the TV.

"Do you remember your father?" he asked, while glaring at Drew Carey.

"No, sir. Not much at all."

"What did your mother tell you?"

"She doesn't talk about him. We never were really allowed to talk about him. I'm not sure why."

He turned and looked me in the face. "Pity," he said. "He was a good man. Very sad what happened."

My father had been a policeman who had a heart attack while walking his beat in the Mission, back when cops walked a beat. He had collapsed on the street and died. I was ten then and Danny was nine. The big priest had been a frequent and formidable presence in our house in those days, and he called us to the rectory just before Christmas to check in. The three of us had sat studiously across from him. I remembered he had smoked cigarettes, talking to us between puffs. The smell had reminded me of my father. I thought God was telling me something. Father Ryan had said that everything would be okay, puff puff, that the worst of it was over, puff puff, that God would take care of us, puff, puff.

"Your brother was a policeman?" he asked.

"Yes."

"He was on the drug task force when . . ."

"Yes."

The old priest nodded. He had a damn good memory for an Alzheimer's patient.

"Are you a parishioner?"

"No, not anymore."

"Married?"

"Yes." Technically, I still was.

He seemed content with my answer.

A large fly buzzed overhead, enjoying the room's tropical climate. It flew past my ear and took another swipe near my neckline. Father Ryan continued to sit quietly, unaware or unconcerned with the intruder.

"Well, I'm sorry, but I can't help you," he said, waving me away.

"I'm sorry, what?" I asked.

"I don't know anything about Pedro."

A slight pain pulsated in my temples.

"Please, Father, he asked for you to pray for him. Does that mean anything to you?"

Father Ryan's face found an intensity that made me step back a bit.

"Pedro said he wanted me to pray for him?"

"Yes."

The priest continued to stare at me. The blankness left his face; he was analyzing me. He smiled and even laughed.

"I'm so sorry, Seamus. I have to be careful, but I will tell you what I know about PG."

He seemed to transform in an instant.

"You're not senile?" I asked.

He laughed.

"You're a fine reporter, Seamus."

"You remember me?"

"Fine runner, too. What did they call you in high school? The Holy Ghost?"

"I haven't been called that in a long time."

"I still remember when you asked me who killed Kenny. I used to tell that story often."

He smiled and pointed at his filing cabinet.

"Drink?"

I was caught off guard. He pulled a key from his waistband and walked over to the gray, dented filing cabinet nestled in the corner of the room. He opened the bottom drawer, which housed a small cooler and two highball glasses. He pulled out the glasses and placed them on the tray table with the medicine bottles. He returned to the cabinet, opened the cooler, and took out a pint of vodka.

I had hoped to hold off on drinking so I could be clear-headed and help PG. But here now, a man of the cloth—God's own emissary—was offering me a drink. Some might have called it a sign from above, a miracle even.

"Drink?" he repeated.

I still didn't answer as he dropped two fingers' worth of vodka in one glass and filled the other near the brim. He held the half-filled one out to me. My mind reminded me that I should just say no. But my mind also reminded me of what those first few sips were like.

My right hand reached out and took the glass. I clinked my glass with his.

"*Slainte*," I said. *The Blood of Christ.*

"*Slainte*, Seamus Shea."

He dropped his head back and opened his throat to swallow a third of his glass.

"Ah, ice cold, pure gold," he said.

"I'd imagine you a whiskey man," I said.

"I am. But that Mara is one suspicious SOB. I have to stay on my toes with her. So, I drink to the Russkies. Little smell. Not bad taste. That warm, fuzzy feeling in my brain. All is good."

He blessed himself with the hand holding the glass.

"I don't see your column anymore," he said. "What happened?"

I stared at the remaining vodka in my glass and swirled it a bit. In one quick motion, I finished it and looked again at the now empty glass.

"Politics," I answered.

Father Ryan smiled and refilled my glass. He didn't pry and seemed content having a drink. I shared his contentment.

After a couple of minutes of easy silence, I asked: "So why do you think PG asked me to see you? To have you pray for him?"

"Kratos," he said.

"Kratos?" I asked. "Jesus."

"You know him?"

"Everyone knows Kratos. I almost did a column on him. He's known as the Robin Hood of the Bayview. He gives money to those in need in his neighborhood but apparently earns his money in illegal ways. My editor didn't go for it."

"I don't know him," Father Ryan said.

"What's he got to do with it?'

"A few weeks ago, Pedro came to me and told me he had learned things about one of his students."

"Monique."

"I assume so. He didn't tell me much, but he wanted me to know that Kratos was wrapped up in it and that if anything happened to her or him, Kratos would likely be the key."

"Why didn't he come to me?"

"I don't think he knew everything, just pieces. We've had a very good relationship, and I listen without feeling the need to act. That's not a knock on you Seamus, but more that Pedro didn't want anyone mixed up in trouble that he wasn't even sure *was* trouble."

"Seems like trouble, now," I said.

"He said if something happened to him and anyone came asking me to pray for him, I should give them Kratos's name."

"Did he think he was in danger?"

He took another swig of his drink.

"No. He seemed to be doing it out of an abundance of caution."

"Odd."

"Kratos is the key. Talk to him, and he'll help you with Pedro."

I nodded and finished my drink. He reached over to refill it. He topped off his own glass and leaned back in his chair. I took a taste.

"Can I ask you, Father? Why the Alzheimer's act?"

He smiled and stroked his chin with his free hand.

"Priests don't get to retire, especially not these days. No one wants to be a priest, and who can blame them? A little eccentricity keeps me from having to say Mass. A small victory."

I laughed.

"When I was a young man, I had an invitation to dinner from nearly every house in this neighborhood. I baptized, married, and buried every Catholic that lived in a twenty-block area of this place. Priests could do no wrong. Nowadays, well, things have changed."

He let out a heavy sigh and finished his drink. He motioned for me to give him my glass. He finished what was left in my glass and put them both back in the drawer. He took the empty pint, dropped it in the cooler, and closed the cabinet drawer.

"The church has lost its way. Pedro is a model Catholic. Devout, thoughtful, kind. And he's shunned from our church? Ridiculous. Stupid men made even stupider by their power. Ah, it would get me so upset that I just gave up. You can't fight City Hall, and you sure as hell can't fight the Vatican. So, I decided to start acting different. I read a few books on dementia and slowly over the last year, my mental health has waned. I've faded fast just like my father did. Or at least like I told everyone he did, when I started my ruse."

He turned his head and coughed.

"And I get to watch a lot of quality daytime television."

I smiled.

"Does Mara know?"

"Oh, yes. She's in on it and all for it, except she doesn't like the drinking." He shrugged. "My one vice."

"You are a bad man, Father Ryan."

"You won't give away my secret, will you?"

"Of course not, Father. My own seal of the confessional."

He smiled again.

"Kratos?" I said.

"Kratos," he repeated. "That's what PG said. See him for some help."

"And you are sure he's not the killer?"

He paused to consider if he was sending me to my death.

"Oh, Seamus, I'm not sure of anything these days."

CHAPTER NINE

I HEADED BACK TO MY APARTMENT ENJOYING THE BUZZ FROM MY HAPPY HOUR WITH FATHER RYAN, but a little unnerved that he gave me the name of the city's biggest drug dealer for a lead. Inside, I fell back on my bed and looked up at my ceiling and Jesus, hoping for some miracle advice to save PG.

Technically, my mother's ceiling. Yes, I lived with my mother. This was not as undesirable or embarrassing as it may sound for a soon-to-be forty-year-old man. At least, I told myself that. After my ex Jenny and I had parted ways—or more accurately, after she left me—we agreed she'd stay in our suburban abode nestled at the end of an oak-lined, peninsula cul-de-sac, and I'd find other lodging. She enjoyed the suburban life. J. J. Johnson had likely taken my place, manned my grill, and tossed the pigskin with the neighborhood kids.

As luck would have it, my mother owned a sizable triangular wood frame with an unoccupied, albeit illegal, in-law unit in a quiet, unassuming San Francisco neighborhood known as Noe Valley.

My mother was one of the few remnants of the Noe Valley I knew as a child. Forty years ago, it had been a working-class ethnic enclave, where everyone seemed to be Irish and Catholic and angry. Soon, waves of gay men, mostly couples, mostly happy, spilled over from the Castro and found quaintness in the Valley of Noe.

In time, the hood became a haven for rich, White, power-couples tapping on laptops as they rode enormous, air-conditioned busses through the neighborhood's narrow streets and down 101 toward

Google and Twitter, while their nannies pushed thousand-dollar strollers along 24th Street. Facebook's founder had lived a few blocks away. It was a real estate agent's wet dream.

Location, location, location.

Therefore, I lived nearly rent free in an affluent, hip hood; quite the upgrade from the generic, suburban no-man's-land where my ex and I settled. And the limited rent was a double bonus given my unemployed status. Yes, my landlady had issues, but you should see the view!

My in-law unit had its charm. It sat below the main house, basement level. We lived on a hill though, so I was above ground. Pockets of sunlight trickled in from the front window. The living room blended into the bedroom. The entire place was veiled in a certain melancholy. Thin films of dust gathered in all the hard-to-reach nooks and even in a few easy ones.

As I laid in bed, enjoying my buzz, my brain was already consumed with where and when my next drink would come. I panicked for a moment, thinking that I was dry. I checked my old standby, and sure enough, there was a nearly full bottle of Jameson under the sink, hiding behind a bottle of Clorox cleaner. I slammed the cabinet doors in joy but accidentally caught my left pinky and jammed the crap out of it.

The pain killed. I carefully opened the doors again and scrounged for any duct tape. I looked in my bedroom closet and in my bureau for any tape that I could use to wrap my fingers and hopefully ease the throbbing. No luck. I headed upstairs to ask my mother.

I found my mother sitting at her kitchen table in all her early evening glory: purple terry-cloth bathrobe, beige Ugg slippers, dyed black hair wrapped in a tight bun. The robe and the Uggs were both Mother's Day gifts from the past two years. Her hair made her look younger than her true age of seventy-two. She could lose a few pounds, twenty according to her doctor, but her sturdy country frame carried the weight well. She was smoking a menthol and tapped it lightly on a bowl in front of her to chase the ashes.

"Do you have any duct tape?" I asked.

"What do you need that for?"

"Never mind, do you have any?"

"Why are you holding your finger like that?"

"Jesus, does everything have to be a question?"

"I could say the same for you."

I should point out that my mother, Mary Shea, was a saint. She'd tell me this often. And there was some truth to it. She did raise two ungrateful boys by herself after her husband had died. It left her a little bitter though. Her life mantra seemed to be that not only was the glass half empty, but it was also laced with arsenic. Of course, if you were Irish, whether off the boat dripping wet—moist as my grandfather used to say—or generationally removed from the old country, like my mother, you usually looked at life through one of two lenses: half empty or half full. There was not an in-between. Every Irishman and Irishwoman that I had met had fallen into one of these two extremes. They were either eternal optimists, forever seeing the wonder of it all in life, or they were pessimists, forever seeing the Great Famine happening over and over again.

There's no point in being Irish if you don't know that the world will eventually break your heart.

"I jammed my finger in a cabinet door by accident and I need some duct tape to support it."

She rested her cigarette on the bowl, crossed her arms, and stared at me. She had a strong bullshit meter. Eventually, she stood and walked to a kitchen drawer. I could hear her rummaging. She returned and handed me a roll of gray tape.

"That doesn't look good," she said.

"It's fine."

"Isn't it duck tape?" she asked.

"I'm sorry?"

"You said duct tape; duc-t tape. I thought it was du-ck tape."

"It's duct tape."

"Imagine? All this time and I've been saying it wrong."

"Wonders never cease."

"Tell it to your psychiatrist!" she said in a huff, taking her seat. She had been using this phrase with me more and more lately. I didn't know if she thought I'd been seeing a shrink or whether it was just a form of insurance in case I might one day.

I ripped off half a foot of tape, took a deep breath, pressed my pinky back upright into my ring finger and spun the tape around both until they were solidly bound in a makeshift splint. I let out a muffled scream of pain.

"That doesn't sound good, either," she said, picking up her cigarette.

"It's fine. And I thought we agreed you'd cut back on the smoking."

"Ah!" She waved her hand, scattering the smoke. "Toughens up the lungs. Anything bad for you makes you stronger. I knew a man who worked in the coal mines growing up, lived to be a hundred. Iron lungs, he had. True."

I tried to imagine how she would ever have known a coal miner growing up in San Francisco, but like most things with my mother, I had to let it go.

"I don't want to fight," I said. "I've had a crappy day."

She pursed her lips and nodded.

"Why crappy?"

"PG was arrested."

"What? What for?"

"A student was stabbed to death in his class. Circumstantial evidence points to him as the killer."

"Jesus, Mary, and Saint Joseph." She blessed herself, bringing the cigarette along for the ride.

"He's also confessed, but it's got to be a false confession."

"The poor dear, I can't imagine he would do such a thing," she said.

"He didn't do it," I said. "I just have to figure out who did."

She smashed her cigarette in the bowl and dropped her hands to her waist.

"You are not a detective."

"I know that."

"Don't get involved, Seamus."

"He's my best friend."

"That's all the more reason. If he's innocent, and I'm sure he is, let those in charge handle it. You'll only hurt his cause if you step into it now."

She was half right. There was a risk of me sticking my nose where it didn't belong. But I knew Rhodes and the others wanted it to be a closed case. This was a PR nightmare. They had other murders to solve without confessions and none as high profile as this one.

"I'm just going to run down a few leads."

"Listen to your mother, stay out of it."

I rubbed my aching pinky.

"I don't need your advice."

"Tell it to your psychiatrist!" she said, dismissing me with a wave of her hand. "I'm going to make some more tea." She stood up and walked to grab her silver kettle on the stove.

I retreated to the living room for a break. Round one was over. My pinky was throbbing.

Mary Shea had inherited her modest house from her Irish immigrant parents. She grew up in it. The neighborhood had been infested with Irish families back in the '50s and '60s. The Irish had loved San Francisco. The city was made for immigrants; the city was built by immigrants. Cool weather, large homes, water views. They would revitalize Our Lady of Angels, open pubs, invest in land and homes, and above all, fear God and government. They had been laborers and maids. Their children would be cops and firemen and work for the city. Their children's children would be doctors and lawyers.

We did our part. Danny had become a policeman. I'd become a reporter. But Danny and I never had kids, so there would be no children's children for this house. No doctors. No lawyers. We'd been only two because my mother had complications after Danny's birth.

She wasn't able to have more children. Danny would carry a burden all his life knowing that fact.

He should have been a teacher, a fireman even, but he became a policeman, trying, it seemed, to right the wrong of my father's death. Friends of my father encouraged and helped him despite the reservations they voiced to me. It didn't matter. He did well as patrolman. He was well-liked by the other cops. He had built up a reputation in the Mission, where he worked as our father had. Neighborhood folks called him the good cop because he was kind and thoughtful regardless of who you were. That stood out. He had moved to narcotics, surprising everyone. He was tired of seeing drugs tear apart families, friends, and communities. He had wanted to end it. An idealist to the end.

We both loved the house. It could have been any house in any city: a limited wood structure with two bedrooms and one and a half baths; a house with its own dressing room; an ample, angled backyard; a small, dim kitchen; and a spacious but illegal in-law unit. A house that had only grown in value despite a dripping faucet, unbalanced stairs, and risky wiring. It was a lonely house too, with that faint odor of solitude. A house where one woman had lived by herself for the last twenty years, a house where no new furniture had been added in at least fifteen years.

I stared at the small bookcase in the corner of the room. It housed only one book: the bible. I remember my father had read from it a week before he died. He'd stood on our front steps, preaching to me and Danny. My father loved the neighborhood. He'd called it the Valley of Noah.

"Let me ask you a question, Little Fella," he'd said. "Where are you from?"

He would call me Little Fella in deference to the Big Fella, Michael Collins, the hero of the Irish revolution. My middle name was Michael, and my father had told me it was in honor of the great hero.

"America," I'd said. It was an early Sunday morning in November. Clear skies. Quiet street.

"Ah, yes. But where, pray tell, in America?"

"San Francisco," Danny said. He was only ten months my junior, blessed with thick, dark hair and darker blue eyes.

"You're Black Irish," my fair-haired father would tease him. "There's Spanish in you, lad; that's why you are so sensitive." And he was sensitive, bookish, kind. The kind of sensitivity that others admired. It wasn't a weakness. Even in our working-class neighborhood, populated with aggressive sons of alcoholics and other abusers, Danny was left alone.

That day, the two of us were sitting on the landing outside our front door at the top of our stairs.

"And where in San Francisco do we live?" my father had asked, standing a few steps below us. I shrugged my shoulders. Danny shook his head.

My father had often been mistaken for the actor Steve McQueen thanks to his honey-brown hair, sensitive blue eyes, and wiry frame. The worry lines that had streaked his forehead gave him a sage look, while his close-cropped hair suggested, falsely, a military background.

"Noah's Valley," he'd said, "you are from the Valley of Noah." He'd reached out and grabbed my face with his cold hands and nodded my head up and down. The odor of cigarettes overpowered me; he would inhale two packs each day.

"Noe Valley is the valley of Noah. That's the truth now." He rhymed "Noe" and "Valley," No-ee Vall-ee.

He'd stepped past us and walked into the house, reaching for the bible, even then, the only book in the small wooden bookcase hiding in the corner of our front living room.

"Here we are," my father had said. He stood in the doorway now, Danny and I sat obediently below him. "The St. Joseph's Bible. St. Joseph. A carpenter, a laborer, a craftsman. The patron saint of workers. A great man. A fine father, or step-father, I suppose.

"In this bible," my father began, "Noah is spelled Noe, N-O-E. That means we are blessed and that this neighborhood is blessed.

God will protect this land and all its inhabitants just as he protected Noah. Understand, lads?"

We nodded.

"You are from the Valley of Noah. Understand?" He leaned toward us, looking for a final affirmation of our faith. I nodded again, and said, "yes, sir," loudly and firmly. Danny didn't move.

"We are blessed, lads," he'd said after a long silence before looking out at the view.

A week later, he was dead. We were far from blessed.

"Can you imagine what will happen to him in there?" My mother's voice carried from the kitchen.

"In where?" I said, rejoining her.

"Prison. A handsome little Hispanic like him. That warm, olive skin. Those large, dark eyes."

"Would you stop? Please."

I took a seat at the kitchen table, resting my wounded left hand on my lap.

"He'll be popular in there, if you know what I mean."

I stared at her. The purple terry-cloth bathrobe and beige Ugg slippers; had she worn them all day? It was nearly 6 p.m.

"Do they all shower together?" she asked.

"What?"

"In prison, do they all shower together, or do they have private stalls? I mean, I'd imagine if they're all together it would be . . ."

"I don't want to talk about this," I said.

"Tell it to your psychiatrist!"

In my Psych 101 class in college, they'd talked about Erik Erikson's social development stages. Basically, there were two paths for an infant: one where they'd received love and nurturing from birth onward and therefore see the world as safe and secure, and the other—I'm paraphrasing—where they were raised by my mother.

I used the back of my right hand to brush away the sweat loitering at my hairline. The kitchen was running a slight fever. Father Ryan and her both set their heaters well into the '80s. I heard it rattling and exhaling in the corner.

"I just met with Father Ryan," I said, changing the subject.

"Father Ryan? Why him? They say he has dementia."

"Alzheimer's."

"What's the difference?"

"I have no idea."

She lifted her chin and her eyes swept the room. They settled on my face and the slight tilt of her neck and the sudden blankness in her eyes gave me an unsettling feeling.

"PG wanted me to meet him; ask him to say a prayer."

"Well, he was always very good to you and Danny. I'll give him that."

I didn't respond.

"Oh, I should call Danny and let him know. He always liked both of you very much. I'll call Danny tonight to tell him."

It was an odd defense mechanism my mother used to help her cope with my brother's passing: she did not acknowledge his passing. She had created a world in which Danny was not dead, but living in Canada, only a phone call away. He didn't come to visit because he was busy with his job. He was a good boy. This line of reasoning started two days after his funeral.

I had not confronted her about it. I wasn't sure I ever would. When you got right down to it, who could blame her?

"Are you seeing anyone?" she asked.

"No. I'm not ready for that."

"What about sex?"

"What?"

"Are you having sex? It's important, you know."

"What is wrong with you?"

"I just want to make sure my little boy is doing okay."

"I'm fine, thanks for the concern."

"Is *your* little boy working?" she asked.

"My what?"

"You know, your willie. Is it working? Stress and age can do awful things."

"I'm not having this conversation."

"Oh, please, I'm your mother."

"Exactly."

"Tell it to your psychiatrist!"

I ran my hands through my hair and brought them back to rub my face. I coughed loudly to clear a touch of mucus from the back of my throat. Father Ryan bringing up my own father had touched a nerve. As my mother questioned me, I wanted to ask her what really happened and why we never talked about my father. There was more to the story; I knew there was. But I knew that any inquiry would end abruptly with: *Tell it to your psychiatrist!*

"I just want you to know they have this little blue pill now. Mr. Banks has a whole supply of them if you need some. It's done wonders for him; I can attest to that."

"Who is Mr. Banks?"

"A nice gentleman who works down at Walgreens."

I shook my head.

"Well, I'm not a nun, for heaven's sake."

I took a deep breath. I could feel my anxiety rising.

"God, help me," I said to no one.

She crossed her eyes and glared at me.

"Tell it to your psychiatrist!"

CHAPTER TEN

I LEFT MY MOTHER AND HEADED DOWNSTAIRS. My buzz was wearing off and my pinky was throbbing. I thought of the bottle under the sink.

My phone vibrated. A text from Madeline Mina:

MM: *Where r u? R u coming?*

In all the commotion of PG, I forgot about Madeline's party. A few days ago, I'd told her that I would attend. Now, it was the last place that I wanted to be.

SS: *Tired*

MM: *Oh please. Get your ass down here.*

U can't leave me alone with these people.

Madeline Mina was a San Francisco socialite extraordinaire. She was pretentious and overbearing and for some reason, I really liked her. She insisted that I attend her parties even after I had lost my elevated social status as a *Chronicle* columnist. We had an odd connection, one strengthened soon after Danny's death. She was there for me in ways I never knew I would need. Funny how the people you least expected sometimes showed up in the biggest ways. I owed her.

SS: *All right, all right. I'll be there in 30.*

Fortunately, one of the two suits I owned was laundered and hanging in the closet. I took a quick shower, found an olive green tie, laced up my Oxfords, and headed out the door.

Twenty minutes later, I pulled into the valet at the Fairmont at the top of Nob Hill. The attendant found my truck compelling like a small-town tourist might find a downtown homeless person. I was pretty sure it would not be part of the display parking in front of the hotel next to the Porsche and Tesla.

My buzz was completely gone now; I knew my first stop would be the bar.

I made my way to the Gold Ball Room, which had all the subtlety that the name implied. The party was a fundraiser for a local nonprofit that helped get homeless youth off the streets for good. A noble cause supported by noble people who had no idea what it meant to be homeless.

I checked in, patted a name tag across my sport coat, and made a beeline for the bar. Bourbon rocks.

I loathed these shindigs at first. Affluent, haughty socialites nattering and gossiping and swilling their trendy cocktails. I still loathed them, I suppose. But Madeline always made them fun. It might have been her mean girls' critique of her guests or her valuable ability to know everything about everyone or, most likely, the endless supply of free booze.

The Gold Ballroom had gold detail along each wall and on the ceiling. Large windows brought in the dimming evening light, and elaborate chandeliers hung every ten feet added a warm glow to the room's golden hue. This was only a cocktail party, so no over-the-top dinner tables with seven different glasses and ten pieces of silverware per person. Next time.

After a few calming sips, I circled the room. The crowd was the usual players that made Madeline's parties an odd mix of San Francisco elite: politicos, old-money titans, tech-trenders, local celebs, big bankers, and at least three billionaires. At last count, San Francisco had seventy-seven billionaires. Seventy-seven out of a city of 870,000. Only New York (113 out of 8.4 million people) and Hong Kong (ninety-six out of 7.5 million people) had more. So, it was surprisingly easy for me to rub elbows with people I had no business rubbing elbows with.

"Seamus, my dear, you have arrived!" Madeline was a good fifteen feet away from me when she started talking. She glided toward me and offered a dainty hug.

"I have arrived. Nice dress."

"This old thing?" She twirled, displaying a thin frame hugged by a sequin dress that glistened in the light. She had been a model in her younger years. Married well. Divorced better. She kept the beauty of her youth with little need for Botox or surgery or whatever procedures other socialites used to revive their appearance.

"I thought you were going to abandon me," she said, hooking her arm with mine.

"Never."

She led me to a side table.

"This is a dreadful party. The guests are even worse," she said.

"Why do you throw these parties when you don't like people?"

"I like you."

"You like the idea of me."

"Maybe."

An elderly woman in pearls and a cheetah print handbag approached. She knew I was someone but seemed unsure who that someone was. Madeline recognized her dilemma.

"Milly, have you met Seamus Shea?"

Milly?

"Why yes, of course, Seamus Shea. I absolutely loved your column. I felt like it brought me close to so many people in the city. It was wonderfully written. Why did you stop?"

There was no bar in the office.

"I needed a new hobby."

"Of course, of course. I'll be anxiously anticipating your next adventure."

She wandered off in search of more important people to bother.

"Milly Weiss," Madeline said. "She's as old school as they get. Her father's father's father was building this city pre-Gold Rush."

"Is she single?"

Madeline laughed, her authentic laugh—not the cocktail party one. It might have been her only authentic laugh tonight.

"What happened to your finger?" she asked. "Is that duck tape?"

"I jammed it in a cabinet door. And yes, it's duct tape."

She let my correction pass.

"Are you doing okay? You seem edgy."

I exhaled.

"You heard about the student being killed? Stabbed by a teacher at Jefferson High School?"

"Yes. It sounded dreadful."

"The teacher is my friend, Pedro Gomez."

"Oh, Seamus, I'm so sorry."

"Known him since the sixth grade. Best friends ever since. I visited him today. He was found at the scene holding the murder weapon. And he confessed."

"Oh my God, Seamus. I had no idea. I wouldn't have asked you to come if I knew . . ."

"I needed a drink," I said.

"Well, you leave whenever you need to. I won't be insulted."

"Thanks. I might be a two-drink minimum tonight. I have some work to do."

"Anyone you want to meet and talk to? I think the chief is here. I know the mayor will be if she isn't already."

"Not sure what I'd ask them. He confessed. I imagine they want it to go away as soon as possible."

"Oh, Seamus. You have not had a good run."

"I found out today Kratos might be involved. Do you know him?"

"Everyone knows Kratos," she said.

"He might be mixed up in the murder."

"Oh, Seamus, baby, run away. You do not want to have anything to do with him."

"I almost wrote a story about him a few months ago."

"Well, be glad you didn't. He is dangerous with a capital 'D.' Stay away."

"Seamus, is that you?" I turned to see the editor-in-chief of the *San Francisco Chronicle*. I last saw him four weeks ago when he fired me.

"Mr. Cronin, good to see you. You know Madeline?" I asked.

"Of course, the world knows Madeline." He was a beefy man with long gray hair and tortoiseshell glasses. His shape led me to believe he was a frequent guest at these parties. I had only met him a few times before the firing. He didn't get too involved in the day-to-day operations. My firing aside, I had no reason to like or dislike him.

"Well, I just wanted to say hello. I hope you are doing okay."

He looked at my bourbon rocks.

"Thanks, Mr. Cronin. I am. I am."

"Okay, then. Always a pleasure. Madeline, lovely party as always."

"Thank you, Dennis. Make sure you try the stuffed peppers."

He nodded and moved on. Madeline glanced at me but said nothing. This town was too damn small.

"So, you'll survive if I get out of here soon?" I asked.

"I will. There's a certain waiter I have my eye on: Henry. Isn't that a manly name? Heeennnrrryyy. He'll keep me busy."

"Have you given up on women?"

"Women are complicated, men are not. Right now, I want the uncomplicated version."

A thin, impeccably dressed man with a tan face and bright eyes approached.

"Madeline, wonderful party as always. But I'm afraid I must leave a little premature. Duty calls."

"Oh, that's a shame. But I know you are a busy bee."

"Yes, always buzzing."

"Do you know Seamus Shea?" Madeline asked.

"Yes, we know each other. Mr. Shea did a splendid column on a charity I am quite fond of. We talked briefly for the story."

He offered his hand.

"We did. You were quite gracious." I shook his hand. Richard Cory was a successful lawyer, prominent in the philanthropic world. He was rich, but I never understood how he made his money.

"You both take care," he said, before leaving us.

Madeline watched him walk away.

"I think *he's* single," she said. "Finding straight men with style in this town is nearly impossible."

I cleared my throat and she turned back toward me.

"Oh, yes. And did you drive your *pickup truck* here?" she asked, looking down her nose.

I took a long drink and looked away.

"I need to make the rounds. Join me?" Madeline asked.

I held up my now-empty highball glass and rattled the remaining ice cubes.

"Duty calls," I said.

Madeline glided around the room, her presence appreciated and admired equally by billionaires and busboys. I made my way back to the bar.

"Bourbon rocks, please," I said to the bartender.

"They still let you in these shindigs?"

I turned to see a hirsute, haughty face: Detective Rhodes.

"I'm very popular."

"I'll bet you are."

"I'm surprised to see one of SF's finest at such an affair."

"My wife. She's on the board of the nonprofit. She's the do-gooder in the family."

"At least there's one of you," I said.

He frowned and ordered a drink.

"Look, Shea," he began. "I get Gomez is your friend. I'm sorry about that. This must be tough for you. I've seen this quite a bit. People snap. It happens. It's terrible."

"You still think he was in love with Monique?"

He laughed.

"No. We know he's gay. But did you know he had been disciplined for how he treated one of his players?"

"What?"

"A month ago, he lost it on a player in practice. Verbal abuse. Threw a ball at her. She ran home crying. The parents, the principal, and Pedro Gomez had a long meeting. Unlike him, they thought. Out of character, they said. It happens, Seamus. It happens more than you think."

He took his drink and nodded to me.

"He's an old-school coach."

"The video makes it look like he's a madman."

"Video?"

"I'm sorry," he said, as he walked away.

This time, I was the one with the long division face.

SATURDAY

CHAPTER ELEVEN

I WOKE UP HUNGOVER, again, and my pinky was killing me.

I checked my mouth for a dirty sock, but no such luck. I still had my suit on from the night before: tie, shoes, and all. I tried to remember what happened, and as I rose, the empty whiskey bottle on my nightstand jogged my memory. I had gone to Madeline's party, had had two cocktails, and had come home to finish off the bottle of Jameson hidden under my sink. No wonder my head felt like asphalt to a jackhammer.

I trudged to the bathroom. The mirror showed an unholy sight: eyes blood red, skin dry and pale, beginnings of a bulbous nose, a swollen face. Slowly my fogged brain remembered that PG was in jail, and I was likely his only hope. *Christ.*

PG never told me about getting in trouble with a player. He wasn't an old-school coach and not much of a yeller. But he did lose his cool at times in practice and games. I could see a new player, not used to his style, getting upset. Or was I just rationalizing away another fact that pointed to his guilt?

I showered, shaved, and brushed my teeth, including my tongue. In the kitchen, I mixed and downed a cocktail of apple cider vinegar, green tea, and cod liver oil. I'm a bit of an expert at shaking off hangovers. Years of experience.

I found my old reporter's notebook in a shoebox in my bedroom closet. The notebook had an ominous blood-red cover, a spiral top, and notes from my last columns. I flipped through it, recalling those stories. The last few were never written.

Outside, I picked up my copy of the *Chronicle* resting on my stoop. Even after being fired they still sent me a copy. The headline of the Jackie James's byline read:

"DECORATED TEACHER, COACH ACCUSED OF KILLING STUDENT"

Man bites dog. There was a picture of PG looking clean-cut and scholarly next to an image of Monique. She was a beautiful girl. Large, intelligent eyes; soft smile; confident expression. There wasn't much in the article that I didn't already know. Rhodes had a quote decrying the tragedy but saying that they believed there was no further threat to the community. They had their man.

I stepped into my truck and sat there, unsure what to try and tackle first. I could talk to one of Danny's old narcotics partners about Kratos. I could drop in at PG's apartment and look for clues. I could try to track down Kratos and confront him. I decided to start at the scene of the crime.

It took me just over fifteen minutes to get to Jefferson High School. I parked in front of a mom-and-pop store across from the school's main entrance. I had a craving for a blue Gatorade, which I thought might further help my lingering hangover. The store had one aisle stacked with dry goods down the center and coolers and freezers forming a U around it. I wandered to the far-right corner past the beer display before I found my favorite ice-blue drink.

The cashier, an older Asian man with oversized Eurostile glasses, stood with arms crossed, staring at a small TV mounted above the entrance. His cash register had two bounced checks taped prominently on its front: a Mr. Henry and Ms. Fall would likely not be returning customers. The TV aired the local news, which was recapping the sad story of Monique Profit.

"She went to school across the street," he said, keeping his eyes glued to the TV.

I nodded, but he didn't notice.

"Did you know her, Monique?"

He turned to look at me and pursed his lips. He seemed to be assessing my worthiness of knowing such a fact. His face lit up.

"Hey, you're that reporter, right? 'City Views.' You here to interview me?"

"Yes, I am," I said, quickly. You never knew who might help. "What can you tell me about her?"

"She used to come in here and get things for her Mamá on her way home. Sweet girl."

"I heard she was an honor student."

"Oh, yeah. Smart as all get-out. I remember one time she bought a few items: milk, bread, ice cream, Pepsi. I totaled it all up and told her the price. She said no without blinking, 'that's not right Mr. Poon.'"

I smiled.

"Smart as a whip. She says it's actually this much. So, I did the count again, real slow, and sure enough she had it right down to the penny."

He uncrossed his arms and rested his hands on the counter.

"It's a damn shame for a girl like that to go so young."

I opened the Gatorade and took a long drink. I wiped my lips with the back of my hand making a blue streak.

"But you know, I hear things," he continued.

"Things?"

"Well, rumors going round."

"What kind of rumors?"

"Before this happened. People asking about her. I heard a lot of different things, but she was the topic of conversation for a few weeks there."

I fiddled with the lid of the Gatorade bottle.

"How do you mean?"

"There was some lady that blew through the neighborhood two weeks back. Said she was Monique's mentor. Most people didn't pay it no mind, but some, like me, found it curious. I hear teachers talk; students talk. And so, people started speculating."

"Like?"

"Maybe Monique's someone important or knows someone important."

"Did she?"

"I don't know. But that's what I mean, just silly rumors trying to figure out why some well-dressed White woman comes to our neighborhood to help this Black girl."

"Did you talk to her?"

"No. I saw her come in the store once and buy some gum. But she didn't want to talk to me. I was fine with that. Less I say, the better."

Right.

"What did she look like?"

"Small. Half-White, half-Caucasian."

I smiled.

"She had blonde hair, blue eyes. Small body but looked pretty fit. Like one of those long-distance runners. She was tan, too. White people with tans stand out around here. And she wore a suit. Nice one. Expensive."

"Did she speak? Did you hear her voice?"

"Uh-huh." He smirked. "Might have said thank you, but I don't remember much about her voice. She was pretty, though. I remember thinking she was quite pretty."

The old man took a rag out and wiped the area in front of him. I guess lust didn't fade with age.

"What about the teacher?" I asked.

He turned the rag over and shrugged his shoulders.

"I think it was him, if you want to know."

"Why do you say that?"

"I see these kids every day. There are some that are good kids, but there are a lot that aren't. Tough job, teacher. Stressful. Maybe he had enough and took it out on Monique."

I tried to imagine what that meant, but let it go.

"We talked a couple of times," he said. "My grandson's been getting in trouble and we talked about it and he gave me some good advice."

PG had a knack for getting people to open up to him. I'd seen it at gas stations, supermarket checkout lines, dive bars. After just a few words of small talk and maybe one innocent question, PG would learn about absent fathers, derailed dreams, alcoholic mothers, cancer, missing cousins, suicides, and all the other deep secrets that haunted psyches. He would have made one hell of a priest. Maybe that was why he and Father Ryan connected. It made me wonder if Monique shared some secret with PG. Some truth that ended up getting her killed and PG in jail. Some truth about Kratos?

"But you still think he did it?"

"Murderers can give good advice. Besides, I heard he confessed. That says a lot."

I finished the Gatorade and he reached out to take the empty bottle from me. He tossed it in a small garbage can behind him and it rattled around, the sharp sound of plastic on plastic.

"Will I be in the paper?" he asked.

"Maybe," I said.

"Come to think of it, how come I haven't seen your column in a while?"

Because I'm a raging alcoholic who can't hold down a job.

"Taking a little break."

He took off his glasses and wiped them on his shirt.

"Too bad," he said. "Some days, I liked that column."

Some days, I did too.

CHAPTER TWELVE

I CROSSED THE STREET AND HEADED TOWARD JEFFERSON HIGH SCHOOL'S FRONT ENTRANCE. I wasn't sure if anyone would be around on a Saturday, but I figured I could find my way in. The school's facade was hard and imposing with a high arch of some famous architectural design that I forgot about soon after my Art History 101 class in college. The front doors were locked. I gave a salute and leaned into the small window in the front door for signs of life. Nothing.

I swung around the side and found a small driveway that led to an unlocked maintenance door. I had been to the school a few times to see PG and had a rough sense of its layout. I knew PG's classroom was on the third floor, northwest corner. I was southeast as best as I could figure, and I found a small set of stairs that would hopefully take me to the third floor.

As I climbed the stairs, I looked out the second-floor window and I could see a security guard smoking near the gate to the football field. This might be easier than I thought.

"Can I help you?" The deep voice came from behind me at the bottom of the stairs. I turned to see a tall, broad-shouldered Samoan man holding a walkie-talkie. He had thick black braids that reached down past his chest. He wore a navy blue short-sleeved collared shirt and slacks. I could see a decorative neck tattoo creeping over his collar that I first thought was a necklace. Definitely passed the curb appeal test for security.

"Uh, yeah, thanks. I'm a little lost."

He lifted the walkie-talkie to his mouth and was about to speak before he pointed it at me and shook it.

"Wait, I know you. You're Mr. Gomez's friend, the writer for the newspaper."

"Got me." I put my hands up to surrender.

"You have to go. You can't be here. No one can."

"Look, I'm sorry. I'm just trying to figure out what happened. I know Mr. Gomez didn't do this." It sounded odd to hear PG called Mr. Gomez.

He tilted his head slightly and nodded.

"I know. I don't think he did it either. I watched him with students. I know it's not much, but you do get a sense of a person."

He walked up the stairs to meet me and we stood at the end of a cold second-floor hallway. Lime green lockers lined the walls on both sides, and there was a bone-white drinking fountain at the end of the hall with a nozzle for refilling water bottles. The hallways of Thomas Jefferson weren't that different from the hallways of the Hall of Justice.

"I'm trying to find out who did kill her," I said.

He held his arms out, palms up, and shrugged.

"That's the problem. I have no idea. I know just about everyone in this building and there are no killers here. Trust me."

"Were there any students that bothered her?" I asked.

"One that I know. Rolando. He had a thing for her, and she ignored him. He turned on her after that. Said some bad things, threatened her even. The principal had to get involved. I've seen him be violent, but killing someone?" He dropped his chin into his broad chest, his braids falling forward. "The cops talked to him, but they didn't pursue it."

"Can I get a drink?" I asked. I still felt dehydrated.

"Sure," he said.

I took a couple of steps and leaned down to get a drink from the fountain. The water was ice cold, and I wiped my mouth with my sleeve.

"I think it's got to be something with Monique, something outside the school," he said.

"Did you know her?"

He shook his head.

"I knew who she was, but our paths didn't cross much. She was an A-plus student. School leader. Those aren't the kids I tend to deal with."

"Who found her?"

"James, our janitor. Walked in and saw Mr. Gomez with a knife, standing over her body."

"He was cleaning the room?"

"No, he goes in each morning to say hi to Mr. Gomez. They talk about sports, politics."

"He goes in each morning?"

"Pretty much."

"Same time?"

"Yep. 7:45 a.m. Classes start at 8:15 a.m. They only talk for a few minutes, but I think they both look forward to it. I would join them sometimes."

"And what did PG, I mean Mr. Gomez, do when James saw him?"

"Look, you gotta get going, I'll get in trouble."

"I understand, but I'm just curious what he did."

The security guard closed his eyes and seemed to count to five. He opened them, and I noticed they were a unique shade of brown.

"He dropped the knife and went and sat at his desk and put his head in his hands. Said, 'she's gone.'"

"She's gone?"

"Yep."

I let the image sink in and felt my stomach turn.

"Time to go now, okay?" he said.

"Just one more thing. I was hoping to just see his classroom. To take a quick look and see if anything catches my eye."

I bit my lower lip and joined my hands in prayer to add to my verbal plea.

"I'm Seamus, by the way."

He looked over his shoulder down the hall and then over my shoulder. He let out a deep sigh.

"I know who you are. How come I haven't seen your column in a while?" He asked.

Because I like whiskey, and it makes me hungover and cranky, and I told my boss to fuck off one too many times.

"The Internet."

We shook hands.

"I'm Mika," he said, "And only because you are Mr. Gomez's friend."

"Thank you."

He walked past me and up the stairs to the third floor. He explained the plan as I followed.

"I'll let you in the class, and I'll be off on my rounds. There is another security guard around who went on some smoking break. The guy's useless but takes his job very seriously. I think he was a mall cop before this. The district sent him over because they thought I'd need extra help."

We turned a corner to the right, and I recognized PG's hallway. It had their school mascot, a golden lion, mid-jump, painted on the far end above the stairwell. There were more lime green lockers on the left and classroom doors on the right. Each door had an image of the teacher and pennants from the colleges they attended. Ms. Sierra, UC Davis and SF State. Mr. Dowd, UCSB and USF. Ms. Walsh, Loyola Marymount and USF. I stopped in front of Ms. Walsh's door. Daniella Walsh, the woman I had met outside the Hall of Justice, the woman concerned with PG's plight, was a petite, pretty blonde with blue eyes and tan skin. This Ms. Walsh was heavyset with dark hair and thick glasses.

"Mika, is this Daniella Walsh's room?"

He stopped and walked back toward me.

"Yep, Ms. Walsh. Daniella. Nice lady."

"Is this how she looks now?" I pointed at the picture.

"Pretty much. She might have put on a few more pounds if I'm being honest. She's always struggled with her weight."

I nodded and continued to stare at the picture. The Daniella Walsh I'd met was petite and blonde and tan. Petite, tan, blonde. The mentor the corner store guy mentioned.

Mika took a few steps and stopped at the next classroom numbered 301. A bright-red Stanford pennant was pinned atop the cork board to the left of the door, and below the pennant I could see PG's picture. He wore a Jefferson High sweatshirt and was holding a copy of *Hamlet* up so that only his large eyes and forehead were visible. Even with the book blocking his mouth, I could tell he had a big smile.

"No crime scene tape?" I asked.

Mika shrugged.

"They had a full crew in here yesterday. All afternoon and all night. Did all the tests and forensic stuff. Cleaned it all up, I guess."

I noticed a camera in the corner above the hallway.

"Did the camera pick up anything?"

"No. It broke a week ago," he said, pointing at the one I noticed. "We never got around to fixing it. There was another one in the stairwell that also broke last week as well."

"Does this stairwell lead to the street?" I asked.

"Yeah. You go straight down, and you're on the back side of the school. There's an exit right at the bottom."

"So, someone could have come up and down this stairwell without the cameras picking them up?"

He thought for a moment. "Probably," he finally said. "It's a straight shot, come to think of it. Not as many people use this back stairwell, and most kids wouldn't have been in the school that early."

I took out my reporter's notebook and jotted down a few notes:

1. *Hallway cameras broke last week.*
2. *Who was the Daniella Walsh at HOJ?*

3. *Who was the mentor mentioned at the corner store?*

4. *Track down James the janitor.*

5. *Back stairwell straight to street.*

Mika unlocked the door and held it open for me to walk in.

"You are on your own now. Get out as quick as you can. Not sure when the mall cop is coming back."

I smiled and patted his shoulder as I walked past.

"Thanks again, Mika."

He offered a faint wave and headed down the stairs.

PG's classroom felt crowded. His desk was off to the right, a small gray metallic job with three drawers on each side. It was empty except for a stack of papers in a small bin and a copy of *Hamlet*. PG had always been a neat freak. The room had eight tables with four blue chairs at each table. Not much room to wander in between them. It was a bright room, with a wall of windows straight ahead that let in the late-morning light and offered an expansive view of the neighborhood. Movie posters including *Romeo + Juliet* (DiCaprio version), *The Lord of the Rings*, and *The Hunger Games* decorated the top of the wall opposite the windows. And the front and back walls were covered with large white boards scribbled with notes in PG's less-than-stellar handwriting. Despite the claustrophobic feel, it seemed like a nice place to learn.

As I reached PG's desk and faced the class, I noticed a wide blood stain in the far-right corner. Why there? I looked back at the door. It would have been a blind spot to the small window in the entrance door. The window was a foot by half a foot in the top half of the door. You could only see a small sliver of the class from the hallway, and that's only if you pressed up against it. Anyone walking by would likely not have seen anything. They should have heard a scream, though. Why didn't she scream?

I walked around the classroom, squeezing between the desks, and tried to recreate the crime. There were papers on a desk in the middle of the room: brainstorms and drafts of college essays. PG and Monique were working on the essays, but how did she end up in the corner? Was someone else with them at the table? It seemed like three spots with the papers, but it wasn't clear. If she was killed in the corner, it was a blind spot; no one outside the room would see it. If it was done quick enough, there wouldn't have been a scream. Brandish the knife, force her to the corner, tell her to be quiet, then attack. But if PG was there, it was two on one, and a knife wouldn't do it. He had to have been out of the classroom. They must have known the killer. Rolando? Holden? They're working on the application, PG takes a bathroom break, and the killer strikes. PG returns, finds the killer, Monique was already down, the killer threatens him, and PG complies. Killer flees. Janitor comes in after that, and off they go. But that was a lot to happen with no one seeing or hearing anything. Why didn't the janitor see the killer leave? Why didn't anyone see the killer enter the building?

What if there was no killer? Just PG.

I shook my head to chase the thought out of my mind. On a basic level, if PG was going to kill her and confess, why not just do it at the table? Why take her to the corner? No, someone else had been in the room and acted while PG was out. They had cornered Monique, attacked her quickly, and left just as quickly. But not before threatening PG.

As I circled the room again, a figure walked by outside. I snuck up under the small window and looked sideways down the hall. The smoking guard stood a few feet away. Trapped. I was no lawyer, but visiting a crime scene must have been illegal, and if Detective Rhodes found out, it would be an easy reason for him to lock me up. My mind thought of options: hide until he left, hope Mika would come back and distract him, make a run for it and hope he was slow.

I was out of shape, but I was a runner once, the Holy Ghost, and I was pretty sure I could outrun the mall cop. I had just seen him smoking.

I looked sideways out the window again. He stood down the hall under the painting of the school's mascot. No cameras. Just me and him. I had to make a run for it.

I put my hand on the cool metal door handle. I gave each of my legs a brief shake to warm up. The Holy Ghost would ride again. Two deep breaths and I rocked on my heels, opened the door, and bolted to the left.

"Hey, stop there," the guard yelled.

I took a quick left turn leaning as if I was on the track. I hit my stride and felt loose and free. I blew through the stairwell and had to slow some to keep my balance.

"Stop," he yelled above me. I listened for "or I'll shoot," but it never came.

I ran through the side door and took a hard right away from my truck. I wouldn't have enough time to get in and drive off. I barreled down the sidewalk. I knew that St. Anthony's Church was two blocks up. We played hoops there in grammar school. If I could get some distance between me and the mall cop, I could make it to the church and hide inside. Catholic churches were never closed.

I looked back to see the outline of the guard at least a half block behind me displaying crappy running form. I tore through the intersection, inviting a horn from an irate BMW driver. I didn't break stride; chin up, knees high, the Holy Ghost: so fast you couldn't see him.

When I was directly across from the church, I stopped running, gulped in some air, and jaywalked briskly across the street. I skipped up the pale white steps and pulled open a side door. Out of habit, I dipped my fingers in the Holy Water and blessed myself. I went through another door and stood in the back of the church, getting a lay of the land. A few blue hairs knelt off to the left, lighting candles at the base of a large St. Anthony's station, praying for their lost items to appear. They turned to look at me but then returned to their prayers. The right side of the church seemed bare. I walked to that side and sat in a row blocked by a large pillar. I dropped to my knees, bowed my head, and prayed.

I heard a door in the back squeak open. I kept my head down and I prayed that the mall cop would not find me. I heard some footsteps up the center aisle. My heart was pounding. I could see a faint image out of the corner of my eye. I was still blocked by the pillar. I kept praying. Eventually, I heard the back door open again and bang close. I counted to sixty and slowly slid to my right and looked behind me past the pillar. No one.

I sat back in the pew and took a deep breath. My heart was still racing. Man, I was out of shape. Just as I was feeling some peace, my phone buzzed.

"Hello?" I whispered.

"Seamus? Seamus, it's Jackie. Can you talk?"

"Sort of."

"Why are you whispering?"

"I'm in church."

There was a long pause.

"I didn't know you were that religious? It's Saturday."

"Long story. What's up?"

"I thought we could meet for dinner tonight."

I knew this was far from a social call. I trained her well. She would pepper me for info on PG. I didn't mind being peppered. And I would do some peppering of my own.

"How about Park Chalet at 6 p.m.?"

"Done," she said.

I put my phone away and stood up.

St. Anthony's was a beautiful church: regal carpet, stained pews, hand-carved wood etchings of the Stations of the Cross hanging along the side wall, the stained-glass windows offering faint light. A near life-size cross hung behind the altar with an impaled five-foot-tall Jesus. It hovered over the altar—a foreboding presence, an ominous sight.

I dropped to my knees again and joined my hands. I said another prayer for Danny and for my father, my mother, and PG. I had not been in any church since Danny's funeral. Now, thanks to a police chase, I was on my knees praying. Maybe God was trying to tell me something. Maybe He had a message.

Let me guess: Don't fuck it up.

CHAPTER THIRTEEN

I LEFT THE CHURCH AND WALKED BACK TO MY TRUCK. No security guard in sight.

I put thoughts of praying and running from the cops in a box in the back of my mind and returned my focus to PG. My next stop would be his apartment. I didn't know what I was looking for. Nothing made any sense. But I had made a promise to Mamá. I couldn't let her down.

I took side streets to PG's apartment, an in-law unit like mine but in the Castro. The unit was part of a house owned by Martin Cohen, a retired executive who lost his partner to AIDS in the early '90s and had lived a solitary life since. His house was a classic Victorian, with large bay windows, ornate columns, and period details at every turn. I knocked on the front door before noticing a small doorbell to the right. I waited another beat and pushed the button.

"Yes?" he asked, not recognizing me, despite having met me a hundred times in the decade since PG moved in.

"Mr. Cohen, I'm Seamus Shea. Pedro's friend?"

He squinted his eyes some, and his face brightened.

"Seamus, of course. How good to see you."

Mr. Cohen barely reached my chest. I looked down at the top of his tan, hairless head toward his heart-shaped face. His hazel eyes and neatly trimmed mustache stood out on an otherwise plain visage. Despite his diminutive size, he had the look and the energy of a man in his mid-fifties, even though he had to be in his mid-seventies. He offered me a broad smile and the whiteness of his teeth stood in sharp contrast to his brown skin.

"I'm so sorry about Pedro. I just can't believe it. I just can't."

"I can't either. I think he's been set up. I was hoping I could take a look in his apartment, maybe see if anything can help?"

He looked up at me and down at the floor. He seemed to be considering the idea.

"Well, I don't see why not. Come in, please."

Mr. Cohen bought the house in the early 1980s and lived above Pedro's in-law apartment. He retired from PG&E a good twenty years ago, just after his partner, Paul Hawthorne, died in the San Francisco General AIDS Ward. Mr. Cohen never had the disease, and he had lived alone here ever since.

He wore khakis, a long-sleeve blue polo shirt, and flip-flops. I followed him through the house, which smelled like boiled vegetables and fabric softener. A pot sat steaming on the stove, which explained the vegetable odor, but I didn't see any laundry nearby. His house was otherwise clean and tastefully decorated.

He led me out his back door into the fresh air. A small dog rushed me and barked with what felt like a personal animosity.

"Oh, that's just Mister Mister. Ignore him. He thinks he's a watchdog, but the worst he'd do is lick you to death."

I reached out to let Mister Mister sniff my hand, but he recoiled and kept barking.

We took the back stairs down a floor and then swung around to the side entrance. Mr. Cohen flipped through the twenty or so keys he had on a large silver loop key chain until he identified the right one. He opened the door slowly, and we tiptoed into the living room; both of us seemed scared of what we might find.

"The police were here yesterday. I was in shock," he said.

"Did they take anything?"

"I think I saw them take a computer, and they had a couple of other bags."

"When was the last time you saw Pedro?"

"Oh, a few days ago. He looked fine. As sweet as ever."

Mister Mister sniffed at my pant leg. Mr. Cohen stooped down and picked him up. The dog groaned, hoping to inspire a petting. Mr. Cohen carried him to the front window, which looked out on the street. He held Mister Mister like a football in his left hand. The drapes were closed, keeping the room cool and dark. He used his right hand to part the drapes and let in a sliver of light. He looked up and down the street. I imagined Mr. Cohen knew quite a bit about the neighbors.

"Well, I will leave you. Just close the door on your way out. It will lock automatically."

"Thank you, Mr. Cohen." I extended my hand and we shook. I gave Mister Mister a soft tap on the head and he growled. Mr. Cohen tightened his lips, nodded, and walked toward the door.

"Take care, Seamus," he said, his voice trailing, followed by the loud thud of the front door closing.

PG lived simply. I entered into a small living room area with a bay window that looked out onto the street to the left. A galley kitchen with a Formica table and dining area took up space on the right. Past the living room, straight ahead, was a small hallway that led to a sizable bedroom with an en suite bathroom.

I didn't see much out of the ordinary, but I also didn't know what I was looking for. In the kitchen, two plates and a mug soaked in the sink. The fridge looked bare except for a carton of eggs, standard condiments, a quart of milk, and two cartons of Chinese takeout. More takeout cartons filled up the trash, giving off a funky odor. I leafed through some mail on the kitchen table. Nothing of note.

As I looked, I thought I heard something. A short series of deep thuds, like plastic rattling on tile. I walked slowly from the kitchen to the living room, then to the back bedroom. I tiptoed around and listened intently but heard nothing. Mr. Cohen shuffled above me, and I realized he must have dropped something.

I continued my search. The living room was dark with the drawn curtains; I flicked on the overhead light and brightened it enough. A few magazines were fanned out on a small coffee table and PG's one large bookcase was overstuffed with books. I glanced at the selection: a typical eclectic mix of literary fiction, detective novels, history tomes, and teaching books.

I felt uneasy rifling through PG's life. First, his classroom, now his apartment. We were close, and I knew he wouldn't care, but it still felt intrusive.

In his bedroom, I scanned some bills and other papers resting on a small desk next to his bed. I picked up a worn copy of *Hamlet* that looked identical to the copy he had on his desk at school. *Nothing is good or bad but thinking makes it so.*

I fanned through the pages until a handwritten note fell out.

Mr. Gomez,

I wanted to thank you again for listening to me today. I took your advice and I talked to him. I think it's all going to work out. And thank you for all your help on my applications. I can't believe we are almost done!

I am so lucky to have a teacher like you!

Monique

I took your advice. Talked to him? Him?

Voices grew outside, and I could hear footsteps on the back stairs.

"Yes, of course, officers. I'd be happy to show you his apartment. Let me just see what key it is . . ." Mr. Cohen said, loudly.

"Today, all right?" I heard Rhodes' taut voice. They were watching the house. They knew I was here. I had to get out.

"Oh, which one is it?" Mr. Cohen said, fumbling with his keys to buy me time.

I stuffed the note in my pocket and rushed to the bathroom. I knew there was a window over the tub that even my plump frame could squeeze through. It led to the backyard, and from there, I could hop a few fences without seeing any police.

"Okay, I'm getting it now," Mr. Cohen yelled. I heard the door creak open. I closed the bathroom door and pushed the lock.

As I did, I noticed a plastic trash can on its side below me. I heard a noise, a rustling of the shower curtain. I turned and felt the cool plastic of a large bottle of Head & Shoulders smack my cheek. I fell back over the toilet, and the shower curtain and rod were dropped over me. I looked up to see a slender figure shimmying out the window.

"Open up!" Rhodes yelled, banging on the bathroom door.

The locked door gave me just enough time to shake off the curtain, get to my feet, and fall out of the window to the backyard. My attacker jumped a neighbor's fence. I followed and hopped it Western-roll style. I scurried down the side path of the house out to the street. I scanned up and down and saw him running toward Castro Street. I ran up 18th Street doing my best to dodge the window shoppers and Castro Street revelers.

He took a hard right onto Castro Street, running through the crosswalk against the light and dodging a UPS van that nearly took him out. I paused to let a couple cars pass before crossing. I lost track of him for a moment. He cut across the street, dodging more cars. I followed.

He disappeared down a wide set of stairs into the Castro Muni Station. If he caught a train before I reached him, he'd be downtown or out at the zoo in minutes. The stairs rushed me, and I stumbled some as I tried to control my speed. I felt my knee twinge.

In the station, I held out my left hand and managed another Western roll over the turnstiles. My pinky flared. A heavyset woman in the attached booth yelled at me through the PA system, but I kept going. I paused by the railing, scanning the inbound and outbound platforms crowded with midday shoppers, tourists, and the unemployed. On the inbound side, I saw him sitting on a bench, hiding behind a small group of Japanese tourists. Squinting, I realized that he was a she. Before I hit the stairs, she stood up and jumped off the platform and into the train tracks. The tourists screamed when they saw her jump. She was already in the tunnel heading downtown when I leapt off the platform and followed. More screams. I felt another twinge in my knee when I landed.

As I entered the tunnel, I heard an announcement blaring through the station: "Downtown train, three minutes." I was breathing heavily and had to squint to make out my path in the darkness. I could see a faint figure moving about fifty feet in front of me. She kept a quick pace, but despite my huffing and puffing and tweaked knee, I knew I could catch her. The Holy Ghost riding again: knees up, chin high, arms pumping.

The rail below me vibrated and a rumbling, whooshing sound surrounded me. Before I knew it, a train heading outbound roared past me. Its momentum nearly knocked me off my feet. I thought about the dreaded third rail. The power of the train forced me to stop and brace myself so that I didn't end up electrocuted. Although, looking down, I had no idea which rail was the dangerous one. I decided to avoid them all.

I looked up at the windows flying past and noticed a few startled faces, as if they had seen a ghost. Not yet. I picked up the pace again as the tunnel bent to the left. I could see her up ahead, her small frame intermittently blocking certain lights that lined the tunnel.

I heard a faint rumble behind me. I remembered the "downtown train, three minutes" call and realized I had less than a minute before the next train would be on me. I had closed the gap and I'd probably be able to reach her right about the time the train barreled over both of us.

"Stop," I called out. "There's a train coming. We both don't need to die. I just want to talk to you."

She didn't stop. The tracks shook as a deep roar grew. I looked for a nook in the wall where I might get out of its path. Ten feet ahead, a neon green EXIT sign glowed over an emergency door. I kicked into another gear; the Holy Ghost: so fast you couldn't see him. I headed for the sign, knees high, chin up. But three strides in, my knee twinged again, and I tripped over the far rail that I had just promised not to touch. The good news was, I didn't get electrocuted; the bad news was, I fell on my stomach and my left foot caught on the outer rail.

I could hear the downtown train roaring through the tunnel. The bright lights of the L Taraval became visible. The rails shook and warmed. I could not hear anything over the roar. I caught the eye of the driver. I think he mouthed, "Oh, shit."

CHAPTER FOURTEEN

I KICKED MY LEFT LEG HIGH TO FREE IT FROM THE RAIL AND ROLLED TO MY RIGHT. I turned, leaving my back to the track and covered my head with my arms. I held my breath as the train powered by, the draft fanning me, bits of pebbles and dirt spraying me. I rolled a few feet more and hit my back against the tunnel wall. I could see the backside of the L growing smaller in the distance. I wondered if I was in shock and maybe the train took my legs. I reached down and felt them both. I looked up at the light above me, still shaking from the passing train. I looked again and realized the light was still; I was shaking. I took a deep breath and pulled myself up.

I walked the rest of the way through the tunnel, expecting to see my prey splattered across the tracks. But no such luck. I popped out into the brightness of the Church Street Station, about three-quarters of a mile from where I started. No prey, only two of San Francisco's finest standing on the platform. They did not look pleased.

A short, stocky female officer led me out of the Muni station in handcuffs. A crowd gathered at the exit, gawking at me and murmuring to each other about my crime. A homeless man leaning over a shopping cart full of crap gave me a toothless smile and a thumbs up. The officers stuffed me in the back seat of a patrol car. I bounced into the seat with my hands clasped behind me and stared ahead through the grate partition that separated me from my captors. My pinky was throbbing. The patrol car smelled like puke.

The female officer drove while her partner, a young male who looked like he should be at a frat party or on *The Bachelor*, took shotgun. We sped off down Market Street, and they even put the sirens on. I was impressed.

"Where are we going?" I asked.

"Shut up," the frat boy said.

"Did you get the other guy?"

"What part of shut up don't you understand?"

"The middle part."

"Smart ass, huh?"

"I have rights, you know?"

The driver offered a Bronx cheer.

"It smells like puke back here," I said.

"Our last customer. Sorry," he said.

"Were you ever on *The Bachelor*?" I asked the pretty one.

"Shut! Up!"

We took a hard left onto Castro Street and my face planted into the screen. Both chuckled. We took another left onto 18th. I realized where we were going and took a deep breath. They pulled into the driveway of PG's home where Detective Rhodes stood on the front steps.

"Seamus Shea," he said, as the driver pulled me from the car.

"Detective Rhodes, always a pleasure."

"Bring him inside," Rhodes said.

Above us Mr. Cohen peaked out his window. Mister Mister was unseen but barking loudly.

My captors kept the cuffs on and led me down the side of the house and into PG's apartment. They sat me at the small Formica kitchen table. Rhodes spun one of the chairs around backward and took a seat, his forearms resting on the top of the chair. He stroked his woolly mustache.

"What are you doing here, Shea?" Rhodes asked.

"Your friends brought me here."

"Before that. We saw you come in the house. We know you were in the apartment and scurried out the window."

I blinked at Rhodes.

"PG had borrowed some things from me. I wanted to get them back."

"What things?"

"Personal stuff."

"Your vibrator?"

The frat boy, a.k.a. *The Bachelor* contestant, enjoyed that one.

"Jesus, you're an angry man," I said.

Rhodes stood up and pushed the chair away.

"Why are you doing this, Shea?" he asked. "Look, I told you he's on record blowing up at a kid. And more stories like that are coming out. He was feared on the basketball court."

"He's a tough, old-school coach. It doesn't make him a killer."

"You seem so convinced. What are you up to?"

"Nothing."

"Bullshit. He's your best friend. You're trying to clear his name. What do you know?"

"I know nothing. I know *nothing*," I said in my best Sergeant Schultz impression.

Rhodes picked up the chair and tossed it at the refrigerator. It thudded against the fridge before sprawling on the floor.

"I'm sick of this shit, Shea. Tell me what you know or so help me God!"

I kept still and studied the thin green vein that ran atop his forehead. I enjoyed watching him lose it. I had issues with authority figures. Some, like priests and nuns, I put my blind faith in. Others, like Rhodes, I only had disdain for. The fact that my father was a cop likely played some role in the psychology of it all.

Tell it to your psychiatrist!

I knew I'd have to give Rhodes something if I didn't want to end up in jail for the next couple of days. I'd be little help to PG there. And if I could get Rhodes to consider that the case might not be closed; it could give PG a chance.

"Have you talked to Rolando?" I asked.

Rhodes raised one of his hairy eyebrows.

"Why should we?"

"He threatened her. He's violent."

"Okay. That's something. What else you got?"

"Look, there was someone else in the apartment when I was here. I chased her out the window into the street. Then down into the tunnel."

"We only saw you coming in here," Rhodes said.

"I don't know. Maybe she went in the way we went out. Pretty easy to sneak around the backyards there. But I'm not making it up. You think I'd run through the Muni tunnel for kicks?"

He smirked. I think he got my point.

"You said 'her'?"

"Yeah. There was a woman who approached me after I met with PG yesterday. She said she was a teacher from the school, but she wasn't. I also heard a woman with a similar description was at the school a couple of weeks ago. Said she was a mentor to Monique."

"Mentor?"

"Yeah, it's when an older person helps a younger person with their career path."

The vein on Rhodes' forehead doubled in size.

"Shea . . ."

"Sorry, I didn't think you knew."

"All right, why was she in his apartment?"

"I don't know. Maybe looking for more stuff to make sure he keeps quiet. So he doesn't take back his confession."

Rhodes stepped back and considered this.

"What did she look like?" he asked.

"Petite. Blonde. Like Swedish: tan and blonde and pretty."

"You think he's being threatened? That's why he confessed?"

"I do. Someone else wanted to get at Monique and PG got caught in the middle."

"Who would want to hurt her?"

I couldn't bring up Kratos. That would raise way more questions than I could answer.

"That, I don't know. It's what I'm trying to find out."

Detective Rhodes rested his thumbs inside his belt. He blinked back at me and waited for me to say more. I kept quiet.

"You look like your brother," he finally said. He picked up the chair he threw and put it back down across from me. He took a seat, properly this time.

"I get that a lot," I said. It was pretty easy to tell we were brothers. Danny was slighter, but the similarities in our faces were undeniable. The Shea shine, my mother called it: wide, wrinkled foreheads, blue eyes, and flat noses.

"We worked together for a bit, early on. Same precinct."

"I didn't know that."

"He was a good man. I'm sorry for what happened."

"Thanks."

"He saved me once. In the station. A guy got loose and picked up a chair. I fell and the guy was about to whack me with it, but your brother tackled him. A clean hit, right in the core; the guy dropped the chair and dropped to the ground. Your brother cuffed him in less than a minute. Like some cowboy roping a steer."

Rhodes ran his right hand through his thick mane. He motioned for *The Bachelor* contestant to take the cuffs off.

"Go on, Shea. Get out of here. You hear anything worthwhile, you sure as shit better let me know." *The Bachelor* contestant leaned down and uncuffed me.

I nodded and made my way out. Rhodes stayed seated but kept his eyes fixed on me as I left.

"You hear *anything*, Shea, you let me know."

I didn't respond. I rubbed my right wrist and tried to understand why he let me go. I made my way out of PG's apartment to the sound of Mister Mister barking angrily from above. I didn't look back. I got in my truck and drove toward Ocean Beach and my dinner with Jackie.

CHAPTER FIFTEEN

I HAD AN HOUR TO KILL BEFORE I'D MEET JACKIE AT PARK CHALET. I parked in the restaurant's lot and crossed the Great Highway. I took a seat on the seawall and looked out at the Pacific.

Another clear November day, but ice cold. The sun dropped slowly above the water. A crisp headwind numbed me. The sounds of crashing waves, barking dogs, and squealing teenagers surrounded me. Tourists and locals were walking, biking, sitting on the beach. All of them wrapped in sweatshirts and long pants and even beanies; not the California beach of the Beach Boys. I wanted to sit there all day and all night and never have to leave.

I loved this city. It was a work of art. Not in the Norman Rockwell sense, more like Dali, a complicated collection bound tightly by conflict and contrast, composed of characters; metaphysical, surreal. Seventy-five years ago, the great columnist Herb Caen had asked in his column, "What is San Francisco?" He'd answered: "It's the indescribable conglomeration of beauty and ugliness that makes San Francisco a poem without meter, a symphony without harmony, a painting without reason—a city without an equal." True in October 1940. True now. Caen died in 1995. I'd read archives of his columns when I was in college. He was a big reason why I became a reporter. I thought I had finally made it when I had my own column, just like the master of the three dots. And then it'd all fell apart. I'd failed.

And now, PG. I couldn't fail him.

We would come out here in high school: Rev, PG, and me. Post-game parties with bonfires, beer, and freezing cold wind. We had braved the chill of Ocean Beach but steered clear of The Grove or Twin Peaks. A more aggressive crowd was known to haunt those locales, and while we were not lovers, we were hardly fighters. I had tried my best to talk to the Catholic school girls but had little luck. They all loved PG. He'd seemed to be friends with all of them. None of us knew then that they were wasting their time. He didn't come out to Rev or me until after college. I remember not being that surprised, like I had known all along. Rev had apologized for being straight. Told PG it must be terrible to have such a good-looking friend who would forever be out of reach. We didn't miss a beat after that.

I couldn't fail him.

I pulled out my notebook and jotted down more notes:

1. *PG tells Father Ryan about Kratos and a student a few weeks ago*
2. *Monique sends PG a note thanking him for advice and a "him" Who? Kratos?*
3. *Who is the Nordic gal that approached me and is she who I chased in the Muni tunnel?*
4. *What about the Rolando kid?*
5. *Was Kratos seeing Monique? Love gone wrong?*

Too many questions and not a lot of answers. I unfolded the note that I took from PG's apartment. While I had been avoiding the thought, I couldn't anymore: I would have to meet Kratos. He had to be the "him" in the note.

I called Super Mario who ran the Willie Mays Boys & Girls Club in the Bayview. I wrote a couple of columns on him in the past, and he was as connected as they got. He agreed to meet me at 10 a.m. the next day. I didn't tell him it was about Kratos, and thankfully, he didn't ask. I called Rev and left a voicemail asking him to go with me.

My phone buzzed and I answered without looking at the screen.

I assumed it was Rev calling back.

"Rev, can you make it tomorrow?" I asked.

"This isn't Rev."

No, it wasn't. It was my ex.

"Hey, Jen."

"Seamus, I heard about PG. My God, what happened?"

"I don't know."

"Murder?"

"Yeah, his student. None of it makes any sense. He's confessed and isn't talking. There is something larger going on, and I'm trying to figure it out."

"Poor PG. Of all people." I heard what sounded like a PA announcement in the background.

"Where are you?" I asked.

"I'm on my way to see my parents," she said. We were in that stage. A few months ago, I knew where she was at all times. Now, she could be 500 miles away and I'd have no idea. I wondered if J. J., the former All-Pro, was with her, off to the side, signing autographs while she called me.

"Where's Billy?" I asked.

"He's with a friend."

"I miss him."

"He misses you. I thought we agreed you'd see him more. Take him for weekends."

"We did, I've just been busy."

"Busy despite losing your job?"

"You heard about that?"

"Everyone keeps asking me what happened to your column."

Drinking happened.

"Layoffs. They're losing money hand over fist."

She didn't respond. She knows.

"Maybe I'll come by next week and take Billy to the park."

"He'd like that. He's getting old."

"What is he, seventy now?"

"We've had him ten years, so yeah."

Our first purchase as a married couple: a loveable golden retriever we named Billy. I wanted to go see him, but didn't want to see my ex. Sometimes, divorce was toughest on the pets.

"So, what are you going to do about PG?" she asked.

"I need to meet a couple of people. Ask some questions. Hopefully something will shake loose."

"You need to be careful, Shea. This is serious. A girl is dead."

A girl was dead. An eighteen-year-old who, by all accounts, seemed to hold nothing but promise. I spent so much time thinking about PG that I let the tragedy of Monique slip by. Or maybe I intentionally blocked it out. If PG was guilty . . .

"I'll be careful. I'm bringing Rev with me."

She liked Rev. He always put her at ease. He put everyone at ease.

"Be careful, Shea."

When she used my last name again, I knew she was serious. I didn't want to talk about it anymore.

"I heard you're dating," I said. It was the first time we talked since I learned she was seeing J. J.

"Yes. Nothing serious. We all need to move on."

"Some move faster than others."

"Don't say that. It's nothing. We're more friends than anything."

"I don't get it, though. You don't like football."

"Football? What does football have to do with it?"

She sounded genuinely surprised. Maybe she rehearsed her response. Practiced this moment to prepare.

"You're dating an ex-football player, no?"

She laughed out loud.

"Football player? No. I don't even like football."

"You're dating J. J. Johnson, ex-49er."

"I'm dating J. J. Johnson, accountant for Levi's."

What the . . . ?

"Seamus, I'm sorry for PG. Please, let me know if there is anything I can do. Talking to you about J. J. is not something I want to do."

I didn't respond and she clicked off. I tried to remember who told me about J. J. and why I thought he'd be the famous football player knowing full well my ex would never date anyone like that.

PG's words returned: *Nothing is either good or bad but thinking makes it so.*

CHAPTER SIXTEEN

I WALKED BACK UP TO PARK CHALET TO MEET JACKIE. I always preferred Park Chalet to Beach Chalet. The view of the park was not quite as glorious as the Pacific Ocean, but it was always easier to get a drink at Park. Serious drinkers didn't look at restaurants or bars for ambience or decor or menu items. They looked for what was on tap, what was on the shelves, and how long it took the barkeep to get it to them. Why were dive bars never empty? No waiting.

I remembered when Jenny and I had gone on one of our first dates. I'd had a long day and needed something stiff. We chose a fish restaurant that only offered beer and wine. I realized it as I read the menu. I had told Jenny with a disappointed voice that they didn't have a bar. She corrected me. "No," I said, "a *real* bar." You would think she might have caught on right there and then. No such luck for either of us, but apparently it worked out for J. J. Johnson, Levi's accountant.

"Drink?" I asked Jackie as our waiter hovered. We were seated at a two-person table in the corner, parallel to the floor-to-ceiling window that looked out onto a small grove in the west end of Golden Gate Park.

"Arnold Palmer," she said.

"Bombay Sapphire and tonic," I said.

The waiter, college-aged, androgynous, and blonde, offered a formal bow.

"What happened to your finger?" Jackie asked.

"Jammed it in a cabinet door."

She grimaced.

"Okay, well, how's it going with PG?" She unfolded her cloth napkin and placed it on her lap.

"Well, I went by the scene of the crime and didn't find much. I got chased away by an out-of-shape security guard. I went to PG's apartment and got hit with a Costco-size Head & Shoulders bottle by someone else canvassing his apartment. I chased them through the Castro and into the Muni tunnel, just missed getting hit by the L. They got away, and two cops took me to see Detective Rhodes for a tongue lashing."

She furrowed her brow.

"You're joking?"

"I wish I was."

The waiter brought our drinks. I told him we'd need another minute to order.

"That's some afternoon. You ran into the Muni tunnel?"

"I did. I think I have some stains in my underwear to prove it."

"Who were you chasing?"

"I don't know," I said. "I think it was a woman who approached me after we talked yesterday. She said she was a teacher at PG's school, but that was BS. I don't know who she is or why she'd be in his apartment."

I let Jackie process my absurd afternoon as I scanned the room. It was probably half full, not too good for a Saturday night. A young baby erupted a couple tables over, wailing at the top of its lungs. Jackie and I both looked at each other and smiled.

"That is loud," she whispered, leaning into me. "Is that why you never had kids?"

"That and a million other reasons," I answered.

"Okay, so some mystery lady is at the Hall and at PG's apartment," Jackie said. "And she'd rather run through the Muni tunnel than talk to you." I could see her wheels spinning. She wanted to reach for her notebook but refrained.

Mother and baby soon swooped by us, headed for the bathroom or fresh air or someplace where the baby's cries wouldn't shatter glass.

"You heard anything?" I asked.

"Not much. They seem to think they have their man. Guess he's on record as having a temper as a coach. Could be a hothead."

"No one else?"

"There was a student who had a thing for her. Monique. He's got a mixed history, some violence."

"Rolando?"

"Yep."

"Yeah, security guard at the school told me. He doesn't think he's a killer though."

"He doesn't even go to school much. Spends most of his time at a park by the school. Fancies himself a great basketball player, though I don't think he plays on any team."

"What park?" I asked.

"MLK."

I knew it. It was about three blocks from PG's school. Modest playground surrounded by an uneven field and a full-court hoop on potholed asphalt with chain nets. Definitely known to be populated by a rough crowd. The kind of place where you wouldn't want to work on your jump shot after dark.

"Anything else?"

"Monique's mom has a boyfriend who is sketchy. He's been a little overzealous talking to the police, railing on your friend. The cops don't know what to make of him. He's trying too hard with them."

"I saw him do that interview in front of the Hall; the one you were at. Seemed odd."

"He works security for a downtown firm, so they're guessing he wants to be a cop."

"Any criminal history?"

"No. He used to be a musician, saxophone player at some of the old Fillmore haunts."

The waiter came back and shared the specials. Jackie went into interrogation mode.

"Is the salmon baked or grilled?"

"Are your French fries cooked in vegetable oil?"

"Is that with sea salt?"

"How much cumin?"

She systematically worked through the seven menu items she was considering, multiple questions per item, before settling on the Cobb salad without eggs and the dressing on the side. I had forgotten that each meal with her was as if she was writing an exposé for the paper. The waiter turned to take my order, and the poor kid looked like he had just walked through a hailstorm naked.

"Burger, medium rare, and sweet potato fries for me," I said. I needed some comfort food. The waiter expected a new beat down, but I just smiled and ordered another gin and tonic. He took our menus and limped away.

"I remember why we don't eat together," I said.

She held her left fist up in front of me and used her right hand to simulate she was unwinding the fist. The middle finger of her left hand slowly rose up. Southpaw.

"Nice shade of nail polish," I said.

"I do like my mani pedis." She held her left hand out, palm down, fingers splayed, to admire her nails.

"The boyfriend have any motive?" I asked.

"Sleeping with her mom. Maybe get the mom all to himself? Maybe had a thing for the daughter and she rebuffed him? Who knows. There are always motives; you taught me that."

I smiled.

"Sounds like he might have an alibi. They're checking it out. I hate to say it, but it keeps coming back to Pedro."

I took a gulp of my gin and tonic.

"You hear anything?" she asked.

"Same stuff as you. But there is one thing. You know who Kratos is?"

"Everyone knows who Kratos is," she said, laughing.

"Well, I think he's connected to Monique in some way. I'm not sure how."

"How'd you hear that?"

"I'd rather not say."

She sipped her Arnold Palmer.

"But if he's connected to her, it could explain a lot."

"Connected like, what? Romantically? Some R. Kelly shit?"

"God, I hope not. I don't know. I'm going to try to set up a meeting with him and see what shakes out."

She looked at me sideways.

"You are going to set up a meeting with the biggest dealer in the city and see if he had a role in Monique's murder?"

"Well, when you say it like that . . ."

"Be careful, Shea." Like my ex, she always used my last name when she wanted to warn me.

Eventually, our food came, and we ate quietly looking out at the views of the park between bites.

"I brought you something," she said.

"I'm intrigued."

She reached into her purse and pulled out a small pamphlet.

"It's not a gift. I know I talked to you in the past about my dad."

Uh-oh.

"He had a drinking problem. We were estranged for a long time. A couple years back, we reconnected. He did AA. It really worked for him."

I took a healthy swig of my drink. A warmth grew in my stomach. She handed me the pamphlet. It was the width and height of a small paperback novel, but only a few pages and folded accordion style. I pulled it open and noticed a couple paragraphs and what seemed like a train timetable taking up most of the space.

"It tells about the program and has meeting days and times in San Francisco and Marin."

"Thanks, Jackie. I appreciate the thought, but I'm good."

I folded it back up. She didn't speak.

"I'm working things out."

"Of course, of course. But just take it. Take a look later. Maybe it helps. Maybe not. Just humor your old mentee."

I nodded and stuffed the pamphlet into my back pocket. We finished our meals and didn't talk much after that. Eventually, Jackie gave me a hug and left to meet a pending deadline that may or may not have existed. When she was out of sight, I ordered another gin and tonic. I was two sips in when my phone buzzed.

"Seamus?"

"Yeah."

"This is Tito."

"How's Mamá?"

There was a long pause.

"That's why I'm calling. She's a mess. Crying nonstop. PG is her everything. It's killing her."

I swirled the drink in my hand, watching the ice cubes collide.

"Well, I got a couple of leads. Kid at school. The mom's boyfriend. Some mystery woman who keeps showing up."

"You give me the word and I'll fix things. Straight up. You understand?" he said.

I did. I was surprised by his bluntness, but it also reassured me. Part of me wanted Tito to fix everything. Use his powers to force a confession. Make the true culprit pay. Set PG free. But that wasn't how it worked.

"I understand. And I appreciate that. But let me handle it my way and see what happens. I don't know who's what yet. We got one innocent man in trouble already. I don't want to add to that list."

"Mrs. G keeps asking for you. She wants to see you. She wants to know what's happening with PG."

"There's not much to tell her yet."

Tito didn't respond.

"Okay, let me track down a couple things. I might have more

tomorrow. Can you hold her off until then?"

"Yeah, I think so," he said. "Good luck and call me when you have something."

I was making some progress with him since he wished me good luck. I thought about Mamá crying, PG in jail.

I finished my drink and called for the check. I was feeling good. My buzz was sturdy, fueled by the expensive stuff. I knew where I had to go next.

CHAPTER SEVENTEEN

I PARKED ACROSS THE STREET FROM MLK PLAYGROUND. Four large lights lit up the basketball court. Two teens were shooting around on one hoop. The other court was empty except for four men leaning against a fence just out of bounds, drinking what I assume were Tallboys in brown paper bags. I should have started my engine and headed back home. What was I doing at MLK park after dark? I needed something for Mamá. Something to be able to tell her. Rolando, at this point, was a real lead. Besides, the gin and tonics were pumping liquid courage through my veins, and I felt a little invincible.

I popped in a few Altoids, took a deep breath, and walked slowly toward the two playing. I hoped one was Rolando. I also hoped the men at the far end wouldn't beat the crap out of me for being in the wrong neighborhood at the wrong time.

The teens stopped playing and watched me. One was tall and lean in baggy jeans and a white Air Jordan hoodie. The other had a medium build and wore a taut white T-shirt and khakis. He had to be freezing.

"Hey there," I said. "I'm looking for Rolando."

"Who are you?" the tall one asked.

I had a sudden sober thought: I'm looking for a murderer, alone, in a rough neighborhood, and approaching teenagers at night. I have to stop drinking.

"My name is Seamus. I'm a friend of Mr. Gomez. I wanted to talk to Rolando about what happened at school."

"Shay-moose?" the tall one asked, laughing. "That's your name?"

"Seamus," I repeated, feeling my buzz and sense of invincibility fading fast.

The smaller one stepped forward. "I'm Rolando, what do you want?" He looked to be a mix of everything: Black, Latin, Samoan, White.

I hadn't thought this through.

"I wanted to talk to you about Monique."

"Monique's dead," he said. "Word is Mr. Gomez did the deed."

I glanced at the other end of the court; the four men watched me.

"I just wanted to ask you a few questions."

Rolando looked at his friend and they both laughed. Rolando had a twitchy quality, a nervousness that came from either a deplorable childhood or a crystal meth habit. I guessed the rough childhood. I knew some violent Irish dads back in the day; drunks who raised their hands often to release their pain and keep their children in line. Rolando had the look of those children.

"Sorry, Shay-moose," the tall one said. "You better be on your way."

One of the men drinking on the other end of the court approached. He was dark-skinned, stocky, and annoyed.

"There a problem here?" he asked.

Rolando shook his head.

"No problem, this is a long-lost relative of mine."

The man took a sip from his brown paper bag and nodded. He walked back to the others.

"How about I play you?" I asked, pointing at Rolando. They both looked at each other again and laughed. "To seven by ones. I win, you answer some of my questions."

"And if I win?" Rolando asked, intrigued.

"Twenty bucks."

"Forty," he countered.

"Done."

"Marco holds the money."

I assumed Marco was the tall one, so I handed him two twenties. He held them each up to the court lights, as if checking if they were counterfeit.

"Clean," he said with a laugh.

The hoop had a worn wooden backboard supported by two metal poles buried deep in the cement. The rim was bent down slightly and had the heavy chain net. The court smelled like weed, but I was pretty sure that was thanks to my company.

I called for the ball and dribbled a bit before taking a short jumper. Nothing but chain net, which made a smooth metallic clanging sound. Rolando smirked. My left hand still had two wrapped fingers that were a bit tender; I'd have to favor my right even more than usual.

Rolando took it out and shot a quick jumper that rattled around the rim and fell through. I would have to play up on him. Luckily, I had on running shoes and loose pants so I could move quickly enough if he tried to go by me.

"Winner's outs here," he said.

"Fair enough," I answered. Marco watched us carefully with crossed arms on the sideline. I wouldn't be getting my forty bucks back either way.

Rolando faked a shot and got me in the air. He went right by me and laid it up. I felt a heaviness in my chest. This would not end well. He was better than I thought. And I was drunk.

He hit another jumper and another layup. I was down 4-0 before I finally got a stop. I turned and kept my back to him. I did the old man back-down until I was a couple feet from the basket. I faked left, and he bit. I laid it up easy on the right—4-1. That was all I had, though. Rolando went by me three straight times after faking the jumper. My defense was always a little suspect.

"7-1, done," he said, walking toward Marco. He held both twenties and admired them before stuffing them in a pocket.

"Good game. Clear ass-kicking. I'm out of my league." I bent over, hands on knees, oxygen depleted.

"You don't look too good," Marco said.

"I'll be all right." I felt like I needed to hurl. "Look, can I just ask you a couple questions about Monique?"

Rolando blinked at me. He held the ball against his right hip.

"A couple," he answered.

"Did you know her?" I asked.

"Maybe," he said.

I took a step toward him. He didn't move.

"I heard you knew her."

"Man, you don't know shit."

He tossed the ball in the air above his head and caught it.

"You got in trouble for bothering Monique, right?" I asked.

He grabbed the ball firmly. I could see the anger grow in Rolando's face. I needed to back off.

"No," he said.

"You sure? I heard you got in trouble. I'm not judging, but you can see how it looks."

"No."

"You weren't bothering her?

"That was nothing. We talked it out. We were cool."

"You liked her, but she didn't like you?"

"No."

He bounced the ball once, hard with both hands.

"What about Kratos?" I asked.

Rolando looked at Marco.

"Do you know who Kratos is?" I asked.

"Everyone knows who Kratos is," Marco answered.

The four men who were drinking on the other side of the court had left. It was just me, Marco, Rolando, and the lights.

"Did Kratos know Monique?"

Rolando didn't answer. Kratos' name seemed to scare him.

"I don't know nothing about Kratos," he finally said.

"Did Monique have a thing with Kratos?" Rolando's eyes lit up.

He gave me a warning stare that I should have heeded.

"You don't know what you're talking about!" he yelled.

He took a step toward me. I had overreached.

"I don't want any trouble," I said. "I'm just trying to find out what happened."

"Fuck this guy, Role. Let's go," Marco said. Rolando ignored him. He stood firm with his right fist clenched, his left hand holding the ball. I missed the warning signs. Rolando moved from yellow to red in a blink of an eye.

"Fuck you," he said.

"Role, be cool, bruh. Let's go."

"No, fuck him. He can't come here and talk about her like that."

Marco repeated that they should leave, but Rolando kept staring at me. I glared back, unsure of what to do. In a flash, Rolando hurled the ball at me, low and angled. I caught it with my crotch, and I buckled over in pain. The ball bounced meekly away. I looked up to see Marco taking a couple steps back. I turned to my right to see a brown mass streaking toward my face. I felt a sharp pain from my chin to my lower lip. I distinctly heard "oh, shit," on my left. I stumbled a few feet, shook my head and blinked rapidly. I hadn't been punched since the fifth grade. There was a hot sensation on my lower lip. My balls were still throbbing from the basketball. I dropped my head to see a small pool of blood growing on the floor. There was a faint stream of red below my eyes and I could see the pool of blood expanding.

It wasn't Rolando's blood.

It wasn't Marco's blood.

It wasn't the blood of our Lord and Savior, Jesus Christ, whose image could clearly be seen on the bedroom ceiling of my mother's modest one-bedroom Noe Valley in-law.

No, it was my blood.

SUNDAY

CHAPTER EIGHTEEN

I WAS HUNGOVER, my pinky ached, and my lower lip was throbbing. Ceiling Jesus was still there but seemed to be looking away. He was disappointed in me.

What the hell was I thinking? Did I expect a confession from Rolando on the spot? Ask me to take him in and book him? This had to stop. I needed to stop drinking if I was ever going to help PG.

I tried to piece together the evening. I remembered Jackie and Park Chalet. Rolando and Marco. They ran off after Rolando landed his punch. I was a little hazy on why I had bothered to even try and find them. I guessed Tito's call about Mamá's concerns spurred me to act. The gin and tonics didn't help.

Stupid.

My shirt was laid out on the floor next to my bed, spotted with blood. My blood. I remembered stumbling to my car and taking it off to stop the bleeding. I headed home after that, stopping at a corner store to buy a pint of Jack. That now-empty bottle was next to the shirt.

I stumbled to my bathroom to see a nickel-sized growth on my lower lip. Red and swollen with a small gash on the inside of it. I washed it as best as I could. I threw on some jeans, a T-shirt, and a Giants hoodie. I glanced at the time on my phone. Rev would pick me up in ten minutes.

The pamphlet Jackie had given me of AA meetings rested on my nightstand. I picked it up and eyed it like a receipt I didn't remember getting. I unfolded it and scanned for Sunday meetings. There were a lot all over the city. I saw one at 5 p.m. at Our Lady of Angels, my old school. I tossed it back on the nightstand.

I headed out and found the Sunday paper at my door, full of useless ads and flyers. I dug into it to find the front page. I skimmed the story on the murder. Nothing new, and Jackie hadn't added any of the other mysteries surrounding the case. I hadn't expected her to, and they were far from mysteries, more like peculiarities.

I took a seat on a step and leafed through the rest of the paper while I waited for Rev. The sports page led with a story on the Warriors' decent start. Below the fold, a story on the Giants' Hot Stove rumors. The cover of the style section had a large picture from Madeline's fundraiser. Madeline and Richard Cory posed with the executive director of the homeless youth nonprofit. Locked arms, cheesy smiles, fake enthusiasm. *We are having too much fun, Mr. Photographer!* I would have to call Madeline and berate her.

Rev picked me up in his 4Runner, and we headed out to meet Super Mario.

"What the hell happened to you?" He was looking at my face. "Your lip looks like something out of a cartoon."

I flipped the passenger-side visor down and had another look in the small embedded mirror.

"It's nothing," I said. I had no interest in explaining that I'd gotten beat up by a high school kid.

"And your finger?"

"Jammed it in a cabinet."

Rev rubbed his face with his right hand; his left hand was guiding the steering wheel. He stayed quiet.

Rev, known formally as Malcolm Calvin Thompson, had a round face with chubby cheeks and a prominent unibrow. His neatly trimmed salt-and-pepper goatee was in stark contrast to his smooth, bald Black head. While he would never admit it, he shaved his head to hide a hairline that had been in quick retreat for the past few years.

I hadn't seen him in two months. He was a busy lawyer, happily married, father of two young girls. He coached one of his girls in pee wee soccer; a sport he detested. There were weekly practices, weekend games, plus birthday parties, playdates, and all those other time-consuming activities that children provided. We were on different life paths, but still bound by a nearly thirty-year friendship. A real friendship that I had taken for granted, like PG's.

"We have an appointment tomorrow with a defense attorney," Rev said. "A friend from law school who is very good."

"That's a relief. If we can't figure out what the hell is going on, he's going to need a good lawyer."

"So, what do we have?" He eventually asked, not needing to be specific.

"PG confessed to killing his student. Monique Profit. Honor Student. Flawless. He was helping her with her college applications and essays. Ivy League. They met Friday morning to go over them. The school janitor, who usually says hi to PG each morning, came in his room and found PG holding a knife and Monique lying motionless on the floor. She was stabbed multiple times. Video cameras outside the classroom and the hallway, broken. No one else was seen. It's a mess."

"Why would he confess?"

"I don't know. When I met with him, he asked me to see his mom and Father Ryan. He wanted me to tell his mom to get Tito and go talk to Uncle Carlos."

"Uncle Carlos?"

"Yeah. A joke between them that she used to say to him. That she'd send him to Uncle Carlos in El Salvador if he was bad. Her brother, but he died a few years ago."

"So, what does that mean?"

"I think it means he wants her to leave the country. To get out of town. She, of course, refuses. But at least Tito took her to stay with him."

"If anyone can protect her, I guess it's him," Rev said. "That guy scares me."

We were stopped at an intersection. An elderly man with a handsome bowler hat crossed in front of us. He was likely on his way to 10:00 a.m. Mass. Rev tapped on his steering wheel as if that might help move him along.

"Someone must have threatened him," I said. "That they'd go after his mom if he didn't confess."

"The killer?"

"That's the only thing that makes sense. The killer wanted to frame him for the murder. I can't see PG being pressured into killing anyone. I just don't think he could do that, even if they threatened his mom. But someone kills Monique. She's dead. They tell him to take the fall. I could see that."

Rev continued driving.

"And if PG's there and someone tries to kill Monique, he isn't going to stand by and watch," I said.

"No way. They'd have to kill him too."

"So, maybe he walks in on the killer who had already killed Monique. Gives PG the ultimatum. He's in shock. Lets the guy get away and takes the fall."

"I agree with the logic. PG is a straight arrow," Rev said. "If Monique is dead and someone threatened his mom, he'd take the fall in a heartbeat."

"I know."

"What about Father Ryan?"

"He tells me PG came and saw him. Told him that if anything happened to him, it would be because of Kratos."

"What is Kratos?"

"Who. Drug dealer. I came across his name a few times. He's a Robin Hood-type. Gives a lot to the community. He's really well known. I almost did an article on him."

"A drug dealer with a heart?"

"Sounds like it. The guy we are going to see now, Super Mario, he gets us to Kratos."

We left Noe Valley and maneuvered our way through the Mission and Excelsior to get to Hunter's Point. As we drove, the simple ride from my mom's house to the Willie Mays Boys & Girls Club got me thinking about Monique and her experience. There was little overt racism in San Francisco, but plenty simmered below the surface and manifested in how your zip code determined your destiny. Not what you'd expect from that shining liberal city on thirty-eight hills. Rev had plenty of unfortunate stories. PG often talked about the striking opportunity gap in the city. Truth was, Monique Profit's life was never going to be easy, with stellar grades or without.

Rev pulled into the parking lot and took an open spot near the entrance. We walked through two sets of light brown double doors into a small but modern gym. The Boys & Girls Club logo was centered on a brand-new hardwood floor. Six teens were playing a game of three-on-three while Super Mario stood on the far side of the court inspecting their game.

A couple years back, I wrote a column about a midnight basketball league at the Willie Mays Boys & Girls Club. Super Mario was the focus, and it was so popular I did a follow-up six months later. He'd spent most of his youth as a gangbanger, but after being convicted of murder at age twenty-two, he spent the next two decades in prison finding Allah and repenting for the error of his ways. Since his release five years ago, he'd been working in his old neighborhood trying to keep young ones from following in his footsteps.

"Seamus Shea!" Super Mario yelled across the gym. "The crazy Irishman is here."

I raised my hand and waved. He crossed the court and held out his paw of a hand to shake.

"It's good to see you again," I said.

He smiled back at me, showing off his fence of giant white teeth. He had that rough-hewn look you see in most people who did significant time. But his wide smile always offset that edginess. He was quite a few inches shorter than me, but he owned a stocky frame that gave him an undeniable physical presence. He had light brown skin, likely the result of a mix of Black and Latino blood.

"This is my friend, Rev," I said.

"Rev?"

"Malcom, but folks call me Rev."

Super Mario nodded. He pointed at my face.

"You got a fat lip, man. Actually, it looks like some bad herpes. What happened?"

Rev laughed.

"I walked into a tree," I said.

Mario paused to consider if I was joking. He seemed to give up and offered a sympathetic nod.

"And your column is gone?" Always with the questions; Super Mario's mouth was in constant motion. "I still got my stories framed at my mom's place. What happened to it?"

Jameson. Three fingers. Neat.

"Budget cuts," I said.

He nodded and showed more teeth.

The players stopped their game. They bent over, tugging on their shorts and breathing heavily. Confused faces. They looked to Super Mario for answers.

"You guys play another one. To eleven by ones. Loser's outs. I'm gonna take a walk with my good friend here."

Mario put his large hand on my shoulder and led me down the end line away from the game. Rev followed.

"How can I help?" he asked.

"What makes you think I need help?"

"I heard about Pedro."

"You hear everything."

"True."

We stopped at the far end of the court, and Mario skipped up the stairs of the sideline stands. He took a seat on the top row and gestured for us to follow. I sat next to him and Rev took a seat one row below us. I looked down the court at the six teens lost in their game. They weren't bad. They set solid picks, made crisp passes, and took smart shots. I played a few nights in this gym in the midnight league when I wrote my column, and I remembered it being a pretty good run. It helped me get to know Mario and the folks in the neighborhood, a special group. That first column was one of my best.

"So, you trying to get your boy Pedro off?"

"Did you meet him? He came to watch me in the midnight league."

"I did meet him. Said you guys played in high school. I liked him. He made fun of you a lot. I liked that."

"He didn't do it."

Mario rubbed his hands together and smiled.

"Yeah. They never do."

"I got a lead I'm trying to track down. Someone who may have info to help me."

"Who's that?"

"Kratos."

For the first time, Super Mario looked uncomfortable.

"I don't like talking about him."

"Is he still running things?"

Mario shifted his weight. He looked good for someone closing in on his mid-fifties and with many of those years trapped in an eight-by-six cell doing God-knew-what to survive.

"He's running things. He's gone all Stringer Bell. Think he's taking econ classes at City, learning all about supply and demand and shit."

I took out my notebook and started to write notes. I looked up and gestured if it was okay, and Mario mumbled an agreement.

"He's got most of the city. Tenderloin, Mission, HP. He's expanding. Fillmore. Club scene South of Market. Rumor has it he's eyeing parts out of SF, too."

"What's his game?"

"Mostly drugs. Coke, molly, some meth, that fentanyl shit. That stuff is nasty. He got a new supplier, and he's got plenty of stuff to move. That's why he's growing. He's taken a few folks out along the way. Sounds like the power is making him more confident."

"I remember him being pretty smart."

"He is. Still is. But smart folks can do dumb things. I tried hard with him, to get him to go straight. Met him often. Thought I had a chance cause I could appeal to his reason. He is very logical."

"No luck?" Rev asked.

"No. He was just humoring me. Leading me along. Finally, he got bored and told me he was done with our chats. That was just over a year ago. I think it was soon after he got this new supplier. We talk every few months or so but not like before."

"Any idea who the supplier is?" Rev asked.

He shook his head.

"They call him Keyser Söze."

"Keyser Söze?"

"Yeah, from that movie, *Usual Suspects*. No one knows him, but everyone's scared of him. He's connected to Mexico and China. Runs a shit-load of product through Kratos. They all must be making a killing."

"How come no one takes Kratos down? He's so public about it all."

"Have to ask SF's finest that one, or the DA. Think the Feds are involved, too. They all want the big player, and they know Kratos is the way to him. Think they're just taking their time till they have something concrete to move on. But Keyser Söze is smart. Not sure they're ever going to get him."

"As I remember, they didn't in the movie," I said.

"There you go."

"He's not a local guy?"

"Shit, no. I heard something about him being a legit businessman living in Marin with a giant view of the city. But that might just be smoke."

"Can you set up a face-to-face for us and Kratos?" I asked.

Super Mario dropped his chin to his chest and crossed his eyes. He looked at Rev and back at me.

"Say what?"

"We want to meet with him," I said. "You can use my name. He should remember me. We talked about an article; he'll meet me."

"You sure about that? Kratos is no joke."

"Yes. We need to see him."

"You are crazy."

"Well?" I said.

Super Mario stood up, picked up a ball lurking in the stands and flung it underhanded toward the nearest hoop. It crashed into the backboard and rolled around the rim before dropping through the net.

"Your lucky day," he said. "Give me a moment."

He retreated from the gym and left us sitting in the stands. Rev and I watched the players. Rolando not only punched me but also showed me that my basketball skills had faded. I needed to shoot around, maybe even play some. These young guys made me long for taking some shots.

"If we get PG out," I said. "The three of us need to get playing again."

"When we get PG out," Rev said.

I nodded.

A few minutes later, Super Mario came back out with a slip of paper that he handed to me.

"He'll meet you. He said he was expecting you."

"Lucky me," I said.

"He's heading to 10:30 a.m. Mass now. He'll meet you after around noon at the church."

"Mass?"

Super Mario shrugged.

"That has the address. Good luck."

"Thanks."

"Be careful, boys. Kratos is no joke."

I nodded. Rev and I started to leave. As I walked down the court, I called for the ball. One of the young men humored me and sent me a crisp pass.

"Don't do it," Rev said. "Don't do it."
I set my feet, jumped, and shot.
Airball.

CHAPTER NINETEEN

WE CLIMBED INTO REV'S SUV, and I handed him the address.

"Interesting guy," Rev said. "What was he in for?"

"Murder."

"Good to know."

We drove for ten minutes before Rev headed down a narrow street that led to a small white church like something out of *Little House on the Prairie*. An actual belfry and bell rested on top of the angled roof. Double-parked cars lined the outside of the church, and Rev pulled off to a side street to find an open space.

"This is it," he said.

"All right. We wait until they start coming out from Mass."

"Easy enough."

"Help me out here, Rev," I asked him. "Young girl. Smart. Very smart. Good student. From a tough neighborhood but a strong mom. Stays out of trouble. College next year, Ivy League in all likelihood. Who would want her dead?"

Rev rubbed his chin.

"Jealousy?" he said. "Boyfriend?"

"Possible. There was a kid, Rolando, who had a crush on her, and she turned him down."

"Yeah, but murder? That's a big leap for teenage heartbreak."

"He's definitely violent," I said, touching my lip.

Rev studied my face. I looked out my side window.

"Wait, wait, wait, did *he* do that to you?" Rev asked. "You got beat up by a high school kid?"

"I didn't get beat up, okay? He's a big dude."

Rev lost it. He pounded the steering wheel with his right hand, laughing uncontrollably.

"He might be a murderer," I said.

"You are a forty-year-old man and got a fat lip from a teenager."

"I'm thirty-nine. And can we stay focused here, please?"

Rev took a couple of deep breaths. He wiped the tears that formed at the edge of his eyes.

"Maybe a random act?" I asked.

"Then why would PG confess?"

"That's the part that gets me. I mean, he's a rules follower for sure. Someone said do this and keep quiet or we'll hurt your mom. He would keep quiet. That's just his way."

"Right."

Three teens on skateboards rode past the church, their boards grating against the asphalt. One jumped the curb, flipped his board, and landed on it on the street. I hated skateboarders, but I was impressed.

"Let's ask the obvious question: if he did do it, why did he do it?" I said.

"Shame!"

"Humor me. No one else involved, why would PG kill her?"

Rev let out a sigh.

"Come on, Rev."

"Okay, okay. He wasn't in love with her, that's for sure. Jealous of her, maybe?"

"Bright minority student, all that talent and bright future, and he's stuck teaching in a rundown school?"

"Maybe she caught him doing something he shouldn't?"

"Walked in on him. But what was he doing?"

"Drugs?"

Rev and I looked at each other and laughed.

"Remember that one time he got stoned?" Rev asked.

"Yeah, he got so paranoid. He locked himself in the closet, slept there!"

"I don't know, Shame; I don't see a motive."

"You're right. Nothing fits."

The bell up above rang. I looked at my watch: noon.

"So, are we just going to ask this guy if he killed Monique? How's that going to go over?" Rev asked.

"I didn't get the sense from Father Ryan that he was the problem. It seemed like PG was telling him Kratos would have the answers."

"What would he be doing with a high school girl?" Rev asked.

"She was pretty."

"Like what, he was sleeping with her?"

"Maybe."

"The honor student and the drug lord? Wasn't that a Lifetime movie of the week?"

"I don't know. Hopefully he can help us."

"Biggest drug dealer in the city is going to open his arms to us and solve all our problems."

"At this point, Rev, he's all we got."

After about ten minutes, parishioners filed out of the church. They stood on the steps and sidewalk and made small talk like after most services. Plenty of smiling and laughing from a well-dressed crowd. Off to the left, I saw a familiar face.

"Oh, shit," I said.

"What?"

"That's Rolando." I pointed toward the left side of the entrance. Rolando was helping an elderly woman down the stairs. He wore a collared shirt, tie, and dress slacks. He looked smaller than I remembered.

"That's the kid that beat you up?" Rev said.

"He didn't beat me up. He threw a ball at me really hard. Then he ran at me while I was disoriented and punched me."

Rev was staring at me, straight-faced, eyebrows raised. He was doing his best to fight back a smile.

"Let's go," I said.

We left the SUV and crossed the street. I followed Rev's lead up the steps and into the church through the mostly African American crowd. Rev stayed clear of Rolando, and I kept my head down so he wouldn't see me. I wondered if he knew Kratos.

Double wooden doors led to one wide-open and unexpectedly large room. Two rows of long, tan pews ran thirty rows up to a simple altar with a caramel-colored podium in the center. Flowers dotted the altar, bringing energy and color. It was warmer than I imagined for such a large, open space, but I guessed the packed house that just left helped heat up the place. Despite all the flowers, the church smelled like a mix of body odor and mildew.

A small group huddled near the altar, but to our right in the back row sat Kratos. I had never seen him before and only talked to him once on the phone, but I knew it was him.

Two large men stood behind him, wide stances, crossed arms. Both dressed in tailored, pin-striped suits and long, black overcoats. They looked like retired offensive linemen. Kratos had both arms stretched out across the pew. He was of medium build but looked like he took care of himself: lean, healthy face; well-formed biceps stretching his dress shirt. I guessed he was in his late thirties. His shaved head looked like Rev's, but I doubted he hid a receding hairline; more likely because it made him look badass.

Rev and I approached.

"Can I help you?" one of the linemen asked.

"I'm Seamus Shea; this is Malcolm. We are here to meet Mr. Kratos—uh—Kratos. Super Mario sent us."

The lineman turned, and Kratos nodded. He stepped aside and let us by.

"Seamus Shea. You know, I actually started to read your columns each week. I started with that one on Mario, and I got hooked," Kratos said. We took a seat next to him on the pew.

"Thanks," I said.

"Then a year ago you called and talked about a story on me?"

"Yeah, my editor didn't go for it."

Kratos watched me with confident, brown eyes. He looked like a slimmed-down version of the Rock. African American and Samoan blood mixed together. The Rock's dashing, Hollywood smile replaced with an intimidating stare.

"Thought I might be famous. And now, no column? What happened?"

Three-martini lunches.

"I quit when they didn't accept your story."

He smiled and rubbed his chin.

"What happened to your lip? And your fingers? You're a mess," he said, pointing at both.

"It's not been the best few days."

He smiled again, or maybe he was laughing at me.

"Got to be careful," he said. "Basketball can be a tough game."

I didn't respond. He was feeling me out. He knew Rolando; they talked.

"So why did you want to meet me?" he asked.

"We need help for our friend, Pedro Gomez," Rev said.

Kratos looked at him.

"This is my friend Malcolm," I said.

"Pedro, the one they say killed Monique?" Kratos asked.

"Yes. Did you know her?" I asked.

Kratos bit his upper lip and nodded.

"I did. She was a sweet girl."

"Do you know who would want to harm her?" Rev asked.

"Besides her teacher?" he shot back.

Rev obliged him, "Besides her teacher."

Kratos ran both his hands over his bald head.

"You boys wouldn't be accusing me, would you?"

The linemen seemed to tense up behind us.

"No, sir. We just heard you might be able to help," I said.

He looked at me sideways.

"I did not have anything to do with it. I give you my word on that. I would like to know who did. I don't like it. Young girl like that. They said she was full of promise."

He coughed into his fist.

"So, who do you think killed Monique if not her teacher?" I asked.

"Shit. The cops think we did it. Already came by here asking. Or at least I guess they're interviewing the usual suspects. But we had nothing to tell them."

"The cops came to talk to you?"

"Yep."

"Which cop? Do you remember?"

"You think I'm on a first-name basis with these men?"

"No, I was just curious." One of the linemen leaned down and whispered in Kratos' ear.

Kratos gave a soft nod and looked at me, debating, I supposed, if he should share.

"Sean Mannion."

Sean was my brother's partner. But he worked narcotics, not homicide. That was Rhodes and Don's world.

"Cops always come talk to me."

"Is it always the same ones?" I asked.

"No. It varies. Any big crime happens around here, they come see me. Like I'm some psychic that's gonna help them solve crimes. Think about that, though. Every time! We're considered bad dudes. Most people see us as a bunch of gangbangers, right?"

I nodded carefully, unsure where he was going.

"You know, we are not dumb, but you think what we do is pretty stupid?"

I nodded again.

"Well, how are we any different than big pharma? They got suits. They got dividends and shareholders. They got lawyers. Is what we do any different than, say, a pack of pharma lawyers?"

"I'm sorry?" I said, confused.

"Lawyers ain't nothing but a legal gang. Some rich guy has a problem, they call in their lawyers who lean on the problem. Someone's business deal goes wrong? Send in the lawyers; make the other person's life hell. Someone disrespected? Attorneys are called; show them they have to respect the man. And for big pharma, man, they're selling shit way more potent than anything on these streets. But they are seen as good and got the lawyers to make sure of it."

"As a lawyer," Rev said, "I have to agree with that assessment."

Kratos stood up and stretched his arms upward. He picked up his wool jacket that was laying on the pew and put it on.

"Right? We do the same damn thing, Mr. Shea. Smaller scale, no JDs, but the same damn thing. I don't have any lawyers, but I got James and Renfro." He pointed at the two linemen.

"So, I heard your name was connected to this," I said, hoping to get him back on track. "I don't know why. Is there anything you can tell us to help us find who really killed Monique?"

Kratos dropped his head toward his left shoulder. He looked at me with a certain pity.

"You really think you can clear your friend? He's Salvadoran, right? You think he's going to get a fair shake in this justice system."

"I have to try," I said.

Kratos kept his head dropped and stared at me in silence.

"I can't help you gentlemen," he finally said. "I appreciate you coming to see me, but I know nothing about Monique, her killing, or the teacher. Someone has given you bad information. Now, if you will excuse me, I need to say my final prayers before I go see my auntie."

"Please," I said, "You must know something. PG mentioned your name. You must have some idea as to what happened to Monique or why."

Kratos walked away, trailed by his two linemen. Rev put his hand on my shoulder and gently kept me from pursuing. I was going to yell Rolando's name, but I wasn't sure where that would get me. I thought of asking if he had a thing with Monique, but an image of his linemen treating me like a wishbone kept me quiet. We left the church and walked back to his 4Runner.

"What now?"

"I have no idea, Rev. No fucking idea."

"This is bad, Shame. This is really bad," Rev said.

"Nothing is either good or bad but thinking makes it so," I said reflexively.

"Yeah, well I'm *thinking* this is pretty fucking bad."

CHAPTER TWENTY

REV AND I LEFT KRATOS' VISIT DEFEATED. I said we should get some rest and tackle it again tomorrow, but even as I said the words, I knew we had little hope of saving PG. Rev, always the optimist, smiled and said we were going to get him off.

"I don't think so, Rev." I admitted my doubts. "I think PG's done for. It's his own fault. He confessed. It makes it impossible for us to clear his name."

"We are going to meet my friend tomorrow, the defense lawyer. We have a good chance."

"We need more, Rev."

"Look, Shame, you know what I'm going to say."

"No, I don't."

"You are special to me, Shame."

"Not now, Rev."

"Very special."

Rev could see my stress, and he moved quickly to comfort mode. Although he'd always had an odd way of comforting me.

"You know what's coming," he said.

"I'm your one White friend."

"You are my one White friend. I can't afford to lose you."

"You work with a hundred White people."

"I know. But they're not my friends. But when I talk to them, I can say 'my White friend thinks this,' or 'my White friend thinks that.' You are very useful."

He looked at me with a straight face. It was just what I needed, and he knew it.

"Now, I can't have you messing this up. I'd have to drop you and get a new White friend."

"You are an asshole; you know that, right?"

"You'll think of something, Seamus. You always do."

"Yeah, well, I wouldn't put money on it."

He reached his hand over to me.

"Sounds like a bet. A hundred bucks you clear his name. You don't, I owe you. Shake on it."

I looked at Rev. Another Jedi mind trick. Regardless, I thought I could use the money. I shook his hand.

He dropped me at home, and once inside my apartment, I stumbled to my bed and collapsed. I was exhausted. I looked up at ceiling Jesus, but He seemed to be sleeping. I closed my eyes and tried to empty my mind of all the concerns that were bouncing around inside of it. I really wanted a drink.

I sat up and called Sean Mannion, Danny's former partner in narcotics. I had avoided calling Sean because I knew he would want to meet at a bar and drink a toast, many toasts, for Danny. But Kratos mentioned Sean visiting him; I couldn't avoid him any longer. He didn't pick up, so I left a message.

The pamphlet Jackie had given me was still on my nightstand. I stood up and leafed through it. The Sunday meeting at my old school was in a couple of hours. How ironic would that be?

I glanced up at ceiling Jesus. He was awake and had a message.

Two hours later, I walked into the basement of Our Lady of Angels. I immediately recognized the worn vinyl flooring of the hall, but little else from my years at the school decades before. The floor had small squares with a yellow and black snowflake pattern that seemed etched deep in my psyche. I had a brief flashback of nuns and school lines and the smell of hot dogs.

There were about thirty metal folding chairs meticulously

arranged in five rows in front of a small wooden table. Twenty or so people sat chatting easily. I took a seat in the back row next to a heavyset biker sporting a beard ZZ Top would be proud of. My heart kicked it up a notch. I took a couple of deep breaths and closed my eyes. I could feel the biker watching me. I opened my eyes.

"How are you doing?" he asked.

"Good," I said.

He smiled. "Well, we're glad you are here."

I nodded. I rubbed my hands together. Icicles might have started forming on my extremities.

"Gets cold down here," he said. "I got plenty of cushion to keep me warm, so it doesn't bother me." He slapped his big belly.

I wanted to sneak out; this was a mistake. I gave myself a few more minutes and looked around the room. I noticed Jesus again. Not the one on my ceiling, not the one hanging behind the altar at St. Anthony's, but the one glued to the support post about ten feet in front of me. A ten-inch wooden cross adorned with a six-inch figure of Christ. A familiar symbol: head askew, hands and feet impaled, covered with a flimsy loin cloth and crown of thorns. Quite a peculiar symbol for some billion people to worship.

A thin man wearing running gear and a Giants cap took a seat at the small desk in front of us. He opened up a white binder before him on the table.

"Hello, everyone. I'm Mark, and I'm an alcoholic."

"Hi, Mark," everyone replied.

Mark systematically worked through the pages in the binder, which included asking those from out of town to acknowledge themselves; those new to the meeting to share their name; and the so-called first-timers, less than thirty days sober apparently, to speak up. Each of the latter, three in all, received a generous round of applause. I listened but did not react. I could feel the giant ZZ Top man to my left glaring at me. Mark asked a few others to read, which they did from laminated scripts. It was too much for me to take.

"Today, we have a special speaker. Many of you know him. I never tire of hearing him speak. And we all know he loves to speak!"

Laughter trickled around the room. I wanted out. This wasn't my thing.

"Bunny, come on up here."

I saw my opportunity to leave, and I stood up, my back hunched over, ready to sneak out of the row and back to the street. The biker with the ZZ Top beard also stood up. He held a Styrofoam cup in his right hand and lifted it toward me as if saying cheers. He leaned in and whispered, "Wish me luck." He walked to the front, shook Mark's hand, and stood to the right of the table. I sat back down.

"Hi, all, I'm Bunny, and I'm an alcoholic." He placed the Styrofoam cup on the table. Mark looked miniature in Bunny's considerable shadow.

"Hi, Bunny," they responded.

"What's up, drunks? So, let's see, how does this work? I talk about how it was, what happened, and how it is now."

Bunny's large bald head was contrasted with a triangle salt-and-pepper beard that reached its apex at his chest. His olive skin had a sandpaper texture with the exception of his flat, shiny nose. Two stud earrings balanced his face horizontally and vertically, while both of his arms were covered with intricate tattoos of what looked like Aztec drawings, a skull with an Indian headdress, and a flaming tree. He also wore a black T-shirt and a black leather vest. If I saw him walking toward me, I'd cross the street. Actually, I'd run.

"I did whatever I wanted with little concern for others or even myself, really. I drank like a fiend. Got in fights, slept with anybody. I did that for years. I pretended like I was someone. I had some questionable friends who were, let's say, big players in the import-export field. I put out this face to the world, but it was all bullshit. Toward the end, I wouldn't even go out. I'd rarely go to sleep if there was a bottle in the house. I would hide bottles under my kitchen sink. Emergency stash. Mix it in with the Clorox and Pledge bottles. Find it, finish it, replace it the next day. Over and over. Makes for a rough morning. Wild Turkey was my bottle of choice at the end. Head back to the liquor store the next day, buy a few more bottles. Hide one or two and drink the other. Go to a different store the next day, since I didn't want anyone to recognize me and think I was a drunk."

He lifted his cup from the table and took a drink. The cup looked tiny in his thick hands, but it seemed to offer support. I scanned the crowd. An eclectic mix of ages and races. I noticed professionals, hipsters, working class, elderly, and college kids, and all of them were laser-focused on Bunny.

"So my bottom? I crashed my bike. The one thing I really loved. How sad is that? A collection of metal and chrome, the only thing I really loved. Crashed it into a cement barrier. I woke up in the hospital. Broken bones. Cut face. Bruised ego. I had no idea what happened. They told me my bike was totaled. They said I was screaming when they brought me in. They had to sedate me. I was whining about my bike. I could have killed somebody or myself, and here I am crying over a fucking machine." He used his index finger to trace circles on the lid of his cup. "A nurse there, who knew what happened to me, told me about a girl that had died the week before. A drunk driver had crashed into her car. She was nine years old. The accident put her mom and dad in intensive care, but they survived. The girl died instantly. Some twenty-year-old drunk driver. That was it. That was all I needed. I had my bottom. I knew I needed to stop drinking or I'd kill somebody. I didn't care if I lived or died; hell, I guess I wanted to die. But I knew I didn't want to take anyone else with me. I vowed right then and there to that nurse that I was through drinking. She came back and gave me a brochure with all these AA meetings in the city.

"I went to my first meeting the next day. I stuck it out. Kept coming back. I volunteered for a couple of commitments and met a good dude who became my sponsor. He was my sponsor until last year when he passed away. He died of old age with forty-one years of sobriety." Bunny nodded his head emphatically. "That's my goal."

He returned the cup to the desk. Mark was looking up at him, mesmerized.

"Now? Life is good, what can I say? I wake up happy, refreshed. I go to meetings and hang out with you fools. A new bike I ride without fear, except for them damn Google busses; they scare the crap out of me. Otherwise, I have a full, rich life. Something I never thought possible. Honestly. Never thought possible."

Mark thanked Bunny and the room erupted in applause.

"What should we talk about today, Bunny?" Mark asked.

Bunny's eyes scanned the room. He seemed to settle on mine.

"Let's do first meetings, I'm feeling a little nostalgic."

"All right, first meetings is the topic, or if you have anything in Bunny's talk that you want to discuss. Or anything that's on your mind. Let's open it up."

Bunny came back and took a seat.

"How'd I do?" he asked.

"Great," I said.

Mark went around the room calling on others who thanked Bunny for his share. Some talked about their own first meetings and how they felt: scared, lonely, angry. Others expanded on points from Bunny's share and how they had similar experiences.

I thought about hiding bottles under the sink; I thought that was just my trick.

Mark said a few final words and the meeting ended. We stood up and Bunny turned to me, holding out his beefy right hand.

"How the heck are you?" he asked. His voice was deeper up close.

"Good, thanks," I said. His grip was vice-like, but his palms were sweaty. I wanted to run away.

"You look like shit," Bunny said, after releasing my hand.

"Well, I'm good. Thanks." I reached into my pocket and pulled out my phone. I flicked it on and hoped that he'd go talk to someone else.

"First meeting?"

"Yes."

"I'm Bunny," he said.

"Bunny?" I stammered. "I liked your speech."

"Sounds like you got a problem with my name?" He curled his fingers into fists.

"No, sorry. It's just an unusual name."

He laughed, shaking his full body.

"I'm just fuckin' with ya. You gots to lighten up . . ."

"Seamus," I offered sheepishly.

"Seamus? And you're making fun of my name? You gotta lighten up."

He laughed again, rolling his head back and shaking his shoulders.

"First meetings are the toughest, my man."

"Well, I don't think this is for me," I said.

"Honesty. Yes!"

I looked again at my phone.

"Let me buy you a cup of coffee," Bunny said.

"Okay," I answered, unsure of what was happening. He put his hand on my shoulder and led me toward a table in the back of the room with a half-filled coffee pot and assorted cookies.

"So, what do you do for a living, Seamus?"

"I was a journalist."

"Ah, that's where I know you. Seamus Shea and 'City Views,' right?"

"Yes, sir."

"What happened to that column? I liked it."

I didn't respond.

"Let me guess, drinking happened?"

I still didn't respond.

"Seamus, the hardest thing is to admit there's something wrong."

I looked around the room. People had started to fold up the chairs and stack them in the corner. Mark was laughing with a man who earlier said he was in his first thirty days.

"I was drunk in the office," I said, turning back to face Bunny. "Multiple times. Missed some deadlines. Generally screwed up."

Bunny had filled two cups with coffee.

"Black?" He asked.

"Yeah, please."

He handed me a cup and touched it with his.

"Cheers, Seamus."

"Cheers," I said.

The coffee was warm but strong.

"You'll hear stories of a lot worse. Amazing what human beings can overcome with a little clarity and a little time."

"How long have you been sober?"

"Eight years."

"Wow, congrats."

"One day at a time, brother. A cliché, but a damn good one."

Bunny blinked back at me.

"What happened to your fingers?" He pointed at my wrapped pinky and ring fingers.

"Long story, luckily not related to my drinking."

He nodded and drank his coffee.

"And your lip?"

I didn't respond.

"Life has a way of veering off the rails. Most of us, hell, almost all of us sleepwalk through life. We go to our jobs, buy our groceries, watch our favorite team. We spend little time thinking about anything, really, until something hits us in the gut: wife walks out, someone you love dies, you finally face an addiction."

My soon-to-be ex, Danny, my former job. Check, check, check.

"We are stronger than we think," he added. "But we want to control everything, and we can't control anything. We need to just let it be."

"Let it be? Like the Beatles song?" I asked.

"Exactly. Stop resisting, just let it be."

"Resisting what?"

"Everything. You want it all to go your way. All us drunks do. You want the world to work out for you and your tiny little vision of how things should be. You still think the world is all about you. But getting sober is about moving away from that."

A tension rose inside of me, a confluence of emotions I had suppressed for too long. *Fuck this biker and his bullshit philosophy.* I was not an alcoholic. *Fuck this program.* Drinking, while it ruined my life and made me miserable, still gave me some pleasure, some happiness, an identity at least. And now I had to give that up just to feel all the pain and regret and anger that I bottled up for so long. That was my reward? *Fuck this.*

"I have to go."

"Where?"

"I have to go help my friend."

He nodded.

"We meet here every day at 5 p.m. Come back tomorrow, okay? Don't drink between now and tomorrow. That's all you have to do. One day. One day at a time."

"One day at a time and let it be," I said.

"Exactly! Paul McCartney knows what he's talking about. Let it be."

He began singing the first line of the popular Beatles song. He had a surprisingly strong voice.

I walked away without responding. I felt the tension building even more, and I wanted to scream. To yell at the top of my lungs and let it all out. Let out the pain, anger, frustration.

Let it be.

I left Bunny and walked to my truck. My rage melted into self-pity. I did not know why I was so angry. Bunny had been cordial, fun even. But I just wasn't ready for some share-your-soul encounter. I had a friend in jail looking to spend the rest of his life in prison, and I felt no closer to finding who actually killed Monique.

As I walked, my phone buzzed.

"Seamus Shea?" a soft female voice asked.

"Yes."

"I would like to talk to you."

"Do I know you?"

"No. We've never met."

"I'm sorry, what are you calling about?"

"My daughter."

"Your daughter?"

"Yes, Monique Profit."

CHAPTER TWENTY-ONE

BRENDA PROFIT LIVED NEAR THE END OF PALOU AVE, a stone's throw from the Willie Mays Boys & Girls Club where I met Super Mario. She lived on the bottom floor of a three-story carrot-colored complex across from an auto body shop. There was a strong scent of industrial cleaner in the air. I couldn't tell if it was the bay a few blocks away or the body shop.

As I walked toward the building, two teens were leaning against a green Camaro, while a red Bluetooth player on the hood pumped out what sounded like Kendrick Lamar. They kept their eyes on me as I approached. I waved; they looked away.

Brenda Profit's apartment was street-accessible on the bottom floor with a row of potted sunflowers on either side of the entrance. A wooden *Welcome to Our Home* sign hung on the front door. I knocked, and anxiety grew inside me. I didn't do well with death, particularly when dealing with the bereaved.

A tall man with a neatly trimmed salt-and-pepper beard opened the door slightly. He was paler than I was. I recognized him from the mini-press conference on Friday. Holden, the boyfriend.

"Yes?" he asked.

"I'm here to see Ms. Profit," I said.

"Who are you?"

"Seamus Shea. She called me earlier."

"She's not here."

"Do you know when she'll be back?"

A graceful woman with bloodshot eyes came to the door and thoughtfully touched the man on his shoulder. She had thick, black braided hair tied up in a fist-sized hair bun, and her skin had a polished light brown tone like caramel. She wore a flowing blue blouse that reached her knees and wide-legged gray wool pants.

"Hello, Mr. Shea," she said.

"Ms. Profit?"

"That's right. Please come in."

I walked into a large, open space decorated with an array of African Art. The room was dark save for the custom lighting that highlighted the artwork. Six wooden masks hung on one wall; long-faced, etched with intricate patterns, and colored tan, maroon, and green. A tall bookcase leaned against another wall displaying ten thin statues of men in fighting positions and women holding baskets on their heads. There was a wall-mounted TV, a Chesterfield sofa, and a brown leather chair off to the right. A dining room table occupied the left side of the room in front of a small galley kitchen. A hallway off the kitchen led to more rooms.

"Impressive art," I said.

"Thank you. I work at the MOMA. I'm a curator."

"Cool, Ms. Profit." It was an odd word choice, but my anxiety was on high alert.

"Call me Brenda," she said, offering me a seat on the Chesterfield. "This is my partner, Holden. He's a little protective, as you might imagine."

"I understand. And let me say, I'm very, very sorry for your loss."

Holden seemed unimpressed.

"Just so we are clear," Holden said. He had a deep, hoarse voice. "I think your buddy is guilty as sin. Okay?"

"Okay," I responded.

Brenda sat opposite of me in the leather chair. Her eyes were looking at the floor.

"Brenda wants to meet with you. Talk to you. But know that I think he did it, and I think he's going to pay for what he did. Understand?"

"I understand," I said.

Holden took a seat next to Brenda on the chair's armrest. He put his arm around her.

"You must wonder why I asked you here," she said.

"I'm a little curious, yes."

"Unlike Holden, I don't believe your friend killed my daughter."

I could only muster a soft nod in reply. I could see the grief in her face. She'd lost everything.

"I knew the man. He was helping Monique. Helping her with her applications, with financial aid. He came by here a few times, and the three of us sat at that dining room table over there and filled out those damn forms." She pointed at the circular wooden table ten feet from us. "I have no idea why a man would do all that tedious work just to turn around and kill my daughter."

She took in a deep breath and hugged herself. Holden rubbed her back.

"And sometimes, you just know a person and know they could not do something so horrible."

"Did you tell the police that?" I asked.

"I did. They listened, but I don't think they heard me."

"Do you have any idea who might have wanted to harm her?"

"She was an amazing child. So bright. So full of life. Everyone knew she was a good girl. Everyone knew she stayed away from trouble."

Holden nodded. He seemed satisfied that I wasn't out to harm Brenda. He leaned down, whispered in her ear, and retreated to a back room.

"Did she have a boyfriend?" I asked.

"Nothing serious. She was too busy. Studying. Sports. The school paper."

Ms. Profit allowed herself a thin smile.

"I used to tell her she was wearing *me* out. She needed to slow down for the both of us."

She looked down at the floor again.

"The pain of losing a child. Of losing one so close. There is no pain like it, I suppose. Do you have children, Mr. Shea?"

"I don't."

"It's a pain I hope you never know."

It was my turn to stare at the floor.

"I lost my only brother a year ago. I can't imagine losing a child, but I do know how painful life can be."

"Dear God," she said. "I'm so sorry."

We sat quietly. I could hear a siren growing stronger outside. It whizzed past the house and down the block. Another one soon followed.

"I grew up here, Mr. Shea. Just a few blocks over." She pointed her thumb behind her as if I could see past her and through the walls. "My mother still lives in the house I grew up in. I love it here. There are challenges, for sure, but I did everything right with my daughter. She was on track to graduate with honors, go to a good college. I protected her all that time and then . . ." Her voice trailed off. "And then this happens."

"I don't know what to say, Ms. Profit. I mean Brenda. I'm so sorry."

"Don't be sorry. Find out who killed my daughter."

"I'm trying."

"Do *you* have any idea who would harm her?" she asked.

"No. There's a student. Rolando. He had a thing for her, but she turned him down. He's a little hard-edged."

She nodded.

"He's actually the reason my lip is like this. Popped me one last night when I tried to talk to him."

"Good Lord. She did tell me about him, but she said he was harmless. All talk but a pussycat underneath."

"There is also a man named Kratos. He might have had a role or knows who did."

She smiled.

"Do you know Kratos?" I asked.

"Everybody knows Kratos."

"Did Monique know him or have any connection to him?"

She paused and considered the question. She looked past me out the front window.

"I don't want to be indelicate here," I said, "but do you think your daughter could have had a relationship with him?"

Brenda jerked her head back toward me.

"Mr. Shea, Kratos is the reason you're here. He let me know that you met with him and that you seemed intent on finding Monique's real killer."

"Why would he tell you that?" My brain started to overheat.

"I assure you, he had nothing to do with her death. He wanted no harm to come of her. He loved her very much."

"I don't understand."

"Kratos, Mr. Shea, is Monique's father."

I sat quietly, processing the information. Kratos is Monique's father.

"We were together many years ago. Both young, naive. I got pregnant. We tried. He tried, but it didn't work out. I mostly raised her on my own as he went down a different path. But he always stayed in touch, always saw her. I mean it when I say he loved her and treated her like a princess."

"Did you tell the police?"

She laughed.

"Tell the police what? That the girl who died was the daughter of a known drug dealer? You think that would help motivate them? Mr. Shea, the best thing for my daughter is that the police think she's as sweet and innocent as any White girl."

"So, Kratos had nothing to do with her death?"

"Of course not. Except . . ."

"Except?"

"He thinks that this was to get back at him. To punish him. He obviously runs in dangerous circles."

She reached for a tissue from the box on the table and dabbed at both eyes.

"If they knew he had a daughter and they wanted to hurt him, that would be the way to do it," I said. "Does he have anyone in mind?"

"He has quite a few. Too many, in fact. The problem is, he is being watched so closely, he cannot do anything. If he were to confront any of those people, it would open up a door for whoever is watching him."

I scratched my chin.

"Police? FBI?"

"I have no idea, Mr. Shea. I stay out of his business as much as I can, and he tells me even less. I only know as much as I do because of my daughter. I hate him for this. I believe his lifestyle led to this. And I'm working on accepting that. I still want to find her killer. I want them to suffer. I want them to pay. That's why you are here. He thinks, as I do, that you can help us."

"Did you ever come in contact with a woman? Small build, tan, blonde hair?"

Brenda looked at me. Her eyes were swollen from tears. She had done everything right, and this happened.

"No. I don't know anyone like that. I do remember Monique met a woman through a scholarship program she got connected with. She was a mentor. Some pretty White woman was all she said. I was busy with an opening. I didn't pay it much mind." She closed her eyes. "My God, do you think she might have been the killer?"

"I really don't know."

"I have a card here somewhere." She stood up, walked to the dining room table, and shuffled a few papers. "Here it is." She handed me a business card: the name "Bright Futures," alongside a phone number and a sketch of a sunrise.

"Thank you."

"Would you like to see a picture of Monique?" she asked. She had grabbed her phone when she picked up the card.

"Yes, please."

She leaned down and held out the phone and began flipping through the hundreds of pictures she had of her daughter. They were all recent and showed Monique in a variety of activities: triple threat at an AAU basketball game, with friends at a Red Robin, standing on the beach facing the waves, a selfie with mom.

"She's beautiful," I said.

Brenda smiled softly.

"Oh, here's a video she did."

She tilted her phone sideways and pressed play. Monique was mugging for the camera, doing vogue-style poses while Madonna played in the background and her mom egged her on. It was clear they had a sisterly relationship as much as mother and daughter. It was also clear that Monique was mesmerizing. She had a charm, a personality that was infectious. Bright, energetic, beautiful.

Brenda placed the phone in her pocket. She wiped a few tears and walked to a side table.

"Here, I want to give you this, too," she said.

She returned and handed me a yellow sticky note with the name James and a phone number written on it."

"What's this?"

"That's the name and number of the janitor who found her. He left me a very nice message. The poor man was crying. He was very shaken. I haven't had the heart to call him back. I thought it might be something for you to follow up on. Maybe he saw something."

"This is helpful. Thank you."

She returned to her seat and crossed her legs.

"We'll be holding a memorial service Wednesday," she said. "I would like you to come."

"Thank you," I said. "I would like to pay my respects. Everything I've heard about her was that she was truly special. Again, I'm very sorry for your loss."

She dropped her head and wept. Holden came in from the back and hugged her from behind. I nodded to him and let myself out.

I was just past the door when she called me back. I turned, and she rushed to hug me.

"Please find out who did this to my daughter, Mr. Shea. Please."

I wrapped my arms around her and let her cry.

"I will," I said softly.

Before I let her go, she leaned in and whispered a name in my ear.

CHAPTER TWENTY-TWO

I LEFT BRENDA PROFIT TO HER GRIEF. I found my notebook in my truck and jotted down what I had learned and what I needed to do under my previous list of notes:

1. *Monique was Kratos's daughter*
2. *A White woman at the Bright Futures program talked to Monique multiple times*
3. *Call Bright Futures to ask about the woman*
4. *Call James, the school janitor*
5. *Keyser Söze*

As I pulled away, one of the two teens who were outside when I first went into Brenda's apartment crossed the street and motioned for me to wait. He was lean and muscular, likely around Monique's age. He wore a red 49ers cap that covered his forehead but not his large brown eyes.

"Can I help you?" I asked him.
"You asking about Monique?"
"Maybe."
"You a cop?"
"No, just trying to help."
He nodded and scratched his cleft chin with his right hand.
"I've been wanting to tell someone this, okay? I don't trust the

cops. I see you go in and talk to Ms. Profit for a while. I see you come out and she hugs you, so that tells me you're okay."

"You see a lot," I said. "What do you want to tell me?"

"Monique and I have been neighbors since she was a baby. She was a good girl. G.O.D."

"And?"

"Well, I ain't saying he did it. It's just that she was arguing a lot with her mom's boyfriend."

"Holden?"

"Yeah. Moms didn't really know. It was more when she wasn't around. You'd hear them argue a lot. She told me she was scared of him. I just think someone should look into it."

"Scared of him? Do you know what they argued about?"

"No. But if we were out front here, we'd hear 'em. He would be loud and would throw stuff. He comes across as Mr. Sweetie Pie, but he definitely has a temper."

"Thanks," I said. "That helps."

"Find out who did it. Put his ass away. She was a special girl." He turned and shuffled back across the street.

I drove a few blocks before pulling over in front of an empty lot populated with overgrown grass and weeds. It was blocked by a chain link fence that had "Keep Out" signs posted every ten feet. Across the street was a small park with a big grass field and a new playground with swings, slides, and climbing structures.

I closed my eyes. An image of Brenda, a strong and proud mom, came into focus. The name she had whispered in my ear was Keyser Söze. Who the hell was this guy?

I heard shouts and screams. I opened my eyes to see a group of kids playing football in the park across the street, and apparently someone had scored. I reached into my pocket and pulled out the card and the yellow sticky note Brenda gave me. I called the Bright Futures number first. A general announcement told me to leave a message after the beep, and I did. Next, I tried James, the janitor.

"Hello?" A nasally voice answered.

"Yes, I'm looking for James. He works at Jefferson High School."

"This is James."

"James, my name is Seamus Shea. Brenda Profit, Monique's mom, gave me your number and asked that I talk to you."

Silence.

"I just wanted to ask you about what happened at the school."

"Okay. Are you a cop?"

"No. I'll be honest with you. I'm a friend of Mr. Gomez's, and I'm trying to figure out what happened."

More silence. The young kids playing football were still screaming and laughing. I looked over, and the largest kid was eyeing me.

"Would you be open to talking about it?" I asked James.

"Yes," he said. "I told the police a few times, but they don't seem to listen to me."

"Told them?"

"About what happened. I don't think it was Mr. Gomez."

"Okay. Why don't you tell me?"

"It was in the morning and I had done my early rounds. I always go see Mr. Gomez to say hello and talk a bit. I think that's why the police don't believe me. They think I'm too close to him. I walked into his class, and I saw him in the corner, leaning over Monique. His left hand was touching her cheek and he had a knife in his right hand. It was red with blood. He looked back at me, and he was crying."

"Crying?"

"Yes, I could see the tears on his face. He dropped the knife and walked to his desk. He put his head in his hands and said, 'she's gone.'"

"What time was that?"

"Must have been around 7:45 a.m."

He paused. I thought of asking another question but held back. The large kid on the field across the street was still eyeing me. He had not moved.

"I asked him what happened," James continued, "and he didn't talk. He just sat there with his head in his hands. I ran to another classroom to call 911."

"Jesus."

"Yeah, Jesus. I don't think I can go back to that school. It was terrible."

"But you don't think he stabbed her?"

"No. Just the way he was standing over her. Touching her cheek. You don't do that to someone you just stabbed to death. Also, I don't know how he could have enough time. I saw him a few minutes before that coming from the bathroom."

"You saw him outside the classroom?"

"Yeah."

"What time?"

"It was like ten minutes before I went to his room. He said, 'I'll see you in a bit,' all upbeat and happy."

"Did you tell the cops that?"

"Yes, but they thought I got the time wrong. I was confused and in shock when they talked to me. I'm sure I didn't make sense. Once they had his confession, it didn't seem to matter."

"Did you see anyone else? Anyone not normally there?"

"No."

"And where was the bathroom you saw him at?"

"It's at the far end of the hall on the third floor. Right by the stairs."

"The stairs next to his classroom?"

"No, the ones on the opposite end."

"He'd have to walk the full third floor to go to the staff bathroom?"

"Yes."

"Someone could have come up the other set of stairs and not be seen by you or him?"

"It's possible."

I looked back at the park and now all of the kids were looking back at me. One raised his arms out and up as if to say, "you want some?"

Fearless. I was afraid of every adult I'd seen growing up. These kids were fearless.

"James, thank you for talking to me."

"Of course. I feel so bad. I know Mr. Gomez did not do this. I feel so bad for the girl and her family. I'll never be able to go back to that school. Never."

The small group of kids had doubled now. They were all looking my way and had stopped playing football. One of the kids drinking from a soda can moved toward me. I started the truck and pulled out as he ran at me and threw the soda can. The liquid trailed out as it smacked against my side door. I sped away and watched them through my rear-view mirror, dancing in the street behind as if they had just won the Super Bowl.

Fearless.

CHAPTER TWENTY-THREE

I PULLED MY TRUCK INTO MY MOTHER'S DRIVEWAY AND GOT OUT TO INSPECT THE DAMAGE FROM THE SODA CAN PROJECTILE. I noticed a small dent high up on the driver's side door. The paint wasn't chipped, and it wasn't visible unless you knew what you were looking for. Bunny's voice singing "Let It Be" came back to me.

I went into my apartment and fell on my bed. I looked up at ceiling Jesus, hoping for help. No reply. I fell asleep and woke up about an hour later to my phone vibrating. Sean Mannion, Danny's old partner in narcotics.

"Seamus, that you? Seamus, you there?"

"Hey, Sean," I answered.

"Seamus Shea! My man. How the fuck are you?"

He was drunk.

"Good. Hanging in there."

"Sorry about Pedro, man. I heard. That's just . . . that's just . . . it just sucks."

He was really drunk.

"Look, I'm at Norty3s. Why don't you come out, and we'll drink a few? It's been too long, Shame. Too long."

I didn't want to talk to Sean. I knew there was a 99 percent chance he'd want to meet me at a bar. While AA didn't seem to be for me, I still needed to stay somewhat sober to help PG. I could take most of Sean's usual haunts at this point, but Norty3s was the type of place that dive bars made fun of. Sobriety was a four-letter word at that place.

They called it Norty3s just so people knew where to tell the cab to pick them up from. Noriega and 43rd Ave. Its clientele was mostly cops. Danny took me there a few times. I had little memory of those nights.

"I can't make it tonight. Could you meet tomorrow?"

"Can't make it? C'mon, Seamus, get your ass down here. There's a live band playing!"

"Really? A live band at Norty3s?"

I heard him shuffle from his seat and put his cell phone up to the paint-splattered boom box circa 1991 they had at the end of the bar. A fast Irish reel was playing.

"They sound great," I said.

"They're fantastic," he said.

"How about tomorrow?"

"I'm working the rest of the week, Seamus. Now or never. Get your ass down here. This band! They're fantastic!"

Every part of me said don't go. I thought of Bunny. I thought of PG. I thought of having a drink.

"All right, Sean," I said. "I'll be there in a half hour."

"Yes!" he screamed into the phone. I could hear him yelling around the bar: "The Great Seamus Shea will be here in minutes, lads!"

"Who gives a flying fuck?" Someone yelled back.

I drove out to Noriega and 43rd Avenue. It was dark and my windshield was fogging up. I hit the defrost, and it whirred to life, slowly clearing the glass. As much as the drive from my mother's house to Hunter's Point felt like traveling to another world, the Sunset was its own unique universe: cement, little grass, few trees. You'd get hardened just driving around seeing all that gray. It was also mostly flat and on a grid that went on and on and on. Avenue after avenue. The view of the ocean was the only thing that kept you from being lost in a maze, like something out of *The Shining*.

I parked on 43rd Avenue and walked up and down Noriega trying to find the intentionally clandestine entrance to Norty3s. The block had only single-family homes pressed next to each other one by one. I could hear the ocean waves crashing half a mile away. I eventually stopped at a nondescript black door with paint peeling at its four corners. I put my right ear up to it and heard the faint sounds of The Chieftains. This had to be it. I took a deep breath and rapped my knuckles against the black door.

"Who the fook is that?" a deep voice cried out.

"Seamus Shea," I answered confidently.

There was a long pause without response. Finally, the door flew open and a giant of a man with a bright-red face leaned down to me and screamed, "Who the fook is Seamus Shea?"

"I'm here to see Sean Mannion."

The giant stood back and looked me over.

"Are you that fucking reporter?"

"I used to be."

"What happened?"

"Jameson's."

He leaned back and smirked. Policemen were not fans of the press in any form. There was little trust between the two groups. Danny lent me some credibility, but for any other cop who knew me as a reporter, I'd find little welcome.

"You Irish?" he asked.

"Yes."

"Bullshit. Where is your father from?"

"Rosmuc," I said.

"A Connemara man?"

"Yes."

"You ever been there, lad?"

"Once."

"Visit Padraig Pearse's cottage?"

"I did. He taught my great-uncles."

The giant seemed to judge my veracity as if I'd actually make something like that up.

"Come in, Seamus, ignore him. You're welcome here," a voice came from the dark.

The giant led me inside to what was essentially someone's garage. There was a round table in the back where Sean, flushed-faced and dazed, sat staring at an empty shot glass and a half-filled pint of Guinness. He stood up from the table and walked around to give me a hug.

"He's all right, Tommy. He's all right. I'll vouch for him."

The giant nodded and retreated back to a stool near the entrance.

Sean, a short, stout Irishman from the rocky West Coast of Éire, came to the city twenty years prior, earning a spot with San Francisco's finest after four years as a carpenter. He maneuvered his way up from patrolman to gang task force to narcotics. The last three years, he worked with Danny. Danny loved him. I was not a fan.

Sean called out an order to Liam Casey, the red-haired proprietor, who was pouring a Guinness from a jockey box at the far end of the makeshift bar. The bar consisted of three sawhorses, strips of sanded plywood, and six backless counter stools. Liam nodded at Sean and continued his pour. Sitting in the corner, the smell of malt and whiskey mixed with smoke made me feel a little nauseous. This might be the only place in the city where you could smoke indoors. How would cops bust cops? So much smoke swirled above my head that I thought for a brief moment the room might be on fire.

"Where's the band?" I asked.

Sean looked left and right.

"Oh, they just left," he said. "We put that thing on there to break the silence." He pointed at the battered boom box, which was now playing Van Morrison.

It was an odd space with a few round tables off to the left and the piecemeal bar of sawhorses and plywood to your right. Behind the bar was a large bookcase that displayed a variety of Irish whiskeys. Looking at those resting on the stools, I could see the usual collection of men, scruffy and worn out after a day's work. The giant who let me in sat at the last stool across from the room's only decoration. Two sleek hurling sticks were mounted to the wall in the form of an X. Liam Casey valued those sticks more than his bar. They were called hurleys and Tipperary's captain gave them as gifts to the bar when he visited a couple years back.

"So, Seamus, how you doing?"

"I've been better."

"What happened to your lip?"

"Long story. Not worth your time."

"How's your ma?"

"She's doing okay."

"I heard about your friend, there. Sad thing. Sad thing."

"He's innocent," I said.

Sean nodded meekly.

"Sure. But tell an American jury that."

He waved his hands as if swatting flies. Man, he was pissed. He turned to look directly at me.

"How are *you* doing, Seamus Shea? I heard the wife left ya."

That was Sean, empathetic and insulting in back-to-back sentences.

"Yeah, didn't work out."

Sean gave an easy smile.

"Ah, don't I know it. I'm on my third one right now. You didn't have kids, did ya?"

"No, we never did."

He nodded furiously.

"That's good. That's good. I got two from the first one and one from the second one. Got my tubes tied before this third go around, so no more for me!"

"Congratulations," I said, not knowing how to respond.

"Thank you," he said, with earnest. I guess I did know what to say.

"You doing okay?" I asked.

"Ah, can't complain. Above ground as they say; a lot better than being below it."

"I'm hoping you can answer a couple questions for me. It has to do with PG and the murder."

"Shoot," he said.

"What do you know about Kratos?" I asked.

He scratched his chin.

"Kratos. Kratos. That fucker supplies drugs for almost all of the city. He's come on real strong the past year. Got some connection that's doubled or tripled his supply. A very big player who's made Kratos a very big player."

"You ever meet him?"

Sean eyed me carefully.

"Kratos?" he asked.

"Yeah."

Sean seemed to sober up in one comment.

"Why would I be talking to him?"

I didn't answer.

"I don't have conversations with a man like that. The only conversation I'll ever have with him is to say, 'you are under arrest.'"

I felt a sharp pain in my temples. Either a well-known drug dealer was lying to me or my brother's old partner was. The pain grew more intense as I found myself believing Kratos.

"I love this song!" Sean screamed, standing up and raising his glass. The Pogues, "Sickbed of Cuchulainn," had just started on the boom box. Sean sang along and tapped his foot. He did not have a good voice; although Shane MacGowan had the same problem, but he made it work.

"I heard he has a big supplier. Keyser Söze? Who is he?" I asked, screaming up at him.

Liam brought over the drinks. Two pints of Guinness and two whiskey chasers. Sean took a seat and waited until Liam left.

"Keyser Söze!" he laughed. "I believe in God and the only thing that scares me is Keyser Söze!"

I vaguely remembered it as a line from the movie.

"So, who is Keyser Söze?" I asked.

"We don't know."

"You don't know?"

"He's a pro. He is just like the movie Keyser Söze. We've been trying to get him for well over a year, and nothing. It was one of the last cases Danny worked on."

Sean closed his eyes.

"I miss him, Seamus. I do."

"I know," I said. "I miss him, too."

"But this mother. Bleaches his asshole; he's that clean."

I let the image pass.

"You know, your brother made some progress on the whole thing. He had some files that he wanted to share with me before . . ."

I nodded.

"Do you have any idea where those files might be?"

"I can take a look and see what I find," I lied. There was a storage locker full of Danny's things in Daly City, but I had no interest in looking for any files for Sean. I wasn't trusting him too much right now and I didn't feel like chasing anything that wouldn't help me get PG off.

Sean closed his eyes again. He kept them closed as he drank his Guinness.

"I really miss him, Seamus. Your brother was one in a million."

"I know, Sean," I said. "You were one of his favorites."

"Enough of this; let's drink."

He handed me the shot of whiskey. The bar was oddly quiet. The smoke had faded some. Sean Mannion's bloodshot eyes glared back at me. He smiled, displaying his crooked, country teeth. This was how I'd been remembering Danny for the past year. Shot after shot. Beer after beer. Whiskey after whiskey. I thought of the big biker named Bunny I'd met today. I thought of this morning, waking up with a swollen lip and nothing to show.

"Come on, man! Have a taste. For your brother," he said, holding his shot glass toward me.

I could smell the whiskey. I could taste it. I heard Bunny's voice tell me to let it be. I thought of the past year of being sick and tired of being sick and tired. Of trying to drink Danny's memory away. Trying to drink all the pain away.

We clinked glasses.

"Just a taste," he said. "For you brother."

Just a taste.

For my brother.

Just a taste.

TUESDAY

CHAPTER TWENTY-FOUR

I WAS DRUNK.

I stood rooted halfway down the eastern walkway of the world-famous, crimson-colored Golden Gate Bridge, freezing my ass off.

I was not a tourist.

I was not a sightseer.

I was a fool.

I had left Sean at Norty3s and stumbled the mile and a half to the famous perch. The bridge held all the good of the city: beauty, power, function. But it held dark memories too.

I had come to face those dark memories.

A tempest swirled around me as could be expected when you were exposed some two hundred feet above the Pacific Ocean. It was a clear November night, but the gusts were relentless. My face was windburned. My hands were numb. My balls were ice cubes.

I sucked in the cold air, blinked at the view, and tried to figure out what the fuck it all meant.

11:11 p.m.

Despite the late hour, the bridge lights and the full moon brightened the green sea and gray sky. Cars careened along behind me. Not many at such a late hour, and yet, there was a rhythm to the few that rumbled over expansion joints, a metronomic hum: da-dum, da-dum, da-dum. Alcatraz loomed ahead, a ghost prison, a dark lump topped with a flickering candle of a lighthouse. To the right, a small forest of boxy gray skyscrapers huddled on the downtown landfill, while the less famous bridge, the silver one, glimmered in the distance.

A postcard image animated by a soundtrack of blustering wind, rumbling cars, and splashing waves. It was all very beautiful except for the stench: a mix of algae, sulfates, exhaust, and whiskey.

My whiskey.

The flat steel railing that kept me from falling into the Bay that ebbed and flowed below couldn't have been more than four feet high. Was this all there was? Was this why it was so easy? To jump or not to jump? One leap and all the fear and frustration and failure would be wiped clean, one small jump for peace.

It would take five full Mississippis to reach the anxious ocean below. I gripped one of the taut steel ropes and edged my head and shoulders over the railing. Even at such a distance I felt a connection to the water. Rooted deep in the DNA of each of my cells were memories of ancestors smoking salt air while tilling rocky land along the jagged western coast of that fat little toddler island, the one that turned from its abusive stepfather, England, and reached across the Atlantic for its big-breasted mother, America. My ancestors—clan-based, Irish-tongued, coarse creatures—would have had little use for the comforts I held so near and dear today. It would've pained them to know that they endured the Great Hunger, English oppression, country Catholicism, and all the other slings and arrows to produce such a coddled, narrow-back Yank with soft hands and a softer will.

I had disappointed the dead.

The dead.

Danny.

I drank to forget the dead. I drank to forget my past. I drank because I feared my future. I drank to manage the river of uncertainty that churned inside me. I drank because life didn't make sense, there was no method to the madness, there was no logical explanation as to why we ate, shit, and slept 365 days a year, year after year after year.

And so, I stood at the railing, cars pulsed behind me, the wind assaulted me, my face numb, my testicles undescended. I wanted to end feeling miserable, to stop wearing such pain.

Growing up, the nuns would tell us that God was the ocean and we were all just fish. Could you imagine the burden to be God? The terrible weight of His profession? Make the impossible possible, help lost causes, almost seven billion asking.

Danny, what should I do? Should I pray? Will you hear me? In the name of the Father and of the Son and of the Holy Ghost, as it was in the beginning is now and ever shall be world without end, Amen.

Danny, my only brother, my Irish twin, my hero in so many ways, the one person in this world I truly and deeply loved. Danny. Brave and gentle and good. Almost a year ago, Thanksgiving night, he'd driven his orange Mazda to the same southeast visitor's parking lot where I parked, walked the same half-mile stretch to stand at the same perch. I imagined that he had braced against the cold, looked out at the view, and thought about the same damn things. He thought of all that he had done and all that he had failed to do.

But unlike me, Danny didn't complain.

Danny didn't waffle.

Danny didn't whine. No, not Danny.

He jumped.

CHAPTER TWENTY-FIVE

I WAS HUNGOVER, AGAIN. Ceiling Jesus looked disgusted. I didn't blame Him.

Another night at Norty3s that was a bit hazy. I had met Sean. We had talked about Kratos. He gave me a shot. Then another. Then another. I ended up walking to the Golden Gate Bridge, mulling over Danny. How was any of this going to help PG? How was me being drunk into the night and hungover each morning going to help my friend?

I stood up and wobbled; I had to brace myself against my nightstand. I glanced at the AA brochure on it. I had a meeting with Rev and the defense lawyer at 11:00 a.m. I had two hours to kill. I showered, ate a bowl of Raisin Bran, and flipped through my notes. Clear as mud.

I left my truck in the avenues, so I took a Lyft to pick it up. I still had time before I'd meet Rev. I decided to do a little surveillance and drove back to Brenda Profit's place. Something didn't sit right with Holden, the boyfriend. Maybe he had an issue with Kratos? Wanted to get back at him? I parked across the street and halfway down the block. My first stakeout.

There was activity in the body shop across the street. A large Black man holding a clipboard seemed to be in charge. He wore dark gray coveralls and had a noticeable bowlegged walk that made me think he had a prosthetic leg. He'd talk to the car owner, walk gingerly around the car to inspect it, fill out the papers on his clipboard, and get a signature. I watched him perform this ritual three times. He never smiled but had a pleasant manner and each car owner seemed happy.

I flipped through my preset radio stations as I waited. I settled on a local talk radio station that was discussing Monique. Callers were disgusted that a teacher would commit such a crime.

"What kind of a city is this where students get killed by their teachers?" Ronald, a first-time caller, long-time listener asked. The host tried to offer an innocent-until-proven-guilty defense, but Ronald was not having it. "I bet he was sleeping with her. And then it got out of control. And he had to kill her." I flipped to FM and a U2 song from *The Joshua Tree*.

I sat there for twenty minutes and was about to pull away when Holden walked out of the apartment, climbed into a red Camaro parked in front of the apartment, and drove away.

I followed.

He turned right on Third Street and drove half a mile before pulling into a mini-mall. I parked on the street outside. He wore gray sweatpants, black high-top sneakers, and a blue long-sleeved Warrior's shirt. Not exactly business casual. He went into the dry cleaners and came out with a stack of plastic-wrapped clothes that he laid down in the back seat.

He left the mini-mall and continued north on Third Street. After four blocks, he pulled over and parked. I stayed back. He jaywalked across Third, holding a handful of letters. He walked into the post office and came back out in minutes. He crossed back, got in his car, and stayed on Third, going north.

If this was surveillance, it was boring as all hell.

Holden stopped again after a half mile. He parked at a meter and crossed the street. As I looked for a space to park, I noticed a black sedan a few cars back. I thought it was the same black sedan that passed by me when I stopped at the mini-mall. I wondered if I was getting paranoid.

I pulled into an open space three spots behind Holden's car. I looked for the sedan and caught it turning right on the street I just crossed over. I *was* getting paranoid. Holden stood outside a flower shop, inspecting the bins of flowers. An older Asian woman in a light blue apron came out and helped him. She picked out a colorful array of flowers and took them inside the shop. Holden followed.

I wasn't sure what I was expecting Holden to do. I didn't get his animosity toward PG. The teen neighbor seemed convinced that Holden did not like Monique. Yelling between stepfathers and daughters was hardly new or cause for murder. But there were crazier reasons.

He walked out of the flower shop and waved back to his helper. He held a nicely wrapped bouquet of flowers. I couldn't make out what flowers because I was too far away. I also didn't know any flowers except roses, sunflowers, and carnations. They definitely weren't any of those, but they were cheery, and I wondered if Brenda had a birthday or anniversary, or maybe it was just because her daughter was killed.

Holden got back in his car and made a U-turn at the next street. I followed carefully. He gave no indication that he knew I was tailing him. I made the same U-turn and stayed a block back. He turned right on Cesar Chavez. I followed. I checked my rear-view again and saw the same black sedan four car-lengths back. I was being followed. The follower was being followed. What the hell?

Holden turned right and right again to merge onto 280 heading south. He wasn't going back home. I didn't want to chase him on the freeway, but I'd come this far. I was also curious if the black sedan would join us. I turned and turned again. Holden stayed in the fast lane, which meant he would likely be taking 101 South. I stayed a few cars behind him. The black sedan had joined us and was three car-lengths behind me.

We merged onto 101. Holden quickly jerked to the right. I thought he might have seen me and was trying to get away, but he was just moving quickly to make the next exit. I followed and nearly sideswiped a cement truck that slowed down as I tried to change lanes. I pumped my brakes to avoid the collision. The sedan still followed.

Holden got off on Third Street and continued straight down Bayshore. He kept driving and eventually turned right on Sunnydale. The sedan was still a few car-lengths back. I put on my blinker to give them a heads up that I was turning. Seemed the polite thing to do.

Halfway down Sunnydale, Holden pulled into an open space. I did a quick U-turn and parked down the street a block back. I thought I'd catch the sedan driving my way, but it was gone. I turned back and watched Holden get out with his bouquet. The block was mostly new construction townhouses. They each had a few steps up to a brightly colored front door.

Holden walked up the steps of a townhouse two doors down from where he parked. I ducked down in my seat in case he looked my way. He rang the bell. A young, busty woman in a Niners jersey and sweats answered the door. She reached out and hugged him. He passed her the flowers, and they kissed.

Fucking Holden.

They went inside and I started my car, disappointed in the frailties of men. Poor Brenda: lost a daughter, and her boyfriend was cheating. I tried to think of what it might mean. It gave him a motive. Maybe Monique knew and was going to expose him? That could have been the arguing. Although murder seemed a little extreme. But it did show he wasn't honest, and it showed he wasn't a good guy, as the neighbor kid pointed out. His anger at PG might have been some type of projection, a way to manage his guilt for cheating.

Tell it to your psychiatrist!

I pulled out and headed back toward my meeting with Rev. I turned up Bayshore and noticed the sedan again. Where had it been? I sped up and weaved through the traffic. I never tailed anyone before, and I thought I did a pretty good job, although I wished I hadn't found what I found. Now *I* was being tailed. What should I do? Lose them? Confront them? An image of the chase scene from *Bullitt* flashed in my mind.

I merged onto 101 and floored it. I made a move for the fast lane.

The sedan picked up speed. I was close to the 101 and 280 split. I waited as long as I could and then pulled the truck four lanes to the right to just get on 280 by barely missing the divider. I looked up and the sedan was right with me. They anticipated the move.

I headed on 280 South. Traffic was sparse. The sedan kept its distance. Whatever I was doing in search of Monique's true killer, it was working. PG was in the middle of something much larger than an upset student or a cheating boyfriend. My heart skipped. My breathing became labored. My mind catastrophized. The DJ on the radio said she was playing a request for Allen in San Mateo. "Let It Be," by the Beatles. I laughed out loud.

I kept an even speed on 280 South and passed Monterey Avenue and Ocean and Geneva Avenue exits. I pulled my truck to the far-right lane and got off on Mission and Alemany. The sedan was behind me now but far enough back that I couldn't make out the driver. I kept an even pace, heading west on Alemany and stayed in the right lane. The oncoming traffic of Alemany was next to us now, and a small curb with flowers kept you from drifting into the other eastbound traffic. Now or never. I jerked my truck to the left, cutting off a van, jumped the divider, and headed in the opposite direction on Alemany. The sedan tried to follow my move, but the traffic and curb kept them stuck. I floored it and laid on my horn as I ran the light and jumped onto the 280 North on-ramp. Plenty of horns and upset drivers, but they'd live. I looked in my rear-view and smiled; I had successfully lost my first tail.

I turned up my radio and sang along, as the Beatles sang, "Let It Be."

CHAPTER TWENTY-SIX

I MET REV ON VAN NESS AVE. I was still buzzing and a little paranoid from my car chase. He led me into the lobby of a regal, elderly office building. I filled him in on what I learned from Brenda Profit, James, and Holden, and the outcome of my recent Steve McQueen car chase.

"You're an action hero," he said.

We had an appointment with a classmate of Rev's from law school who was a well-respected criminal attorney. Rev got him to take the case.

"Can we trust this guy?" I asked.

"Yeah, we can trust *her*. I'd tell her everything you know."

"Apologies for my gender bias. I assumed she was a man," I said.

"You know what happens when you assume? You make an ass of you and . . ."

"I know, I know."

We checked in with the portly security guard sitting at the front desk.

"Fourth floor," he said.

We braved a rickety elevator with a black accordion-style metal gate for four floors. It lurched and rattled as it passed each floor. I thought I heard it sigh after the third floor. The cramped space smelled like an old folks' home, and the capacity limit was written in large type over the floor buttons: *No More Than Five People at A Time.*

"You sure she's good?" I asked. "This place doesn't exactly scream high-powered lawyer."

"She's frugal," Rev said.

We exited the elevator and entered a modest, modern office space. The secretary, a husky, dark-haired young man with dimples, led us through the maze of cubicles to a back office with double-hung windows that looked out on Van Ness.

"How's it going, Maria?" Rev asked, walking around the desk for a hug.

"Malcolm, it's so good to see you. How are the girls? Pam?"

"Growing up fast. The girls, too."

Maria chuckled. She was of medium build with a youthful face and straight, dark hair. She wore a sensible but stylish navy pantsuit with fashionable open toe heels. She was pretty but approachable. I could see her engaging a jury.

"Maria, this is my good friend Seamus," Rev said.

"Maria Luna," she said.

We shook hands, and she gestured for us to sit. Her office was simple and clean. Two wooden armchairs, a wooden desk, and her ergonomic office chair on rollers. There were a couple of bookcases and file cabinets against one wall, but the opposite wall was bare, no pictures or degrees. It was like they had just moved in. I couldn't decide if that was a good thing or bad thing. Somewhere, PG was yelling: *Nothing is either good or bad but thinking makes it so.*

"I looked over the case, talked to a couple people. I don't get it," Maria said.

I looked at Rev then back at Maria. She had a file folder and a marked-up yellow legal pad open on her desk. She looked at a sheet of paper in the file.

"Everything about this guy says unsung hero. Stanford grad. Goes into teaching and coaching. Stellar rep. No one says a bad word about him. He's helping this girl. He's helping this girl with college apps. Then he kills her? No motive. With a knife? That's personal; that's intimate. And he confesses?"

"We think someone is threatening him," I said.

"Yeah. That's a plausible explanation." She flipped through the yellow legal pad on her desk. "But who? And why?"

"That's what we're trying to figure out," Rev said.

"And how's that going?"

"Like Tort Law 550," Rev said. They both started laughing. "But we have some leads."

"I don't get the sense the police have any other real suspects. They just think he snapped. They point to an incident he had with a player. Hothead coach, snaps with student." She closed the file and looked at us. "And it does happen."

"Not PG," I said.

Maria nodded and leaned back in her chair.

"I'm not worried about the coaching thing. That's pretty thin. But I'll be honest with you guys. Given what we have, if he keeps insisting he did it, I'd have to go for a plea."

"Such as?" Rev asked.

"We'd try for second-degree murder. No guarantee they'd go for it. Fifteen years at least, likely a lot more."

Rev and I sat silently while hefty sounds from Van Ness filled the void. Construction equipment, busses, horns, shouts, and screams all combined in the room like some discordant orchestra.

"I know it seems harsh, but I'm just being realistic. This is a teacher killing a student. They're not going to give him a break, even in SF."

She dropped her elbows on the desk and leaned toward us.

"What leads do you have?" she asked.

Rev looked at me and tilted his head toward Maria.

"So, I've been doing some research to try and see what might have happened," I said.

"Research?" Maria asked.

"Yeah, like my own detective work."

"Okay, what did you find?"

"Well, Monique is the daughter of Kratos. Do you know who Kratos is?"

"Everyone knows who Kratos is," she said. She leaned back in her chair. "That is an interesting fact. What else?"

"Well, I talked to the janitor who found PG in the room. He said he saw PG near the bathroom on the other side of the third floor like ten to fifteen minutes before he found PG with Monique. Said he was fine, friendly, told him to stop by."

Maria didn't speak. She grabbed her legal pad and started jotting down notes. She asked a number of clarifying questions: the janitor's name and number, how I learned about Kratos and Monique, and more. I told her about Holden's infidelity and Rolando's right cross. I also told her about the Daniella Walsh imposter and Bright Futures and my run in with her in PG's apartment. I saved the car chase for last.

She leaned back again, tapping her pen against her left palm.

"Nice work, Magnum," she said.

I shrugged. She looked out the window.

"Well, damn," she said.

"What does that mean?" Rev asked.

Maria glanced at Rev.

"It means, damn. But don't worry, it's a good damn. There is a lot there. A lot to put some doubt in a juror's mind. We can work with this. Nice job."

"But," Rev asked, reading his friend.

"The confession is the real sticking point," she said.

"We are going to see him after this meeting. You think we should try and get him to take it back?" I asked.

"Yes. If he recants, I think we have a shot. Our odds will increase significantly."

"But won't that be in the back of the jury's mind?"

"You let me worry about that. If we can get him to recant, the jury might not ever hear about it. And even if they did, I can pass it off to stress and shock and have expert after expert point out similar experiences."

"So that's a thing, false confessions?" I asked.

"Absolutely."

"Okay, we'll get him to take it back," Rev said.

"Good. And are you going to do more 'research?'" she asked me, using air quotes when she said research.

"Yes, ma'am."

"Great, but don't call me ma'am. I hate that." She handed me a business card. "Keep me in the loop with what you find. There's a lot here. We need to connect the dots, but I see a glimmer of hope, gentlemen. It's all about doubt in the minds of the jurists, and there is doubt here."

Maria stood up and held out her hand to me. She leaned over her desk and gave Rev a hug.

"When do you see him?" Rev asked.

"Later today. Like 4:00 p.m. They scheduled the arraignment for Friday."

"We'll talk to him," Rev said.

"I know I sound cold, Malcom," Maria said. "I realize this is your close friend." She looked at me. "But that's what makes me a good defense lawyer. You immigration guys are all heart. We're all stone."

Rev smiled.

"You were all stone long before you became a defense lawyer," Rev laughed. "Just ask Jeremy."

Maria's cheeks reddened.

"That's a low blow, Malcolm. Low blow."

She walked us out. Rev and I thanked her again and got back in the unsteady elevator.

"Jeremy?" I asked as we rode down.

"Apparently, they never found his balls," Rev said, straight-faced.

CHAPTER TWENTY-SEVEN

PG HAD BEEN MOVED TO THE COUNTY JAIL IN SAN BRUNO. I followed Rev down 280 and practiced my now-familiar routine of rear-view mirror sedan spotting. No luck. Of course, I wasn't worried about if they followed us to jail. That might have been the one place we'd be safe. Still, I dreaded the drive. I didn't want to see PG. I kept imagining him as bruised and battered. He was on the smaller side, gentle, and accused of killing a young Black girl. That couldn't make him a hero inside.

I parked next to Rev, and we formulated a plan as we walked to the entrance.

"We tell him mom is okay," Rev started.

"That we have a couple of leads that could pan out and clear him," I added.

"The key is mom. He needs to know she's safe."

As we approached the entrance, I heard a voice call my name. I turned to see Don's giant frame jogging toward me.

"Shame, how you doing?" he asked.

"Been better," I said. "You ever meet my friend Rev?"

"Don't think so, I'm Don Johnson." He held out a hand to Rev.

"Really?" Rev asked, shaking his hand.

"Yes, really."

I held back a laugh. Don was a little sensitive about his full name.

"You going to see PG?" he asked.

"Yeah."

"What about you?" I asked.

"I had an interview with a potential suspect. No luck, though. Fucker had an alibi."

Don looked toward the entrance.

"How's PG doing?" he asked.

"Not sure. Haven't talked to him since that first day. There's a lot going on here, Don. I've been followed."

"Followed, huh?" He tilted his head as if looking at a scared child.

"Yeah. This is bigger than some English teacher."

"Shame, let us do the detective work, okay? I know you are trying to help. But this is pretty open and shut. Okay?"

"Open and shut?"

"Look, Shame, I don't want to tell you what to do. And I can't talk to you about the case and all."

"I know."

"It's just . . ." he looked down at the path. "I would encourage your boy to plea out. The less he fights this, the better. I mean, he confessed; he didn't resist. He's got a lot of good things going for him in the eyes of a judge."

"What about being followed?"

"Murder cases do strange things to folks, Shame. People get paranoid. You want to help your friend. It's understandable. People create these larger-than-life scenarios all the time. They don't want to believe what's right in front of their face. It's human nature."

I had lost Don.

"Rhodes is all over this, Shame. He's convinced. He's convinced the DA. Time to make a deal. I'm sorry, I wish I could be of more help."

Don looked at the entrance again.

"Nice to meet you," he said to Rev.

He headed out to the parking lot and left Rev and me standing on the path.

"Don Johnson?" Rev said. "Like Nash Bridges and Miami Vice?"

"Yep. How would you like that name as an SF cop?"

Rev shook his head as we shuffled up to the jail, which with its curved facade and rows of large windows looked more like a college library than a prison. We made our way through the processing stations to a scene out of any cop TV show. A small room with five stations, each with privacy partitions and a glass wall looking out on a mirror image. A phone handset was mounted on each side of the partition. Rev took a seat on the one stool and I leaned down above him.

"Don said the same thing as Maria. Plea out," Rev said. He was tapping his right hand on his right knee.

"Yeah. Twenty-five years, Rev."

"Jesus. How did we get to this?"

Eventually, they brought out PG. I'd been bracing myself for a bruised face, black eyes, cut lips, but he looked pretty good. Tired and worn out, but no physical marks. He wore the same wrinkled, oversized orange jumpsuit that I saw him in on Friday.

Rev started talking, but PG motioned for him to pick up the phone. Rev scooted over and we shared the stool while we both leaned into the handset.

"It's good to see you guys," he said. His eyes were heavy and red.

"Good to see you. How's it going?" I said. Probably the dumbest question I could ask.

He shrugged.

"How's my mom?" he asked.

"She's good. She didn't go see Uncle Carlos, but Tito is with her. She's safe."

I could see relief on his face.

"Also, I saw Father Ryan, and he's going to say that special prayer for you."

PG furrowed his brow. I didn't know how cryptic I should be.

"What happened to your lip?" he asked.

"He got beat up by a high school kid," Rev said.

"I didn't get beat up."

"Who?" PG asked.

"Rolando, I was asking him some questions."

"Rolando? From Jefferson?"

I nodded.

"He's got nothing to do with this, Shame, nothing."

I stared back at him through the thick glass.

"Tell us who does then."

PG looked away and held the phone against his chest. He turned back to us and brought the phone to his mouth.

"Me, just me," he said.

"I met with Brenda Profit, too."

PG raised an eyebrow.

"She's a nice lady," he said.

"She thinks you're innocent."

PG scoffed. "Yeah, well, she's wrong."

"I met Holden, too."

"Her boyfriend?"

"Yeah."

"He's got problems," PG said.

"Something I should look into?"

PG scratched his scalp.

"No. He's cheating on Brenda. Monique found out. Was going to talk to him about it. Don't think she got the chance."

An image of Holden shopping for flowers flashed through my mind's eye. I thought of the note from Monique. *I took your advice and I'm going to talk to him.* That must have been about Holden, not Kratos.

"You safe in here? Anyone bothering you?" Rev asked.

"I got a friend, an old student of mine. He's been taking care of me. Protecting me, I guess. He's well known. I was good to him when he was a student. Guess being a teacher finally paid off."

"That's good," I said.

"Yeah, but he's getting sentenced. Going to be transferred Friday. I don't know what to do after that. There were two guys that came up to me and said once he's gone, it's open season. They said they aren't fans of wetback Mexicans killing young Black girls. They were huge. Scared the shit out of me. Didn't have the heart to tell them I was Salvadoran."

"My friend Maria is going to represent you," Rev said. "She's got an appointment with you this afternoon."

PG closed his eyes and nodded. He didn't have the heart to argue.

"She's good. She'll walk you through your options. One thing to consider..." Rev looked at me for support. "Is to recant that confession."

I nodded.

"Mom is safe. She is." I leaned into the mouthpiece and whispered. "Tell us who's threatening you."

He shook his head.

"Nobody," he whispered back.

"PG, we've learned some things. A lot of things that can help you clear your name," I said.

"No way," PG said immediately. "No way." His eyes were fiery and intense. We were not going to change his mind.

"Okay, okay. Just think about it. We're doing stuff on our end that can help you. You have to think about helping yourself in here."

"I appreciate what you guys are doing. I do. But it's over."

I wanted to make our case. Lay out what we had and get him to see that we'd keep his mom safe, get him out, and find whoever did this to Monique. But I could see from his eyes he wanted no part of that. Whoever was behind this had scared the crap out of him, and he was in survival mode. Surviving by taking a murder rap.

"I love you guys," he said. "I want you to know that. I don't say it enough. Hell, not sure I ever said it. I'm sorry this is happening and that you guys have to deal with it."

"I love you too, PG," I said. "You and Rev are the only reasons I made it through a year ago with what happened to Danny. The only reason. It's your turn now, and we are here for you."

Rev was fighting back tears.

"I don't want to say I love you," he said, wiping at his eyes. "You might get the wrong idea."

PG let out a nervous laugh.

"You are such an asshole," he said.

"We're all going to get through this, PG. Together," Rev said.

PG stood and put his hand on the glass. Rev and I mirrored him. I wondered if I'd ever see him again on this side of the glass. He gave a final wave before a guard led him away.

Rev and I walked out into the gray overcast haze of San Bruno. We grasped hands and did a chest-to-chest hug but didn't speak. We were both fighting back tears as we got in our cars and drove our separate ways. We had just visited our best friend in jail. He told us he was being threatened, and he still refused to do anything to help his cause. We were both despondent, but I felt something else: anger. I let out a primal scream as I drove. I pounded my steering wheel. I'd had enough. Enough of being lied to by some Nordic girl, of following a cheating boyfriend, of almost losing my legs to the L Taraval, of being taken out of a Muni station in handcuffs, of being punched by a high schooler, of almost crashing while being tailed. Enough. Enough. Enough. I had to do something. I had to act.

So, I made a phone call.

CHAPTER TWENTY-EIGHT

TWO HOURS LATER, I was staring at the off-white facade of Our Lady of Angels.

A young man in a black parka with a tan fur hood stood to the left of the church, guarding the basement entrance. His hands were stuffed in his pockets, and he greeted people as they arrived.

"Afternoon," he said as I approached.

"Technically, evening," I said, pointing at my watch.

"Ha! Good one."

I headed down the stairs and into the basement. I took the same seat as I had one day ago. Those around me smiled and waved. Everyone seemed so damn friendly. They all wore heavy jackets and hats, wrapped up against the basement's chill. I made a note to dress warmer if I made it to a third meeting.

The room was set up the same. Table on one end and about thirty chairs in rows facing the table. Half of the fluorescent tubes above us were on, spreading an uneven, pale light throughout the room.

I kept an eye out for Bunny, but no sign. Heather, an aged brunette with a weathered face and smoker's voice, ran the meeting. She flipped through the same white binder and asked the same questions. This time, when they asked for newcomers, I raised my hand.

"Hi, yeah, I'm Seamus, and I'm an alcoholic."

The room erupted with applause. An older man to my right reached out and shook my hand. A woman behind me patted me on my shoulder. I had to admit, it felt pretty damn good.

The meeting was structured differently. Heather read a short passage from what she called the Big Book, and then everyone took turns sharing their thoughts on what she read. About ten minutes into the meeting, I noticed Bunny sneak in. Although it was tough to sneak in when you were over 300 pounds. He took a seat in my row and gave me a big smile.

"Seamus Shea!"

People kept sharing. An older man who must have been in his eighties, did a long share about pitfalls. A woman in her thirties talked nervously but thoughtfully about her setbacks. Bunny even chimed in. He liked to talk. I kept quiet and listened.

After the meeting, Bunny gave me a big hug.

"I knew you'd come back!"

"Yeah, well, I made a promise to a friend that I'd go to a meeting tonight," I said.

"Good friend."

"Yeah, she is. But you were late," I said.

"I'm a busy man. Looking this good doesn't just happen. Takes time, effort."

"I see."

"How 'bout I buy you a *real* cup of coffee? I know a great place just a block away."

"If you're buying," I said.

Bunny led me out of the church basement, and we walked about a block to a corner coffee shop called Assaf's Roastery. As we walked in, a stately Middle Eastern woman with raven-black hair and inky black pupils yelled "Bunny!" He walked toward her and kissed both of her cheeks. We ordered black coffees and took our seats at a two-person table by the window. Within a minute, the older woman brought us the coffees.

"To-go cups, as you like it," she said.

"Thanks, darlin'" Bunny said. She smiled.

Behind the register, the cafe had five large, clear bins that each housed beans from the far corners of the earth: Ethiopian, Indonesian, Kenyan, Turkish. The strong aroma of the beans floated around us. I liked the smell. It beat the smoke and malt odor of Norty3s.

"So, Seamus? You got any nicknames or anything else you want to be called?"

He took the lid off his coffee.

"Friends call me Shame," I said.

Bunny raised his eyebrows.

"That's an appropriate name for an alcoholic."

I grimaced.

"Guess I didn't think about it that way."

"Not sure that's the best name for our purposes . . . anything else?"

"The Holy Ghost."

Bunny blinked at me.

"They called you what?"

"The Holy Ghost. I went to a Catholic high school, and I was a runner. So fast you couldn't see me . . . so the Holy Ghost."

He nodded and stroked the tip of his beard. I found myself staring at it. I had never grown a beard. Wasn't sure I could. It would be patchy and miscolored. Bunny's was impressive. I felt a little jealousy creeping in.

"Didn't the priests find that . . . what's the word?"

"Blasphemous?"

"Yeah, blasphemous."

"Not really. It was in good fun. There was a deeper joke in there, that I was pale as all hell. Irish tan. I knew the guy writing the article. But the nickname stuck. They called me that in college, too."

"You ran in college?"

"Yep. Didn't have much success. I was hurt most of my freshman and sophomore years. Didn't do well until my senior year. Made the NCAA Championships. I was second in my first heat, on the final turn, looking good to move on, but two guys came on my right, and one fell, his hand shooting out in front of me; killed my rhythm. I stumbled, tumbled, and found myself on the track looking up at skinny legs flying by."

"Damn, what'd you do?"

"Got my bearings, stood up, and finished the race. Dead last."

"Dead last?"

"Dead last. They ruled that the other runner wasn't at fault. So, I was out."

"Man, that sucks."

"It was fine. I wouldn't have made it out of the next round anyway."

"At least you had that. I didn't do much in high school except drink. Never went to college. Took a couple JC classes once. Told myself I was going to get into it. Go back and get some degree. Lasted a week!"

"Where did you grow up?" I asked.

"Up north. Eureka. Small town, pretty. You?"

"I grew up in the city. Here in Noe Valley."

"Ah, a native. I love it. I don't know many natives."

"Yeah, well I know a few."

"School in the neighborhood?"

"Yes. I did the Catholic school thing. Our Lady of Angels, believe it or not."

"Ha! Now you're going to meetings there. How poetic."

"I don't know if I'd call it poetic."

Bunny flung his head back and let out a cackle.

"Good stuff Seamus, a.k.a. the Holy Ghost, a.k.a. Shame. So, how have these last couple of days been? You drink?"

"I haven't had a drink since last night."

"That's something."

"I had a lot of them, though. I've been dealing with some shit."

"Ah! The famous shit. Yes, the shit will always be there. How we deal with it is what changes. What's the shit this time?"

I took a long drink of my coffee.

"My good friend was arrested. He's a teacher and was accused of killing his student."

"I read about that. That was your friend? Terrible. Poor girl sounded like she had a bright, bright future."

"Yeah, she was amazing."

"And the teacher they said did it, that's your friend?"

"Best friend since elementary school."

Bunny put the lid back on his coffee. He held the paper cup with both hands.

"That's some tough shit, man. Not the usual kind."

"Yeah. He didn't do it. I know he didn't. I've been trying to prove that these last few days."

"Any luck?"

"Nope."

"Anything I can do?" His question surprised me. I just told him my friend was accused of murder and rather than politely excusing himself, he asked if he could help.

"I appreciate that, but I'm not sure about my next steps. Somehow the city's biggest drug dealer is involved."

"Kratos?" he said.

"You know Kratos?"

"Everyone knows Kratos."

"I'm beginning to see that."

"How's he involved?"

"Well, I found out he's the father of the girl that died. I think someone wanted to get back at him. I keep hearing there is some big supplier he has, but no one knows anything about him. Everyone knows Kratos, and no one knows his supplier. They call him Keyser Söze."

"Keyser Söze, huh?" Bunny stroked his beard.

"Yeah. If I could find out who he is, I might have a chance of finding who's behind all this."

Bunny sat back in his chair. I could see he was thinking about something.

"There is a memorial tomorrow for the girl that was killed," I said.

"You going?" he asked.

"Not sure. Her mom told me about it. She wants me to go."

"You met the girl's mother?"

"Yeah."

"Nice job, Magnum," he laughed. "Did it help?"

"I don't know. The mom has a boyfriend who seems a little too eager to blame my friend. I also found out he's cheating on the mom. And a neighbor kid told me the boyfriend always argued with Monique."

"Complicated," Bunny said. "Kratos," he said, more to himself than me.

"It's all a bit of a mess," I said, and exhaled.

"You know what I'm going to say, don't you?"

"No," I said.

"Yeah, you do."

I thought for a moment and nodded.

"Let it be," I said.

"Let it be."

"Easier said than done."

"I know."

"I appreciate you listening."

"That's what I do best. If you can, don't drink. Focus on helping your friend. Focus is good, but keep your stress down. Stress is bad. Remember to just let it be."

"You're not going to sing for me this time?"

"Ha! That's a one-time deal. Just keep going to meetings as another distraction. One meeting to the next and no drinking in between. Can you do that?"

I thought about it and answered yes.

"Good," he said. "The Holy Ghost, huh?"

"So fast they couldn't see me!"

Bunny laughed.

"So fast you couldn't see him!"

TUESDAY

CHAPTER TWENTY-NINE

THE NEXT MORNING, I woke up in a sweat to a loud, consistent pounding. Ceiling Jesus looked afraid.

I threw on a sweatshirt and a pair of jeans. For the first morning in a long time, I wasn't hungover. I had a decent night's sleep and felt pretty good except for the constant pounding. Some angry person was assaulting my front door.

As I walked to the door, thoughts of PG and car chases and rumbling trains flooded me. I had two days before PG's protection would be gone. People died in jail.

The pounding on the door continued. I grabbed the baseball bat that I always kept by my door. Forty years of city life, and I learned to always be prepared. I closed one eye and looked through the peephole. Sean Mannion stood on the other side of the door, holding a newspaper. He did not look happy.

"Sean," I said, after opening the door.

"Seamus, what the hell is this?"

He threw the paper at me. I scanned the front page until I saw the source of his ire: *Police Turning Blind Eye to Alternative Leads in Student Killing.* Jackie had come through.

"Looks like a reporter doing her job."

"Bullshit. You don't know what you're playing at, Seamus."

I held the paper in my right hand and the bat in my left.

"I'm playing at clearing my friend's name. He's innocent."

"You need to be careful."

"That sounds like a threat, Sean."

His face lost its intensity. He took a deep breath and smiled at me, displaying his crooked, country teeth.

"Ah, I couldn't threaten you. You're like me own brother," he said. Twenty years in the US and he still confused pronouns. "Aren't you going to invite me in?"

I stood back from the door and extended the bat, directing him inside.

"You gonna hit me with that?" he asked, looking at the bat.

"Considering it," I said.

He walked into the apartment.

"Nice place," he said.

Sean took a seat on my small couch. My living room modeled Interior Design 101: a couch and two club chairs facing off with a four-foot-by-four-foot coffee table in between. A faux Persian rug underneath bringing it all together. I put the bat back near the door, dropped the paper on the coffee table, and took a seat in a club chair across from him.

"Your ma's upstairs?" he asked.

"She is."

He wore gray slacks, a gray sport coat, and blue Oxfords. He had a light blue tie stuffed in his jacket pocket. I couldn't tell if he was just coming home or getting ready to head out for the day.

"That was a fun Sunday night," he said. "At least what I remember of it."

I nodded. His face had lost its anger. He was the good cop now. I did not really know Sean. Danny did. I joined him and Danny for a few dinners. Drinks after. Usually a blackout. A couple of times at Norty3s, but in other places around the city, too. I enjoyed those outings. Sean was fun and funny. But I didn't really know him, and now he'd shown up at my door complaining about press coverage?

"What's the latest with your friend?" he asked.

"Not much," I said. "Seems like the focus is still on him. Don't see your pals looking anywhere else."

"So that's why you did this?" he said, pointing at the paper. A hint of anger coated his words.

"I'm all for a robust press keeping everyone honest," I said.

He smirked.

I called Jackie yesterday after visiting PG in jail. My anger had boiled over. I laid out everything I knew: the Daniella Walsh impersonator, Monique was Kratos's daughter, Holden's infidelity, me being tailed. She wasn't sure if there was enough for a story, but she promised to dig deeper and run with it if she found anything. In return, I had to promise her I'd go to an AA meeting that night and participate, which I made good on. I was amazed she got it written and in today's edition. I hadn't read the article, but she obviously hit a nerve if Sean Mannion was pounding on my door at 8:00 a.m.

"So, you think they should be looking past your friend?" he asked.

"I do."

"Like?"

I shrugged my shoulders.

"Kratos, maybe."

Sean leaned forward on the couch and looked around my living room.

"You went and saw him, I heard."

"Yeah, so?"

"So? He's a fooking drug king. Is that who you want to be spending time with? Getting involved with? What do you think Danny would say?"

"You went to see him too," I said.

Sean rubbed his chin.

"So, what?"

"You told me you never met him."

"What are you, me first wife? I have to tell you everything I do?"

"What's going on, Sean? Something's not right with all this."

Sean stood up and paced the length of the room. He looked down at the paper and rubbed his eyes with his palms.

"I need you to back off, Seamus. Let this play out in the court. If your friend is innocent, he'll have his day in court to prove it."

"I'm sorry?" I said.

"You need to back off. You're upsetting some people. Dangerous people. It won't end well."

"What are you saying?"

"Let the court handle your friend's fate."

"My friend is in county jail. Come Friday, the one guy that's been protecting him all this time will be gone. My friend will be on his own to deal with real murderers and rapists and who knows what the hell else. They've already told him come Friday, he's done."

Sean took a deep breath.

"I'm sorry to hear that. Prison can be an evil place."

"And you want me to back off? To let him get his ass handed to him? My best friend? That's what you got the nerve to come here and tell me."

He raised his hands to calm me.

"I'm very sorry about your friend, Seamus. And I know you want to help him. I'm just saying he seems to have gotten wrapped up in something pretty big. You poking your nose around in it likely means you could get wrapped up in something big. I don't want that. You're not your brother."

"What does that mean?"

"It means you're a reporter. He was a cop. He could handle himself. He knew this world."

I let the comment go. He wasn't trying to insult me, but my ego still felt a little bruised. Of course, a high school kid did give me a fat lip, and the L Taraval almost amputated my legs.

Sean noted the picture of me and Danny on the side table.

"Your brother was one in a million, Seamus. One in a million."

"I know."

"Did you know he kept me from quitting the force?"

"No."

"I'd had enough of my old boss. A real asswipe. I was going to quit, go back to working construction. I was on my way to his office after our shift ended, and Danny grabbed me. We went to the pub down the street from the station. He let me vent and vent and vent. He convinced me to stay. I owe him that."

He looked away from the picture, staring at a spot on the wall, gathering his thoughts.

"He was just . . . he was just too good for this world. You know?"

I nodded.

"His focus was always others. Helping others. But he took everything in; held on to it all. Me? I don't give a flying fuck about anyone. That's how you need to be in this job. You have to let it go. Junkies. Dealers. Overdoses. You let it go."

He looked back at me.

"Danny never could. He could never let it go."

I didn't speak. I didn't know what to say. I thought of "let it be." Was it that easy? If I told Danny to let it be, all would have been okay with the world?

I thought of Rhodes's words when he let me go: *he saved me once.* In the year since Danny died, I had scores of people approach me, send me notes or emails, all with the same theme, just like Rhodes and Sean: Your brother helped me. For someone only on this earth for a few decades, he made an impact. Sean. Rhodes. The volunteer at SFPCA he helped get a job with the city. The junkie he connected to a rehab center in Marin. The neighbor whose yard he cleaned out. On and on and on. A life of service to others. And I failed him.

"That reminds me," Sean said. "Any luck with those files? The ones Danny had."

"You know, I haven't had a chance to look. I'll let you know what I find."

He kept his eyes locked on mine; his own lie detector test. I ran my hand through my hair. I was lying. I put all of Danny's stuff in a locker in Daly City. The last thing I'd want to do was to go there and stir up those old memories.

"Ah well, who knows where they went off to. If they do turn up, let me know. They could be of some help."

"I will," I lied.

"And will you be careful, for me? Stay out of all this shite."

I nodded, but he didn't seem convinced.

"Don't do it for Danny, okay," he said.

"For Danny? What do you mean?"

He closed his eyes and exhaled.

"I think you're trying to help PG because you couldn't help your brother. I can't tell you how many times I've done the same this past year."

"That's not true."

"None of us could help him, Seamus. He was suffering on the inside, and none of us knew. We didn't. If we did, we'd have helped him. You would have. I would have. But this with your friend is different. You can't help him. You need to back off."

"This has nothing to do with Danny," I said.

I was lying. It had everything to do with Danny. Anything I'd ever do in my life going forward would have to do with Danny. I had been sleepwalking through life when he took his own life. I was on autopilot. With work, love, family. In those moments, when you are not paying attention, that's when life screams at you to pay attention. Unfortunately, it doesn't knock gently or politely. It reaches down your throat and pulls out your fucking heart.

Danny's death registered 9.9 on my Richter scale. It was my reckoning. How could someone I knew so closely, so intimately, my Irish twin, be gone? How could my brother—someone I'd just eaten thanksgiving dinner with; who'd left me a voicemail hours before; who'd sent me emails, texts, and all these communications—leave no sign of what was to come? How could it end just like that? The pain was distant at first, like the moment you get the wind knocked out of you. You have a few seconds to process before you realize you can't breathe, and you fall to your knees and suck air into your body, tight and constricted, only now feeling the pain. But it was more than pain—it was anguish, sheer mental, physical, and emotional distress.

I fucked up, too. I failed my Irish twin. I thought about him every day. I thought about my failure. I walked slowly through the memory of those last days and tried to break down where things went wrong. I tried to identify a moment I could have been more aware, less selfish, more understanding of the pain he felt. A pain that would lead him to do something I never imagined from my little brother. Someone brave and gentle and good. I thought about his death every day. I had analyzed every scenario, every situation, every experience that led him to that final leap on that fateful day. I had done this over and over again in my mind, and I had nothing to show for it.

It was simple: I fucked up. I didn't see it coming; I let it happen.

Sean walked over to me and put his hand on my shoulder.

"You need to be careful, Seamus. That's all I'm saying."

"That's what I used to tell Danny. You're a drug cop. Be careful."

Sean smiled.

"Be careful, Seamus." He looked down at the paper. "Sometimes when you stir shit up, you end up covered in shit."

I didn't say anything as he left.

CHAPTER THIRTY

A WEEK BEFORE HE DIED, I met Danny at Finnegan's Wake, a dive bar on 24th Street, just down the street from Our Lady of Angels.

Danny had been nervously tapping his right fingers on the bar.

"Will you stop that shit, already?" I had said.

He stopped, looked at me, and continued.

"Why are you so restless?"

He took a deep breath.

"I don't know. I don't know."

He had not aged well. His dark hair, while not receding, was thinning and dominated by a lot more salt than pepper. He had a beer belly, a small volleyball bulge from his gut that gave him a certain unhealthy sturdiness. The weight in his belly was mirrored by a swollen face and fleshy neck. Despite the wear and tear, he was still handsome. His soft blue eyes countered his edginess. We both still had the Shea shine, as my mother called it: wide, wrinkled foreheads. I was taller than him. I was thinner than him. My hair had more pepper than salt. I didn't know if these truths bothered him. It never did in the past. We had never been competitive with each other, mostly because Danny seemed above such things. He only wanted the best for me. I was less noble. As we hit the midway point of life, I started to count the chips, and it was clear to me that I had been winning. We were on two opposite paths. I was a columnist, minor fame, married, living in suburbia. He was the crime-fighter, single, living alone in an apartment in Mission Bay. I tapped away at a computer, got invited to every big party Madeline and others threw, knew billionaires and other important people. He got his hands dirty, worked with drug dealers, lowlifes, troubled souls. I didn't know he was in pain. I didn't know he was suffering. Maybe I did and just didn't care.

"Another round?" Susan, the bartender, asked. She had dyed blonde hair, wore bright red lipstick, and exhaled smoker's breath.

I nodded. She grabbed two pint glasses from below the bar. She tilted one under the Guinness tap and poured it three-quarters full. She did the same for the next one. She kept both just under the tap and walked down the bar. I took a twenty out of my pocket and pushed it across the bar. Susan came back and topped off both drinks. She placed them next to our empty ones.

"You all right?" she asked Danny.

"Yeah, why do you ask?"

"Haven't seemed yourself lately. Seen you in here a few times this past month. You don't say much, just drink."

I finished off my old pint and handed the glass back to her.

"It's a bar, ain't it?" he said.

Susan shrugged and left us.

"Think she's sweet on you," I said. "You should talk to her."

Danny rolled his eyes. The bar was mostly empty save Susan and an elderly lady sipping Jameson in a corner booth. It was just past noon, and I was two drinks in and about to start my third.

"She's right," Danny said. "I've been struggling."

"Struggling? What do you mean?"

"I don't know. Just struggling. The job. All the shit."

I drank my Guinness.

"I'm onto this guy now. Thinks he's a big shot. And he's just a drug supplier. A huge one. Connected to China and Mexico."

"Wow. You going to take him down?" I asked.

"I don't have enough. Not nearly enough. It's more a hunch than anything. And I can't accuse a guy like that without solid proof. He's killing people, Shame. Killing people with all the crap he's putting on the street. And I can't touch him."

He took a long sip of his beer.

"And I don't know who I can trust," he continued. "I have to keep my files with me, not in the office. I think we got a rat. I don't know how else to explain how this guy stays so clean."

"Who is he?" I asked.

He looked at me.

"I've said too much, Seamus. I'm sorry. I've said too much."

"You never have to say sorry to me, Danny Boy."

"You know I hate that nickname."

I started singing the famous ballad, soft at first, and then my off-tune voice filled the bar.

". . . the pipes, the pipes are calling! From Glen to Glen and down the mountainside."

"Shut the hell up," the old lady in the side booth said.

I offered a faint wave of apology.

"It's demoralizing," he continued. "I see this guy do whatever he wants, and there's nothing I can do."

"You'll get him," I said. "Just takes time."

He let out a heavy sigh.

"I guess I was expecting more," he said, staring at his pint glass. "I was expecting something to have happened by now. That I'd have made an impact. That I'd done more, you know?"

This was where I should have paid attention. This was where I should have understood what he was trying to tell me. But all I did was drink and offer platitudes.

"You've done plenty, Danny Boy," I said.

"Do you ever think of Dad?" he asked.

I nodded.

"I still relive that day in my mind. When the policeman came to tell us he was gone. I can't shake it."

Danny fingered the rim of his pint glass.

"And his funeral? All those cops lining the church."

"You have to forget about that," I said. "I know that's easy to say, but it's been what, thirty years?"

He gripped his glass and took a drink. I watched him wipe his lips with the back of his hand. I sipped my beer.

"Remember he used to call this place the Valley of Noah?" he said.

"That's right. He thought we were blessed."

We kept drinking. I soon felt uneven, like I had dropped into a river thick with sediment and algae. Danny had laughed at the bartender or me or nothing. My head had seemed to be spinning extra fast. I had asked Susan for some water. Danny told me everything I needed to know in that meeting at Finnegan's. He had been struggling. He had been anxious. He had been down. He had told me everything I needed to know. I didn't do anything. I had forgotten. I would just drink.

One week later, he would be dead.

I should have listened. I should have paid attention. I should have sensed something. But I had failed. I did. When your conversations center around drinking, not much gets noticed. In those last few years, all our conversations had been around drinking.

"The Valley of Noah," Danny had said, laughing.

My father had thought that our neighborhood was blessed, that Noah would protect us.

We had been far from blessed.

CHAPTER THIRTY-ONE

AFTER SEAN LEFT, I picked up the paper and read Jackie's article. It outlined all the reasons why PG might not have killed Monique: their track record together, no motive, Monique's mom didn't believe it. It didn't dodge any reasons he might have, including his fiery coaching style. It shined the light, vaguely, on other options and how the police seemed singularly focused given a confession. Even James, the janitor, was quoted. It was good news. It brought doubt and would likely make Rhodes and his team work a little harder.

I flipped through my notes again. Keyser Söze was the key. Danny had mentioned some big supplier to me that day at Finnegan's. He must have been on to Keyser Söze. He knew who he was. He talked about files he kept. Keyser Söze's real name might have been in those files.

I had packed up Danny's apartment a week after his death. I moved everything worth keeping to a storage locker in Store Your Stuff Storage down by Pier 80. I hadn't been back since. I would have to go there today.

I called Maria, PG's lawyer.

"See the paper?" I asked.

"Yeah, I figured that was your doing."

"I do what I can."

"How was your meeting with PG?"

"He won't recant."

She exhaled.

"I may have another angle," I said. "I think I found something."

"You want to share?" she asked.

"Not yet. A little early."

"Okay, well, go for it," she said.

I made my way upstairs to find the key to Danny's storage locker.

"Well, hello, stranger," my mother said. She sat at the kitchen table, smoking.

"I need the key to the storage room with Danny's stuff."

"Why do you need that?"

"One of our high school yearbooks is in there. I need it."

She took a drag of her cigarette and kept her eyes fixed on me.

"High school yearbook?" she asked.

"Yeah, I can't find mine, but I know his is with the stuff." I would lie to my mother often. It was an unwritten agreement we seemed to have. If I was to tell her that I wanted to look through Danny's things to find information on an unknown drug supplier they called Keyser Söze, she would make clear that that was an idiotic idea. By telling her I needed a yearbook, she'd have a reason why I needed the key, and I could avoid the shaming.

She stood up and walked to the side drawer where she found the duct tape last time. I heard keys rattling. She came back and handed me the storage key attached to a square plastic keychain that listed the address and locker number.

"Give it back to me when you finish."

"Of course."

"And you need to make sure to put the yearbook back. He'll be home soon enough and will want all of his things."

"Uh-huh."

"He can't make Thanksgiving, but maybe Christmas this year."

"Maybe."

"That reminds me. I was going to invite Mr. Banks to Thanksgiving this year. It would just be the three of us."

"Mr. Banks?" I asked, not remembering the name.

"My friend. He works at Walgreens."

"Ah, the guy with the little blue pills."

"Tell it to your psychiatrist!"

"I intend to."

She blushed.

"Do you have any objections?" she asked.

"Nope. The more the merrier," I said.

My phone buzzed. She shooed me away, and I walked into the living room to answer.

"Seamus Shea. How ya doing?"

"Bunny?" I asked.

"Yes, sir."

"I'm good. I didn't recognize the voice. You sound different on the phone."

"Well, I was never one for phones, to be honest. But the program is all about calling and talking and calling and talking. So, I've been doing a lot of calling and talking for the last few years. I guess I developed a telephone voice."

"It's lovely," I said.

"You staying sober?"

I hadn't even thought of drinking in the past day.

"I have. Keeping my mind busy."

"Your friend?"

"Yeah."

"Well," Bunny started, "I'm calling because I may be able to help. I asked an acquaintance about the big player you said was maybe behind all this."

"An acquaintance?"

"Let's just say he's connected. He told me the guy they call Keyser Söze is a lawyer, works at 555 California, who is thought to control most of the distribution of coke, heroin, amphetamines, fentanyl, you name it, in NorCal."

"This acquaintance would know such things?"

"Yes. I know him from a past life, when I was a little deeper in the motorcycle club business."

"Why would he tell me this? Or you?"

"The guy is bad news. He's taken out a few friends of my acquaintance. He'd like nothing more than to be rid of him."

"555 California? Isn't that the Bank of America building?"

"Yeah, I guess it's called 555 California now. Not sure when they changed it."

I didn't know the city anymore.

"I know it's not much, there must be a thousand lawyers working there, but hope it helps."

"It helps, Bunny, thanks.

"Yeah. Just be careful. Again, he's bad news."

"I will."

"And remember, Seamus, get to a meeting and let it be!"

CHAPTER THIRTY-TWO

I LEFT MY MOTHER TO HER SMOKES AND HEADED TO STORE YOUR STUFF STORAGE. I made it two blocks, and Tito called.

"How's she doing?" I asked.

"Not good. She's stuck here. PG is in jail. She wants to go see him. That's why I called you. She wants to leave."

"She can't leave. We don't know if anyone is after her."

"I know. Can you come over and see her? Talk some sense into her? You know how she gets."

I did know how she got. Mamá might have been the sweetest person I knew, but she had a fire inside her that you did not want to let out. There was a reason PG was a straitlaced, polite young man. You listened to what Mamá told you.

"Send me your address; I'll be there in fifteen," I said.

I was careful driving to Tito's house. I kept my tired eyes peeled for a familiar black sedan or any other car that might be tracking me. I made a point to take multiple turns the closer I got to Tito's house. He lived in the Mission on 21st between Valencia and Guerrero. I parked a block from his house, circled the block with eyes peeled, and finally knocked on his door.

Tito answered. I recognized him right away. He was wiry and muscular with tight, cropped hair and sharp, dark features. He exuded confidence and a certain toughness that I admired. He looked up and down the street as he put his hand on my back and led me in the house. I followed him into the kitchen, where a stocky young man with tattoos covering both arms sat playing solitaire. Tito ignored him and I tried to do the same. He gave me a quick once-over and then returned to flipping his cards.

Tito led me to a back room with pinkish wallpaper, two twin beds, and a white six-drawer bureau. Mamá sat on one of the beds, clutching wooden rosary beads. She jumped up and ran toward me as I entered.

"Seamus, oh Seamus."

"It's okay. It's going to be okay."

She wore a long blue skirt, a beige sweater with a mock turtleneck, and sensible shoes. Her eyes were puffy and red. She looked even smaller and frailer than when I'd seen her last. I imagined she had not been eating. She buried her head in my chest.

"I saw PG yesterday. Rev and I went to see him. He's okay."

"He is?" She wiped at tears forming on the edge of her large brown eyes.

"Yes. He told me to tell you not to worry." Lie.

"Why is this happening?"

I looked directly into her eyes; they looked so much like her only son's.

"I don't know. I think the girl who was killed had some troubled family members. I think PG might have been in the wrong place at the wrong time."

"Why would he confess?"

"I think..." I remembered the only way was through. "...I think someone may have threatened you."

"He's doing this to protect me?"

"It's the only thing that makes sense. So, you need to stay here and listen to Tito."

Her face went blank. She sat back on the edge of the bed, processing the news. The grip on her rosary beads tightened.

The doorbell rang: a dull, grating sound.

Tito looked at me. I shook my head.

"Stay here," he said. He closed the door behind him and left Mamá and me alone in the room. I put my right ear against the door.

It rang again.

"Who is it?" I heard Tito yell.

"Package delivery," came the reply.

"Leave it at the door."

"I need a signature."

Tito came jogging back into the room.

"Something's wrong. Were you followed?"

"No," I said. "I was really careful after this morning."

"This way."

Tito led us out of the room to the back door and down a rickety set of wooden stairs. We followed him to the backyard, and we rushed in single file away from the house to a back fence that had loose board you could remove. He pulled the board off and gently led Mamá through. He pushed me behind her just as gunfire erupted in the house.

"Get her somewhere safe," Tito said. He pulled a 9-millimeter from his waistband and ran back toward the house.

I held Mamá's hand, and we walked briskly through the neighboring backyard and down a side alley that led to a small gate and out to the street. It was Hill Street. We went right and headed to Valencia Street. I could hear sirens. We were blocks away from where I parked. It wouldn't be safe to be on the street. I checked my phone and clicked for a Lyft. Four minutes. We hid in the doorway of a restaurant. I kept Mamá behind me. We were back from the street, and the awning above us gave a little more cover. Every car that sped down Valencia looked suspicious. I checked my phone again, and the Lyft was on 18th Street, one minute away. Longest minute of my life.

Mamá was quietly reciting the Lord's Prayer. I was about to join her when I saw the black sedan pull up to the stop light at Valencia, diagonally across from us. In the passenger seat sat Daniella Walsh, the Nordic beauty, or whatever her name was. She was scanning the streets. I ducked down more. Her driver looked like an extra from an Eastern European prison movie: tall, wide face, angled chin. Even in the large sedan, his head nearly touched the roof, and his massive hands covered the steering wheel. As their light turned green, our Lyft pulled up: a yellow Toyota Corolla.

Christ.

I turned my head as fake Daniella and her giant passed. I waited until they were half a block down and rushed toward the car, leading Mamá.

"Hello there, I'm Mark, your driver."

"Hit it, Mark. Let's go." I looked back and they were turning around.

"Let me just confirm your . . ."

"Go, fucking go!"

"*Madre de Dios!*" Mamá screamed. "Go!"

Mark was unphased. He pulled out and punched it through a yellow light.

"Get on the freeway," I said.

"But your destination . . ."

"Change of plans. There is someone following us, and we need to lose them."

"All right!" Mark said with a newfound enthusiasm.

The car smelled like a citrus air freshener had exploded in the back seat. I told Mamá that it would be okay; we would get her somewhere safe. She nodded, but her face showed only terror and disbelief.

"Get on the freeway for now," I told Mark. His dashboard was decorated with Star Wars action figures, glued down. Han, Luke, Chewbacca, even Vader.

Christ. Christ.

I called Rev and filled him in.

"Okay. I'm out the door," Rev said. "I'll pick you guys up. Send him to Stonestown. I'll meet you in the Target lot, bottom floor."

I told Mark our plan.

"No problem. I'll take 280," he said. He sounded a little disappointed that the chase was over.

"I was looking forward to letting this baby loose," he said.

"This baby?"

"Yeah, the Millennium Falcon." He patted the small space on the dashboard free of action heroes.

"The Millennium Falcon, a Corolla?"

"You've never heard of the Millennium Falcon? It's the car that made the Kessel Run in twelve parsecs."

Christ. Christ. Christ.

As I debated how to respond, the sedan was back. It was a lane over and gaining speed. I told Mamá to duck down. Fake Daniella looked right at me.

"This black sedan," I said to Mark. "Can you lose them?"

He looked in his left side-view mirror.

"This little baby doesn't look like much, but she can fly. Hold on."

I braced my arm against the side door and covered Mamá. Mark jerked the car into the left lane, forcing the sedan to brake hard. He jerked the car back two lanes to the right, narrowly splitting a big truck and a Prius. Horns all around. The sedan was two lanes over now and sped up to be parallel with us. Mark jerked over two lanes to the left, nearly sideswiping the sedan, which was forced to veer into the fast lane.

"Hang on!" Mark screamed, as he pulled the car to the right hard, covering all lanes and veering onto the 280 off-ramp, just missing the dividers. He cut off multiple cars and more horns blared, but I could see Daniella and her friend speeding south down 101 as we headed west on 280.

"You are a genius!" I yelled, slapping Mark on the shoulder.

"Woo-hoo!" he screamed. "Sometimes I even amaze myself."

"They're gone, they're gone," I said to Mamá as I helped her sit up.

"Seamus, why is this happening?" she asked. Tears were streaming down her cheeks.

"I don't know. But I'm going to get you somewhere safe, and I promise you, I'm going to find out."

CHAPTER THIRTY-THREE

WE MET REV AT THE BOTTOM LEVEL OF THE TARGET PARKING LOT IN STONESTOWN. The only cars were Rev's 4Runner and Mark's Corolla. I thanked Mark and promised him a five-star rating and a generous tip.

"May the force be with you," he said, before driving off in his yellow Corolla Millennium Falcon.

Rev put Mamá in the back of his SUV. It was just the two of us standing in an empty parking lot.

"How is she doing?" Rev asked.

"She's shaken up. Hell, I am too. What the hell is going on, Rev? Who are these people?"

"I don't know. PG got in some deep shit."

"I saw the two that were chasing us. One is the woman I told you about. The small blonde who pretended to be a teacher with PG; the one I chased in the tunnel. And some big East German-looking dude I haven't seen before."

"Who is the blonde working for?" Rev asked.

"Must be Keyser Söze."

"This goddamn Keyser Söze. Who the hell is he?"

"I'm guessing he and Kratos had a falling out that Kratos doesn't want to share," I said. "Bunny told me the guy works at the Bank of America building, which I guess is now called 555 California."

"Yeah, been that way for a while. And Bunny? Who's Bunny?"

I froze. I was not ready to talk to Rev about my drinking.

"An old lead from the paper," I said quickly. "Keyser Söze is key.

That's the name Monique's mom gave me. He has to be the one trying to punish Kratos. The trick is finding out who he is."

"I don't mean to add to your anxiety Shame, but we got a couple days before PG's friend is gone. We have to get him out."

I leaned against the 4Runner and rubbed my face.

"I know, Rev. I know."

A blue Toyota truck pulled into the parking lot. Rev took a step closer to the driver's side door. We eyed the truck as it did a three-point turn and headed the other way down the street.

"So, what's the plan?" Rev asked.

"We get Mamá somewhere safe. And we find out who the hell is doing this."

"Should we take her to the cops?"

"I don't trust the cops," I said. "Sean Mannion gives me a warning, and then this happens?"

"Well, that's just great."

"Danny had some files. I think they might tell us who Keyser Söze is."

"Files? You still have Danny's things?"

"I packed up the stuff at his apartment and put it in a storage locker. There was a lot of stuff I kept. It might be in there."

My phone buzzed. Tito.

"You guys okay?" he asked.

"Yeah, we had an eventful car chase, but we are okay now. How about you?"

"My friend sent a little message. I grabbed him, and we snuck out the same way you did. Called a friend to pick us up. With her now."

"They must have followed me. Sorry. I was careful, but not careful enough."

"Whatever. It's over. Just get Mamá somewhere safe."

"I have a place in mind," I said.

I told Tito my plan, and he agreed. I shared it with Rev and Mamá. They were on board, too. I made a phone call, and fifteen minutes later, we pulled up in front of Our Lady of Angels. Mara greeted us and took Mamá to a spare room in the back of the rectory.

Rev dropped me back at my car. It was near dark when I made it back home. I decided to wait until the morning to hit the storage shed. Partly for better lighting, but mostly because I was exhausted.

WEDNESDAY

CHAPTER THIRTY-FOUR

I WOKE UP WITHOUT A HANGOVER FOR THE SECOND DAY IN A ROW. I had an undeniable energy, a certain clarity that was unusual for me in the early morning hours. I made myself a smoothie, showered, and got dressed. I was out the door by 7:35 a.m. and on my way to Store Your Stuff Storage off Cesar Chavez.

I did my obligatory rear-view mirror check for any black sedans or any cars that seemed out of place. None. Of course, I thought no one followed me to Tito's, and that didn't work out so well.

After a twenty-minute drive and no visible tails, I pulled into the small parking lot of Store Your Stuff Storage.

Danny's locker was number 107. I looked at the large display map at the front and determined a path. After a right, left, right, I was rolling up the gray metal door. There was a single light bulb and string hovering in the center of the space. I clicked it on. There was less stuff than I remembered. In truth, I didn't remember much. Those first few weeks after Danny left, I was a mess. Unable to focus, to think, to talk. I was amazed I got any of his stuff here.

There were about twenty boxes spread around the room. Danny's beat-up mountain bike leaned against one wall, next to a set of new golf clubs. Some duffle bags, a few lamps, minor tables.

I started looking through the boxes. Almost a year ago, I wrote headings in black sharpie on each box to give me an idea of what might be in it if I ever came back. *MUSIC, PICTURES, CLOTHES.*

The memories came back like an avalanche. I found a box full of his CDs. He'd loved country and western for some unknown reason. There must have been 200 CDs left over from buying binges in the '90s and early 2000s. A Carrie Underwood CD almost brought me to tears. He had a crush on her, obsession even. It started on American Idol and continued well into her career. Anytime I heard "Jesus Take the Wheel," I'd lose it. Another box had a stack of his favorite books. He had a small library in his apartment, and I dumped the books into a couple of boxes. He'd been a fan of police procedurals, as you might expect. Michael Connelly's Harry Bosch was a favorite. He had at least five of those books, well-worn and dog-eared. Danny hadn't believed in bookmarks.

Another box was filled with framed pictures that I had found scattered around his apartment. Most of the framed ones had him in it with friends or family. There were two of just him and me. Three originally, but I kept one with me the day I packed up. He had just graduated from the police academy in that photo, and I had my arm around him, my face full of pride.

There were other items: familiar clothes—jackets and jeans and sweatshirts that I couldn't bring myself to throw away or donate. Some kitchen items that I thought one day I might use: pots and pans, knives, plates, mugs.

I found a box in the far corner that just said *WORK*. I opened it up, and it was full of manila file folders. There were headings on the top flap of each folder: *Operation Green Frog, Operation Blue Deck, Operation Orange Plane*. What the hell kind of names were these?

Some files had maps with locations circled, some had receipts and invoices with names I did not recognize. A few had pictures of what I imagined to be perps. One file had a couple of images of Kratos, but there was nothing about anyone connected to him.

Bunny said Keyser Söze worked at the Bank of America Building. All residents of the building must have been listed. If I could find a name, a simple Google search might lead me to him.

I pulled out the last file, and it had "Ed Robinson" scribbled in purple ink across the top of the folder. I knew that name. Where had I heard it before? I Googled Ed Robinson and the Bank of America building on my phone. Nothing. I tried with 555 California. Still nothing. I tried just Ed Robinson, which brought up a few random businessmen with LinkedIn accounts and the actor Edward G. Robinson. There was also an Edward Arlington Robinson, a poet from a century ago.

Maybe it was an anagram. I wrote out Ed Robinson, then under it: Son O'redbin, Bornes Rone, Nos Niborde. It didn't take me long to realize I was terrible at anagrams.

I tried another tack. I looked up Edward Robinson and his movies and major movie roles. His real name was Emanuel Goldenberg. He played Caesar Bandello in Little Caesar, Johnny Rocco in Key Largo. None came up with 555 California.

I tried the poet. Edward Arlington. Arlington Robinson. Nothing. I looked at a list of his best-known poems with names: Luke Havergal, Ben Travoto, Miniver Cheevy, Richard Cory.

Richard Cory? I knew a Richard Cory.

I clicked the link and read the poem. It was only sixteen lines but had a brutal ending.

I'd just seen Richard Cory a few days ago at Madeline Mina's party at the Fairmont. Could it be him? I Googled his name and 555 California. It was a hit: The Law Offices of Cohen, Conte, and Cory occupied the 44th Floor. Richard J. Cory, Partner. I clicked on the firm's website and scanned the list of partners. I found Richard J. Cory, Esq., the well-dressed forty-something with dark features and an unsettling smile who shook my hand Friday night. Could he be Keyser Söze? He was well-known across the city. Philanthropist, a player in the city's politics. Could he be the guy? It would explain the clandestine approach Danny took. If he was the guy, you wouldn't want to act too soon. You would need a mountain of evidence before you'd ever want to go public.

I grabbed the file and put the box back in the corner. I would have to pay Richard Cory a visit.

As I turned to leave, I could see a sizable shadow in front of the opening.

"Who's there?" I asked. I reached down and grabbed the bowling trophy Danny won five years ago. I stuck it in my pants at the small of my back.

A hulking figure stood in front of the opening. It was Daniella Walsh's driver, the giant who looked like he just got out of an Eastern European prison.

"Can I help you?" I asked.

He didn't speak, just stared at me.

"Are you lost?" I tightened my grip on the file.

"What you got there, Seamus?" he asked, pointing at the file. His English was perfect.

"A family recipe. Southern fried chicken. From my Irish Grandmother."

He didn't react, missing my humor.

"Why don't you give it to me," he stated more than asked. He had a faint accent that I couldn't place.

"Are you a fried chicken fan?"

I edged my way toward the opening so I wouldn't be trapped in the locker. He did not seem to care. I couldn't see a gun or any weapon, but he looked like the kind of guy who preferred to use his hands. He was at least six-foot-four and two hundred and fifty pounds, with hands the size of volleyballs when he made a fist.

"Give me the file," he said.

I debated my next move. No one else was in the storage place this early, so screams for help would go unheard. He was too big for me to fight. I had, after all, just been beaten up by a high school kid a few days before.

"Look, I don't want any trouble." I had a flashback of saying that to Rolando right before he gave me a fat lip. This guy could behead me with just his hands.

"I don't either, just give me the file, Seamus. I don't want to hurt you."

"I appreciate that," I said. "Where is your friend? The blonde?"

"She's busy with other things."

"Too bad, she was beginning to grow on me."

He took a big step toward me. We were a few feet apart. I could see his next move would be to grab me and likely pull me apart, piece by piece.

"You guys an item?" I asked.

He ignored me.

"Okay, okay," I said. "You want the file, here it is . . ."

I threw the file at him low, so he had to bend down to get it. I pulled Danny's trophy out and swung it as hard as I could, the heavy base connecting just above his left ear. It was a good hit and it caused him to drop to his knees. Before he could react, I swung it back and connected with his right ear. He let out a yelp and crumpled. I tossed the trophy and picked up the file and now scattered papers. He had fallen just inside the locker, and I jumped out of it and pulled the door down and smacked the bolt in. He was on his feet now and pounded on the door. I fumbled with the lock in my pocket and eventually clasped it closed.

"It's locked now, jackass. I suggest you keep quiet. The police will be on their way. Think about giving up your blonde friend and anyone else."

"I'm bleeding," he said, through the metal door. "And you don't have to call me names."

"Sorry about that," I said. "But I love this recipe."

"I know it's not a recipe," he said. He seemed quite despondent.

"I'm going to give you some advice I was given just a few days ago."

"Yeah, what's that?"

"Let it be."

I didn't bother singing the line. I had already hit the poor guy twice with a trophy.

"Like the Beatles?" he said.

"Exactly, let it be, my friend, just like the Beatles."

CHAPTER THIRTY-FIVE

I LEFT DON A VOICEMAIL ABOUT THE EASTERN EUROPEAN GIANT TRAPPED IN DANNY'S LOCKER. I figured he'd send someone to pick him up and ask a few questions.

I called Jackie to see if she knew anything about Richard Cory. No answer, so I left a voicemail. I called Madeline Mina next. She was the only other person I knew who might be able to tell me more about Richard Cory.

"Seamus, darling, you finally call?"

"Wonderful party Friday. I enjoyed it."

"Liar. Such a liar."

"It was real. It was fun. It just wasn't real fun."

"Remind me why we are friends, again?"

"I have no idea. You invite me."

"I will have to reconsider that."

"I want to ask you about a guest who was there Friday."

"Okay."

"Richard Cory? What do you know about him?"

Madeline paused. I couldn't tell if she was choosing her words carefully or was distracted with something else.

"He's a bit mysterious. Not in an interesting way. Lawyer. You know I loathe lawyers. Not sure what law he practices. He's very generous and very good about attending the right parties, being seen. He has a gentlemanly quality you don't see much of these days."

"Any red flags? Anything that might make you think he's not a good guy?"

"Oh, I didn't say he was a good guy. As long as I've known him, there's been a Great Gatsby quality to him."

"Gatsby?"

"Yes, as in he might make his money in questionable ways. I think for Gatsby, it was bootlegging. And there were rumors he killed a man. I've heard similar talk about Richard Cory. But again, my experience is he's always been a gentleman."

"You heard he killed a man?"

She paused again.

"I don't remember that. But I just got the sense he was not someone you wanted to cross."

"Thanks, Madeline. As usual, you're a big help."

"I'll refrain from asking why you are asking."

"And as usual, discrete."

"Take care, Seamus. I'll see you at my next shindig."

"I wouldn't miss it."

"Liar."

Madeline had given me enough to offset any doubt. I headed to the Bank of America building, also known as 555 California, to ask Richard Cory some questions.

It took me twenty minutes to make it across town and park. The building's lobby was a cavernous ode to excess, with thirty-foot ceilings supported by glass walls on all sides. Sunlight walked in from every angle. I wondered what that famous son of Italian immigrants, Amadeo Pietro Giannini, would think of such a creation.

I tried to remember what movie was filmed here. *Towering Inferno*? That sounded right. My father's twin Steve McQueen as the gutsy fireman.

I checked in at the security desk. A trim Asian man with dyed blonde hair stood behind a maple wood desk. He scanned my driver's license and asked me to sign in.

"Who are you here to see?" he asked.

"Richard Cory."

I swear one of his thin, pale eyebrows rose.

"Okay," he said. His eyes moved to a list on his desk, and he ran his finger down the page, stopping a third of the way down. "That's the forty-fourth floor." He handed me a name tag.

"Say, when did they stop calling this the Bank of America building," I asked.

He blinked at me.

"I have no idea, sir. You are going to want to go over to that bank of elevators and ride it all the way up." He pointed past my nose. I nodded and headed off.

A minute later, I stepped into the first open elevator and pushed the number forty-four. The elevator took off in a rush; my ears popped. I grabbed the waist-high runner behind me, feeling a little wobbly at the quick ascent. Skyscrapers made me anxious. I watched the numbers: none yet, just two blinking yellow dashes. Still below forty, an express. Then forty, forty-one, forty-two, forty-three, and the elevator stopped with a sudden jolt, and my heart jumped with it. There was a pleasant ding, and the doors opened wide.

I walked out of the elevator and turned left to face glass doors with The Law Offices of Cohen, Conte, & Cory frosted at eye level. A Jew, an Italian, and a drug dealer walked into a bar. A petite blonde in a ruffled white shirt sat behind a silver desk on the other side. I waved. She looked me up and down before buzzing me in.

"I'm here to see Mr. Cory," I said confidently.

"Name?"

"Seamus Shea."

"Is he expecting you?"

"I don't believe so, but I think he'll want to see me."

She raised her eyes to take another look at me. I smiled. She picked up a phone and talked briefly and quietly. She nodded and hung up.

"All right, Mr. Shea. Mr. Cory will be with you shortly. Please make yourself comfortable in our lobby."

I nodded and turned to see a lobby bigger than my in-law. I took a seat on a right angle covered with thin strips of leather and waited. I wasn't sure if him seeing me so easily was a good or bad sign. After fifteen minutes, a familiar, clean-favored, slim man walked into the lobby.

"Mr. Shea, a pleasure to see you again."

He was perky and healthy-looking, with bronzed skin and a lean frame. His smile seemed oddly warm and unsettling at the same time. He wore a neatly tailored navy blue suit with a patterned silk tie and polished wingtips. He would have been called a gentleman in days gone by.

"Nice to see you, Mr. Cory. Thank you for taking the time to talk to me."

"Of course. Let's go back to my office."

I followed him down a wide hallway, eyeing the overwhelming views in each office on the left and admiring the no-doubt pricey but confusing artwork lining the hallway wall on the right.

We settled into a corner office with floor-to-ceiling windows and views from the Golden Gate Bridge to the Bay Bridge.

"Please, have a seat," he said.

"You have some view," I said.

"Yes. A little overcast today, but still inspiring."

He took a seat behind a sleek silver desk, a more petite version of the one in the lobby. I wondered if it might actually be made of silver. The desk was bare except for a phone, legal pad, and three pens sticking out of a small silver cup.

"So, Mr. Shea, how can I help?"

"Seamus."

"Seamus. I always liked your name. Did I ever tell you that?"

"I don't think so. You know there is a famous poem with your name?"

"Yes, yes. Mr. Robinson made my name famous long before I joined this world."

"Unfortunate ending," I said.

He ignored me.

"It was nice seeing you Friday night. That was quite the soiree."

"Madeline knows how to party."

He lifted his firm chin and smiled.

"Yes, she does."

He reached for one of the pens and started to write on his legal pad.

"What can I do for you? Are you looking for legal advice?"

As he asked, I noticed something moving to the left outside. We were on the 44th floor, so my brain had trouble processing outside movement. Multiple ropes hung the length of the window, and a white cage connected to the ropes gradually rose up to be level with the floor. The cage was about six feet long and three feet wide. Two men stood inside the cage, holding what looked like brooms, and I realized they were window washers.

Richard Cory followed my gaze.

"Ah, yes. The window-washing crew. Quite a sight, huh? I never quite get used to them." He waved and both men waved back. I waved too, although I did not want to distract them.

"That's a real job?" I asked. "I guess I've never seen one up close."

"Oh, yes. Quite the job. They get paid handsomely as I understand it."

"Not something I would ever want to do."

"Really? I don't know. Working outside, looking down on the masses? Might be kind of fun."

The washers sprayed a mist on the glass and used wide squeegees to clean up the spray. Richard Cory looked back at me.

"So, what can I do for you?" he asked again.

"I'm actually here about the murder of a young girl. A student at Jefferson High School."

Richard Cory looked nonplussed.

"Monique Profit?" I said.

He glanced at his watch: silver and expensive.

"I would like to help you, but I'm afraid I didn't know Monique Profit. I read about it in the paper. Tragic. I believe her teacher is in custody."

"Do you know a man they call Kratos?"

"The Greek god of strength?" he laughed. "I'm afraid we've never met."

"No, Kratos, the importer-exporter who supplies, let's say, certain illegal products to much of San Francisco."

His face lost its charm.

"I'm afraid I'm not that familiar with illegal products, Mr. Shea."

I leaned forward in my chair.

"Really? I hear you know a lot about the business." I was being rash, desperate. But I didn't know what else to do. PG only had a couple days of protection left. Sitting on the 44th floor of a successful lawyer's corner office looking at a million-dollar view of the bay; I had to go for the Hail Mary.

"Mr. Shea, I don't take kindly to being insulted by people I've welcomed into my office."

He had a reserved, almost polite anger. I doubted his heart rate rose above sixty.

"Look, Mr. Cory. I have it on good information that you know exactly who Kratos is, and I believe you sent him a message through Monique. And my friend got in the way."

Richard Cory pursed his lips. He smiled. I looked out at the window washers who were slowly rising up to the next floor, leaving a clear pane of glass in their wake.

"Well as enlightening as this has been, Mr. Shea, I'm afraid I can't help you. I am sorry for your friend, but I had nothing to do with what happened to him. And I know nothing of this Kratos person. I think you've been given some wrong information, and I'm sorry."

I didn't move.

"You seem like a nice person. I appreciated the article you did on my favorite charity last year. I actually enjoyed your columns."

I looked out at the view and the Golden Gate Bridge.

"What happened to that column?"

"I'm an alcoholic who drank himself out of a job," I said.

Richard Cory laughed nervously. He straightened the legal pad on his desk and stood up.

"Well, again. Thank you for stopping by, I'm sorry I couldn't have been more help." He held out his hand to shake.

I stood up and shook it. The washers were a floor above now.

"They move fast," I said, pointing at the lingering lonely ropes.

"It's quite amazing," he said.

"Impressive what you could do in so little time," I said.

He looked at me.

"You could ruin a life, multiple lives, in just a couple of minutes."

He kept his eyes on me but did not speak as I left his office.

CHAPTER THIRTY-SIX

MONIQUE PROFIT'S MEMORIAL WAS AT 6:00 P.M. Rev was on his way to pick me up.

I searched my closet, but the only suit I found was the one I'd worn to Madeline's party Friday night. The same suit I slept in until Saturday morning. I had at least hung it up, but it still had wrinkles that a Shar Pei would envy.

I headed outside to wait for Rev on my steps and considered Richard Cory. If he played a role in Monique's death, he gave no indication. He was guilty of being a self-assured asshole, quite comfortable in his own skin, but I wasn't sure what else. In hindsight, my poetic deduction seemed like too big a leap in logic. Why would Danny name the file Ed Robinson? How could a rich society type like that be a drug supplier?

As I waited for Rev, Don called.

"How are you doing, Shame?"

"I've been better, Don. Did you pick up our friend?"

"Uh, yeah. Think he's in holding. Haven't had a chance to talk to him yet. You think he's involved?"

"He's involved."

"I just wanted to check on you. I know this is tough."

"Yeah, well, the guy you have can help."

"There's a memorial for Monique tonight. You going?" he asked.

"I am. Friend is picking me up. Not looking forward to it, but I want to pay my respects. You going?"

He was quiet for a moment.

"No, Shame. This job is hard enough without going to victims' funerals."

"I get that," I said.

"All right, well, I just wanted to check in with you. I'll let you know if this guy talks. Hang in there, and I'm here for you if you need anything."

"Thanks, Don."

Rev picked me up in his 4Runner.

"Nice suit," he said. I didn't respond.

I was a little anxious about attending the memorial. Funerals always reminded me of my father. I remember grainy images from that day: the hundreds of uniformed policemen lining the Our Lady of Angels Church, the dark casket anchored at the foot of the altar, the same casket being lowered into the ground as I watched everyone I knew in the world toss dirt onto it.

In some ways, I'd been chasing that lost man all my life. I knew Danny had been. I looked for him in my teachers, coaches, priests. Most of the decisions I'd made in my life could be traced back to that fateful day when they told me his heart had exploded. I had never let him go. Danny hadn't either. It didn't help that our mother wanted nothing to do with the mention of his name or of what happened to him.

Tell it to your psychiatrist!

As Rev and I approached the New Bright Baptist Church, a few of San Francisco's finest were milling about, though not nearly as many as during my father's funeral. There was a line of TV news vans and a section where reporters were watching and trying their best to get someone to talk to them. I didn't see Jackie.

Rev and I walked up the stairs and quietly entered into the back. The foyer between the stairs and the inside of the church was thick with people. I noticed a side set of stairs and imagined the balcony might be our best bet. I motioned to Rev and apologized as I pushed through the crowd and made my way upstairs to the balcony.

We squeezed into two seats with a clear view of the altar and a blown-up image of Monique resting on an easel. Three other easels held photo collages, but we were too far away to see any detail. Tall flower bouquets, bright with blues and whites, violets and reds, crowded the altar. No roses or sunflowers or carnations. A small choir stood to the right, dressed in robes, humming softly and chanting "Yes, Lord" in a peaceful harmony. Every pew was filled below, and most spaces on the side were occupied by people standing.

The service was a moving, nonstop expression of love for Monique. The pastor, a tall, lean African American man with fashionable glasses and unending energy did a good job of celebrating Monique without letting the weighty grief that we all felt take over the service. Two classmates spoke, and each stopped repeatedly to try and compose themselves. The last speaker, her aunt, spoke with humor and compassion on the curious little girl she watched grow into a beautiful, confident woman. I kept my eye on Holden, but he held and comforted Brenda the entire service. He was still a cheating asshole, but that wasn't my concern right now.

The memorial lasted nearly two hours. When it was over, Holden led Brenda down the center aisle and out of the church.

"Her boyfriend's White?" Rev asked.

I nodded.

More family followed them, and the rest of us slowly emptied the church in a somber shuffle.

Rev put his hand on my shoulder, and we made our way down the narrow staircase to the open space outside the church. It was nearly 8:00 p.m., but the church was well-lit. Rev saw someone he knew and went to talk to them. I stood alone, scanning the crowd.

My phone buzzed and I looked to see that Jackie had called while I was in the church. I listened to her voice mail: *Seamus, don't do anything until you call me. It's about Richard Cory. Call me right now, okay? I mean it.* I started to call her back, but I looked up to see Rolando standing in front of me, face tense, fists clenched. Jesus, was I going to get beat up at a funeral?

"What are you doing here?" he asked.

"I came to pay my respects."

He wore a navy blue suit with a black tie. He could just as easily have been going to an interview for an entry-level job or a more selective college. But he wasn't. He was at the funeral of a classmate. Probably not his first, definitely not his last.

PG said he had nothing to do with it. I could have seen him stepping in for Rolando, protecting him, even. His first instinct would always have been to protect a student. But I believed PG. This whole thing was much bigger than some lovestruck bad boy.

"Hey," I said, "I don't want any trouble." I held both hands up, fingers open, showing my surrender.

He slowly relaxed.

"Sorry about your lip, man," he said. "I have a bit of a temper sometimes. I'm working on it."

"Yeah, I know all about tempers," I said. "I'm Irish."

The joke was lost on him, but it eased the tension between us.

"What up with your suit?" he asked.

"My tailor's under the weather."

He scratched his chin.

"Nice memorial," I said.

"She was special," he said. "It really sucks."

"You had a crush on her?" I asked.

He smiled.

"Everyone did. But she was a good girl. She didn't want anything to do with someone like me."

"I doubt that," I said. "Bad boys always get the girls. Especially the good ones."

As we talked, I saw a familiar face about fifty feet away. I pretended I did not see her. I shook Rolando's hand and wished him well. I gradually made my way in her direction. When I was about twenty feet away from her, she bolted. I looked back, but I had lost Rev in the crowd. I didn't want to lose her, so I followed.

She was fast and agile and took a hard right turn at the first intersection, hugging the curve admirably. I remembered our chase at the Muni station and hoped this pursuit would not involve me dodging street cars. My wrinkled suit was not helping my speed. I let my stride out and gained on her. *The Holy Ghost rides again!* She stopped suddenly next to a familiar black sedan.

"What are you doing here?" I asked, standing a few feet from her.

"I'm a teacher at the school."

"Bullshit. You aren't Daniella Walsh. Who are you?" I stepped toward her and grabbed her right arm. She was athletic, but I felt like I could hold on to her with no trouble. What I would do with her was another matter.

"Let go of me."

"Why did you run?"

"Why did you chase me?" We were both sucking in wind, trying to lower our heart rates and regain our composure. We stood on a quiet side street, far away from the funeral crowd.

"Look. I just want to know who you are. Why did you follow me? Why did you tell me that you were a teacher with PG? That's obviously not true."

"Lying to you is not a crime."

"Who are you? Why do you care about PG?"

"You are so goddamn naive, Seamus Shea."

I reached forward and grabbed her other arm. I held her firmly with both hands. Keeping a tight grip on each upper arm. She held keys in one hand.

"You know me, huh?" I said.

"I know all about you."

"Well, I feel at a loss. Please, tell me about you."

She looked at me and frowned, as if disappointed.

"I'm Lily," she said.

"Lily? Really?"

"Enough of this," she said. In a quick motion she kneed me in the crotch. I bent over and released her arms. She clicked a button on her keys and the trunk of the sedan popped open. I stood up, dazed and in pain. She reached into her jacket and took out an object that I did not recognize until she stuck the stun gun up under my left rib cage and shocked the shit out of me.

CHAPTER THIRTY-SEVEN

LILY PUSHED ME INTO THE OPEN TRUNK OF THE CAR. My first experience with a stun gun. All my muscles spasmed at once and I felt frozen. The pain from the shot to the groin paled to the electric charge pulsing through my body. I was easy pickings for her.

She grabbed my keys, wallet, and phone and slammed the trunk shut. Rev would have no idea what happened to me. Lily had baited me, and I fell for it hook, line, and sinker.

The large empty trunk smelled like motor oil and mildew. I heard a door slam and the engine start. We rode side streets, stopping every hundred yards, before turning. With each hard turn, I rattled around in the back, tossed like jeans in a dryer. My suit would be even more wrinkled.

I patted the floor and back wall to see if the trunk had a release latch. I knew some cars had them, but I had no luck. I remembered Jackie's voice mail. I wished I would have called her. I was toast.

The ride steadied and we accelerated. I could hear a siren and hoped for a moment I'd be saved, but it was an ambulance siren and seemed to be going in the opposite direction. We rode along and I soon felt a jerking every thirty feet that made a familiar sound: da-dum, da-dum, da-dum. We were on a bridge. It ended after a few minutes, and I guessed it was the Golden Gate. We were in Marin. We climbed and kept a high speed for at least ten minutes before we pulled off and slowed. There were more winding side streets, and I tumbled around the trunk. We turned left and climbed a steep hill.

The car jerked to the right and then down another twisting road before stopping. I could hear an electric gate churning open. We drove again, slowly up a long driveway. The car stopped and Lily cut the engine. She opened her door and closed it. I waited. Silence.

Eventually the trunk opened, and Lily stood over me, pointing a revolver at my forehead.

"Out, slowly," she said.

I climbed out of the trunk and kept my hands high. I stood with the back of my knees brushing the bumper, my arms vertical. We were in the shadow of an enormous off-white Mediterranean home complete with high arches, large windows, and a red tile roof. The length of our drive, the bridge, the size of the house, the long driveway, the gate: Marin, probably Ross.

"Seamus Shea!" a voice said from the side. "Nice suit."

I blinked to see Richard Cory standing with his arms crossed ten feet from me.

"Please, do come in," he said.

Lily kept the gun pointed at me and directed me through a side door that led to a sizable, clean, and well-lit kitchen. She pointed at a single Windsor chair parked in the middle of the kitchen.

I sat facing a California king-sized island with a farmhouse sink and overflowing fruit bowl. Lily took a seat at the island on a high stool. Richard Cory leaned against a Sub-Zero fridge, arms crossed, smiling at me.

"You must be impressed with Lily?" Richard Cory said.

"She's a peach," I said.

"Yes, she's an actress and an assassin. Quite the combination."

"An actress?"

"Yes. In college, in Europe."

"Multi-talented."

"She's a retired Mossad agent, believe it or not. Quite skilled. She's worth every penny I pay her."

Lily's face stayed expressionless. How would you hire someone from the Mossad?

"She was quite busy with you. You kept getting in the way. Your friend Pedro agreed to so much. He does love his mother. But you wouldn't accept that. Then you showed up in my office yesterday. Well, that was enough."

"Lovely office, by the way. I told my friends all about the office and your secretary and everything else."

"Oh, I'm sure you did. But when you came to see me you were so distraught. So upset about all the tragedies in your life. We knew each other. You interviewed me in the past. And we reconnected Friday at the party. You asked me about your will and your retirement. I was worried about you."

I crossed my arms. He was impeccably dressed.

"You see, Seamus Shea, we have a simple solution that will solve all our problems. The year anniversary of your brother's death is almost upon us. Tragic. You've just lost your job—fired, actually. Your wife has left you. Your best friend is going to jail for murder. These are tough times for you, Mr. Shea."

"Thanks for the recap."

"I knew your brother, or at least, knew of him. Narcotics Officer Daniel Shea. I thought he might be a problem. And then, to my surprise—luck? Fate? He, well, you know how that story ends."

My stomach tightened.

He looked down at his phone.

"Oh, isn't this lucky. A friend of yours has just arrived. It's like *This Is Your Life*," he said.

I heard the front door close.

"Should we play the guessing game? Don't come in just yet," he yelled.

My heart pounded. I had been wondering since Saturday who that friend might be. Why were these guys always one step ahead of me?

"Come on out, Don," I said.

"Hi, Shame," he said. He walked into the kitchen with the giant from Eastern Europe behind him. No cops had picked him up. There had been no interview.

"How'd you know?" he asked.

"Not sure I did until just now. I wondered why you let me see a murder suspect so easily. You wanted to see what he'd tell me. And Daniella was always one step in front of me. She knew I was at the Hall of Justice that day, that I was going to see Mamá, that I would be at the memorial. You knew all those things, too. I also wondered why you didn't have any questions about our big, Eastern European friend here."

"I'm from Canada," he said. "And my head still hurts from where you hit me. I think I have a concussion."

"Remember to let it be, my friend," I said.

He frowned.

"I tried to get you off this, Shame," Don said. "Multiple times. But you wouldn't listen. Let PG plea out. You wouldn't listen."

"Tell it to your psychiatrist!" I yelled. They all looked at me.

"You are an odd one, Seamus," Richard Cory said.

He walked to the corner of his kitchen and opened a cabinet door that displayed a fully stocked bar.

"Do you have a preference?"

"A preference?"

"For what you drink."

"I don't drink anymore."

"Oh, getting sober, are we? Good for you. Well, I hate to enable an addict, but such is life. Whiskey it is! Canadian."

"Seven and Seven, the good stuff," the giant said.

Richard Cory took down a bottle and grabbed a drinking glass from another cupboard.

"Lily thinks this is all too much for you to take." He walked across the room and handed me the glass. He unscrewed the bottle, tipped it and filled the glass half-way.

"Drink," he said.

Lily kept her pistol trained on me. Don looked away.

"She thinks you're overwhelmed by it all." Richard Cory leaned down and whispered in my ear: "That you will tragically, like your dear brother, end it all." He stood up and walked behind me. He put a gun that I didn't know he had to the back of my head. I could feel its cool weight above my neck. Lily did not stir.

"Not likely," I said.

He patted me on my left shoulder. "Oh, I think it's very likely, Mr. Shea. See, if you do that, we won't bother your mother. Or your friend Rev, or your ex Jennifer, or anyone else. We make deals, Mr. Shea. We made a deal with Pedro, and you upset that deal."

I had a sudden flashback to my mother telling me not to get involved.

"Now, make this deal with us, and I promise you, it will all end."

"Just drink it, Shame, it'll be easier for you," Don said.

"Don't call me Shame!"

Richard Cory used the barrel of his gun to push my head forward. "Drink," he said.

I didn't see any other option, so I drank. My brain lit up and my body felt a rush of warmth.

Lily hopped off her stool.

"I'm going to get a jacket," she said.

Richard Cory pointed at Don and the giant Canadian. They both left the kitchen. The giant rubbed his left temple as he left; Don didn't look at me. Richard Cory and I were alone in his massive kitchen. He refilled my glass.

"Drink up, it'll make it easier," he said.

"Why bring me here?" I asked.

"I did not enjoy our meeting yesterday," he said. "I found you a little rude. Cocky, even. And I didn't appreciate you surprising me in my office."

"You were quite amiable," I said. I threw back the whiskey.

He smiled.

"I had Lily bring you here so you would know I was the one responsible for your untimely end. You have been a thorn in my side all week, and you show up in my office. Too much, Mr. Shea."

Lily returned wearing a large parka with a furry hood. Where the hell was she taking me? Alaska?

"One last good glug there," Richard Cory said. I held out my glass. I thought of crashing it into his head, but he was still holding the gun.

He filled the glass halfway. I threw it back and let out a large belch.

"Goodbye, Seamus Shea," Richard Cory said.

"We'll see each other again," I said. The alcohol was swirling around inside me now. I felt that liquid courage, even though I was likely in the last hour of my life.

Richard Cory took an apple from the fruit bowl, twisted off the stem, and flicked it at me. He laughed and left.

"Stand up," Lily said, gesturing with her gun.

I stood up and stumbled a bit, feeling lightheaded. I grabbed the chair for balance. Lily gave me a moment and then led me back out of the house to her sedan. She opened the trunk and motioned for me to get in.

"Really? I get car sick easy."

"Funny man," Lily said, offering the first hint that she was human.

"I make lame jokes when I'm about to die, sorry."

"In," she said, pointing the gun at me.

I climbed in and met the familiar stench of motor oil and mildew. I would have to burn this suit if I made it out alive. Rev and Tito and even Jesus told me not to fuck it up, but it seems I had. You'd think I would at least have listened to Jesus. I shouldn't have forced Richard Cory's hand. Following Lily was a mistake. My fate was now clear: I was going to die.

We backed down the driveway and onto the main road. Lily drove a good ten minutes before we slowed and stopped. She exited the car again. The trunk popped open. She kept the gun pointed at me.

"Hurry up," she said.

I crawled out of the trunk and felt a cold blast of wind. It took a moment for my eyes to adjust, but I realized she had parked in a dark corner of a familiar parking lot.

CHAPTER THIRTY-EIGHT

I WAS DRUNK.

I stood rooted halfway down the eastern walkway of the world-famous, crimson-colored, Golden Gate Bridge, freezing my ass off.

I was not a tourist.

I was not a sightseer.

I was a fool with a snub-nosed revolver pointed at my back.

Lily was twenty feet behind me with said gun under her thick jacket. We were alone on the bridge. Lily kept her distance, wrapped in the parka she took from Richard Cory's house. She had pulled the hood over her head and added a scarf over her mouth. Any cameras would not be able to identify her. Smart and thorough. Lucky me.

I thought of Don. He had been close to Danny, but he sold me out. For what? Money? I had trusted him all along, and he betrayed me.

My heart was pounding. My head was cloudy. I was drunk and in that uneasy haze from drinking too fast. Lily gave me a simple choice in the parking lot: walk the bridge and jump and no harm would come to my mom or Jenny or Rev, or don't jump and she'd shoot me, toss me over the rail and go kill them all. I had no reason to doubt her.

"I think I'm going to be sick," I said, trying to buy time.

"I don't give a shit. Just jump."

The heavy darkness and limited traffic made me think it was near midnight. Lily forced me to walk at gunpoint from the parking lot to a spot halfway down the span. We had to jump on the roadway briefly to pass the closed gate of the walkway. I debated my options as we walked. I could run into traffic and hope that I wouldn't be run over and instead rescued and whisked away. That would leave Lily free to hunt my family. There had to be people who guarded the bridge; maybe they'd come get me.

My last thought was that I could try and get close to her and wrestle the gun away. She kept a good distance and seemed better trained with firearms since, apparently, she was in the Mossad, and I had never touched, let alone fired, a gun. I considered an appeal to her softer side, to plead with her to let me go, but from what I could tell, that might actually lead her to just shoot me. I accepted that I might have to jump.

"Get it over with," Lily yelled. "It's cold out here."

The wind was relentless.

"I'm so sorry you're uncomfortable," I said. I turned to look out at the bay, windswept crests of blue-green water swirled below, the hunk of land that was Alcatraz, the city skyline in all its modern glory further off.

The steady drone of cars whizzing by brought me back to a few days ago when I stood nearly on this same spot. The thump, thump, thump of those same cars driving over expansion joints every thirty feet. My problems then: Danny, Jenny, being fired. Somehow, in the short course of one week, my problems had gotten worse. PG was either going to be tortured and maybe even killed in prison, or he'd spend the rest of his life there, and I was going to be dead.

"I just have one request," I said softly.

"What?"

"One request I'd like you to do for me. After."

"Jump off the fucking bridge, Shea. I do not have time for this shit."

"Please, you know what happened to my brother. I'll do it, I just need you to do one thing for me."

"Climb over the railing," she said.

It wasn't part of my plan, but I could tell she was getting impatient, and she did have a gun. I climbed over the railing and stood on a thin lip facing Alcatraz, my arms behind me holding on.

"Will you please . . ." I spoke softly again. The rumble of cars and the strong wind made it impossible for her to hear me. She came closer.

"Jump."

"I just ask you to please . . . my mom."

She was only a few feet away now.

"Please, Lily. It's just my mom. Please . . ." Even Lily must have had a mom once.

"What?" She said, annoyed.

"It's just." I turned toward her. Both my hands were back behind me, gripping the railing. I locked both feet into the small groove where I stood. I had to splay them out, but there was enough room to jam my feet. I needed a solid base.

"Just what?" She asked. She was almost within arm's reach. Just a little closer.

"Oh, God. I don't want to die. Will you tell my mom?"

"Oh, God. You are a wimp."

She was a few feet from me now. Gun barrel visible.

"Jump, will you?"

I wondered if some CHP or Park Police person might be on patrol and could swing by to save me. I considered that I could jump. I remembered reading that some people did survive. Go feet first. You'd break both your legs, but you'd keep your head safe. I'd be a paraplegic, but I'd be alive. No! I just needed her a few feet closer.

"Just tell her . . ." I was wailing now, a mess. If she had any bit of sympathy, this was my opportunity.

"The drunk Irishman crying for his mother, really?"

"Tell her . . ."

"Tell her what? Tell me and jump, or I swear to God, I'll kill her right after this."

"Tell her . . ." I said. I was whimpering, my body language pointed to my defeat.

"What?" she screamed. The wind whipped around us. It shook the large square light above.

Lily was leaning over the railing now. Easily within reach. She looked up to see the light sway. I only had a moment. I kept my feet pinned in the groove and used my left hand to hold onto the railing. I reached up with my right hand and grabbed her by the jacket and pulled. She must have weighed no more than a hundred pounds, because I easily brought her over the railing. She fired a shot but missed wildly as I pulled her. I kept my feet pinned in, bent my knees some and pushed her out away from the bridge. She fired again. I felt a bullet whiz by me and heard it ricochet off the bridge. I saw her face for a moment, shock and awe that I outsmarted her. I wondered if for a moment, for just a few seconds, she thought of all that she had done and all that she had failed to do. I couldn't tell, because in an instant, she dropped.

THURSDAY

CHAPTER THIRTY-NINE

I HAD NEVER WATCHED SOMEONE DIE.

I heard Lily scream as she dropped and wouldn't soon forget it. Her flight over the rail and into the turbulent waters below was at once triumphant and horrific.

I stood on the bridge, unsure of what to do next. I buttoned up my suit to fight the chill. I eventually took a seat and rested my back against the railing. I was exhausted mentally and physically. After some time, I had no idea how long, a patrol car drove up with lights flashing and double parked in the right lane.

"What are you doing out here?" one of the cops asked. "Bridge walkway is closed."

He was dark-featured and older, probably in his mid-fifties. His partner was young and tan. Bridge and tunnel.

"I'm just . . . it's just . . ." I still felt pretty drunk, and the reality of police and a dead woman were doing little to sober me up.

"Stand up and hands up," the tan cop said.

I did as he asked. They both approached me, hands on their holstered guns.

"Turn around slowly, face the water."

They handcuffed me and directed me to sit back down. One officer went to the patrol car and put out flares to direct traffic. The older officer asked me questions. He pulled out a small flip notepad and pulled a tiny pen from the spiral top.

"What are you doing here?"

"I got brought here by a woman named Lily. She kidnapped me and then was going to force me to jump."

"Uh-huh," he said, writing down notes. I could tell he didn't believe me.

"You need to find her."

"We will, we will. What's your name?"

"Seamus Shea."

He looked at me.

"The newspaper guy?"

"Yeah."

"'City Views,' right? What happened to that column?"

"I got drunk one too many times."

He nodded.

"Are you drunk now?" he asked.

"No. Well, yeah. I am. They made me drink."

"They made you drink? Who's they?"

"Look, I pulled her over, and she went in the water."

He jerked his head from his notepad to look at me.

"You're telling me there's a body in the water?"

I nodded. He frowned and looked over the railing before walking back to his car. He said something to his partner and leaned into his car and grabbed the radio. His partner walked back to me and glanced over the railing.

"You threw her in?" the tan one asked.

"She was telling me to jump. She had a gun. I didn't have a choice."

"Who was she?" he asked.

"Lily. Don't know if that's her real name. I don't know her last name. She worked in Mossad apparently and was an actress of some type."

The first officer returned.

"So, Lily is a Mossad agent and an actress," the young one said to his partner. They exchanged looks.

"And why did she want to kill you?" The older one asked.

"I found out she killed Monique Profit. The girl from Jefferson High School."

The young one laughed out loud.

"Look, I know it sounds crazy, but it's true."

"Of course," the older one said, calmly. "You're safe now, and that's the important part. You rest here, we'll be right back."

They walked back to their patrol car and talked. The older one grabbed the radio again and made another call.

After a few minutes, another police car showed up. Two officers got out and joined the others. The older one walked back to me with the two new cops.

"Okay, Seamus. We're going to take you someplace safe. This is Officer Wu, and this is Officer Butler. They're going to take you, okay? And I'm going to look for Lily."

"You better jump in the water, because I told you she went over."

"Of course, of course. We have the Coast Guard on it."

He took his handcuffs off, and Officer Wu put her pair on me.

"Just being safe, okay?" she said. "We're just going to take you somewhere safe." She read me my rights. I didn't have the energy to question it. I just nodded and they led me to the car and put me in the back seat.

"Where are you taking me?" I finally asked.

"There, there. You're going to be fine. Everything is going to be okay," Officer Wu, a young, sympathetic female officer said.

"I'm not crazy," I said. But they were both silent.

CHAPTER FORTY

WE DROVE TO THE RICHMOND POLICE STATION. They put me in an interrogation room. Officer Wu took off my handcuffs and had me fill out a statement form. She talked to me in a calming, even tone. She took the statement from me and put the handcuffs back on.

"There, there," she said. "This is just to keep you safe."

I didn't respond. I sat there quietly in handcuffs for at least an hour with no word. The room was similar to the one where I met PG. Eight feet by eight feet, beige walls, small table, a couple of metal folding chairs, and dust. This room had no mirror, but it did have a small video camera in the upper right corner that looked right down on me.

Like PG, I rested my handcuffed hands in the center of the small table, as if I were praying. I supposed I could use a prayer or two.

Finally, Officer Wu walked in with Sean Mannion trailing.

"What the hell, Shame? It's 5:00 a.m."

"What are you doing here?"

Sean looked at Officer Wu. "Tatum here knew Danny. And she knew Danny and I were friends, so she called me."

"She tried to kill me, Sean."

"Who did?"

"Lily. She's a Mossad agent—former agent. She killed Monique."

He looked me up and down and leaned in to smell my breath.

"I'm not drunk. I mean, I am somewhat. They made me drink. I know it sounds crazy, but it's true."

"Like they held you down and forced it down your throat?"

"More or less. They had me at gunpoint."

"Like the movie," he said.

"What movie?"

"The Hitchcock one, where they get the guy drunk and then have him crash his car."

"*North by Northwest*?" Officer Wu asked.

"Yes!" Sean said.

"I didn't see it. Look, she was working for a man named Richard Cory. He's Keyser Söze. Don Johnson is in on it. Cory had Monique killed because she's Kratos's daughter. He was sending a message."

"Okay, Shame, slow down, now."

"It's true, Sean."

"This Richard Cory is Keyser Söze, and Don Johnson's in on it?" he asked.

"Yeah. I thought it was you. I thought you were rotten. I knew they had someone on the inside helping them. But it was Don. Don all along."

Sean breathed in slowly, expanding his chest and rolling his shoulders back. He motioned for Officer Wu to take off the cuffs.

"Give us a moment, will you, Tatum?"

She nodded and left the room.

"Are you okay?" he asked.

"Yeah," I said, rubbing my wrists. "She was trying to get me to jump. She had a gun. Wanted it to seem like I took my own life. Like Danny. I was on to her and Richard Cory. They set up PG, but I got in the way."

"I need to call Jackie. I need to get her to expose this guy."

Sean held his hands out in mock surrender.

"Slow down, Shame. Okay? We don't need press right now. There are a lot of moving parts; let's take it one step at a time."

I took a deep breath. I was lingering between being drunk and hungover. My head was killing me.

"So, you threw her over?" he asked.

"I was over the rail holding on. I pretended to be crying, and she came closer. She got careless, and I grabbed her and threw her over the railing. She wasn't that heavy, and she was wearing a parka, so it was easy to grasp onto. She shot at me; there might be a bullet around there. I'm not sure where it landed. I've never killed anyone, Sean."

Sean, not one to be surprised, looked befuddled.

"What's her name again?" he asked.

"Lily."

"Lily, the Mossad agent?"

"Yes."

He adjusted his pants and looked around the room.

"Did they find her?" I asked. "I told them to look."

He rubbed his chin.

"They found someone," Sean said. "Gonna take a little while to identify the body."

"It's her, you'll see."

"I sure as shit hope so, Shame. Your story is pretty fucking wild. I can only do so much."

"Her car is in the parking lot. It's a big black sedan. I think that's where my wallet and stuff are. I didn't want to kill her, Sean. I didn't. It was self-defense."

"How did you get to Richard Cory?"

"The poem."

"The poem?"

"Yeah, Danny had a file on an Ed Robison. All this stuff, but no name except Ed Robinson. But that got me nothing. Then I looked up the poet Edward Robinson, and he had a poem called Richard Cory. I knew Richard Cory, and I knew Keyser Söze worked at the Bank of America Building.

"I knew a Richard Cory. Society type. I had interviewed him for a column a while back. I saw him at a party Friday. He worked at B of A, I mean 555. I went to see him, and he got pissed. Kidnapped me the next day."

"I told you to stay out of this, didn't I?" he said.

"Yeah."

"But you didn't listen?"

"Nope."

"And now you killed someone?"

"Who was going to kill me."

Sean walked to my side and put his left hand on my left shoulder.

"I know, Shame. I know. This is a mess, and you were trying to help your friend. We'll get it cleared up. But I'll need you to hang out here for a bit," he said. "They want to lock you up, but I'm vouching for you for now."

"Lock me up?"

"5150. Mossad agent. Forcing you to jump and drink. Monique's killer. It's like some rip-off Hitchcock movie. They think you are a little off."

"Well, at this point, guilty as charged."

CHAPTER FORTY-ONE

I STAYED IN THE SMALL ROOM FOR ANOTHER HOUR. Sean brought me a bag of Doritos and a cup of terrible coffee and told me to hang tight. He eventually came back with good news.

"Ok, Shame. We identified the body. Her name is Lilian Gretchen Weis. There was no record that she worked for the Mossad. She did have a Norwegian passport."

"See?"

"See what? I have to deal in proof, Shame. We found her car. Your wallet and phone were in it. That's good news. We're going through her hotel room. We'll know more soon. If it all pans out, you'll be in the clear."

"How did they identify her so fast?"

"I can't tell you that, but you'll know soon enough."

I was too tired to probe.

"So, I can go now?" I asked.

"Sorry, we gotta keep you longer. They're some other folks that want to talk to you."

"Who?"

He dropped his head.

"Feds. Apparently, she was known."

"Feds? You mean FBI? And what does 'known' mean?"

"I'll let them tell you. They'll be here soon. You want some more coffee or a bottle of water?" he asked.

"So, I can't leave?"

"I think for PG's benefit, it would pay for you to stay and talk to them. They're the reason I was pushing you to stay out of all this. You ended up smack dab in the middle of a major operation."

Sean looked at me directly. He nodded slowly. I did not understand what he was trying to tell me, but I realized I should listen to him and wait it out.

"I'll take some water," I said.

Sean left and came back after a couple of minutes. He tossed a plastic water bottle at me, and I caught it, unscrewed the lid, and took a long drink.

"Sit tight," he said.

"I don't have much choice."

Sean left and closed the door behind him. I put my arms down on the table and rested my head in the crook of my right elbow. Within minutes, I fell asleep.

I woke up to the sound of the door opening and two men entering the room. I wiped my mouth to clear away a splash of drool. Both men were dressed in tailored suits. Both clean-cut with sharp, angled faces; buzzed haircuts; and little emotion. One was slightly taller and Black, but otherwise, they seemed to be indistinguishable.

"Hello, Mr. Shea. I'm Agent Woods and this is Agent Holly," the Black agent said.

Holly Woods?

"We'd like to hear from you about what happened tonight," Agent Woods said. He took a seat on the folding chair and sat across from me. He seemed to be in charge.

"I was at Monique Profit's memorial. I recognized a woman who approached me a couple of days ago outside the Hall of Justice. She said she was a teacher at Monique's school. I saw her again in my friend PG's apartment. She attacked me and ran out. I chased her all the way into the Muni tunnel, but I lost her. She also was following me in her sedan. I saw her again at the memorial. I followed her and she ran. I chased, and before I knew it, she tased me and threw me in her trunk."

"And why do you think you kept coming across her?"

"I think she killed Monique Profit at Jefferson High School and was trying to make sure my friend, PG, took the fall."

Agent Woods stood up and walked over to his partner. He whispered something to him before walking back to me.

"Okay, she's got you in her trunk, then what?" Woods asked.

"She drove me for about half an hour. I think to Marin. To see a guy named Richard Cory."

Both agents looked at each other.

"Did you know this Richard Cory?"

"I met him a while back. Interviewed him for a column. I saw him again at a party on Friday night. He's a big philanthropist, a player in the society world of SF. I went to see him yesterday. I had reliable info that he was not a good person and could have been behind Monique's death. So, I asked him."

Officer Holly chuckled.

"What did he say?"

"When I met him in his office, he said he did not know anything about it. When I met him at his house, he said he brought me there to make sure I knew he was the one who was going to have me killed. He apparently didn't like me going to his office."

"Apparently not," Agent Holly said.

"And then?" Woods asked.

"They got me drunk. Cory left, and Lily drove me to the bridge. Had a gun on me the whole time and told me to jump or they'd kill my family."

"How did you get away?" Holly asked.

"She made me climb over the railing. I started to plead with her, hoping she'd let her guard down. She got annoyed and left me an opening. I grabbed her by her jacket and threw her over the bridge."

Both men looked at me but didn't speak. I let the silence linger.

"Can I go now?" I finally asked.

"Mr. Shea, I'm glad you are alive."

"Thank you."

"But you just single-handedly fucked up an investigation Agent Holly and I have been working on for well over a year."

"I did?"

"You did. Lily was an informant for us. We worked long and hard to get her to be one. We were one step—one fucking step—from getting Richard Cory. And you go and kill her."

"I didn't want to kill her. And what kind of informant is she? Kills Monique and tries to kill me? Great company you keep."

"We did not know about Monique. Lily was not the most reliable informant in some ways, but she was ready to give up Richard Cory. Nothing is perfect in this world, Mr. Shea."

"She tried to kill me!"

"The fact is that Richard Cory runs an operation that supplies drugs to most of California. San Francisco was just a small part of it."

"I'm sure you have more than just Lily."

For the first time, a flash of anger crossed Agent Wood's face.

"More? Do you have any idea how slippery this guy is? Or how important he is? His connections run deep both politically and financially. You can't just go accusing him without rock solid evidence. Lily was that."

"He seemed like an asshole to me."

Agent Woods took a deep breath. He pinched the bridge of his nose.

"Well, unfortunately, we can't arrest people for being assholes."

"Did you know she killed Monique?" I asked.

Woods stood up and glanced at his partner. He rubbed his face with his right hand.

"Not at first. Later, we had a suspicion."

"You let my friend take the fall? He's in prison, fighting for his life. English teachers don't do well in prison, you know?"

"It was a delicate situation. He likely would have been in the clear very soon. We were very, very close."

I didn't respond.

"We have a federal case, a very good one. We don't want this derailing it."

I was pissed. I'd had enough.

"I'm sure my friend Jackie James at the *Chronicle* would like to hear all about your case. I can see the headline now: *Federal Informant Kills High School Student*."

Woods and Holly glanced at each other.

"Now, why would you go and do that?"

"Because I'm tired of the bullshit. I'm not exactly Perry Mason, but I seemed to figure out this shit in the past few days. You gentlemen are working on some big case that I solved in a few days."

"You hardly solved it. You did well, I'll give you credit. But putting someone away requires evidence. We can't just throw everyone over a bridge."

"Pity."

We each stayed silent for a few minutes. I crossed my arms and looked at the camera in the corner of the wall.

"What do you want, Shea?" Agent Woods finally asked.

"How about we make a deal, Holly Woods?" I said.

Holly motioned for Woods to step back.

"We're listening," he said.

"You get my buddy cleared as soon as possible, and I won't mention Richard Cory or Lily to my friend Jackie. Lily is Monique's killer and will go down as Monique's killer, and my friend goes free. Deal?"

They looked at each other.

"You won't mention Richard Cory?"

I put an imaginary key in my mouth, twisted it, and threw it away.

"We have your word?"

"Yes, you have my word."

"Okay," Woods said. "Seems like the right thing to do."

"We're way past the right thing to do, Holly Woods."

"Can you stop calling us that?" Holly said.

"When will PG be free?" I asked.

"I'll talk to the DA. We'll get him a hearing this afternoon, and you'll have dinner with him tonight."

Both agents stood over me, and Woods held out his hand.

"Agreed?" he said.

"Agreed," I said and shook his hand.

CHAPTER FORTY-TWO

I WAS ALMOST SOBER.

PG was almost free.

After our deal, Holly Woods sent me on my way. I was able to recover my phone, keys, and wallet. I was going to call Rev, but my phone was dead. In the waiting room, Sean Mannion was asleep in a chair. I gave him a nudge.

"Seamus, they let you out?"

"Yep. Did you wait for me?"

"Sure, I had nothing better to do at 6:00 a.m. in the morning. Come on, car's out front."

I followed Sean out into the overcast morning. He led me to a neon yellow Mustang.

"Subtle," I said.

"What did they tell you?" Sean asked, as we pulled onto Geary Boulevard.

"They're going to let PG go. Lily will go down as the murderer. I can't touch Richard Cory. They have a big case on him they don't want touched."

We drove on in silence save the hard rock radio station playing Guns N' Roses.

"You did good, Shame. Danny would be proud," Sean eventually said.

"Doesn't feel good, but at least PG will be free."

"I'm sorry I didn't tell you about the Feds. None of us knew what was going on; they just told us to stay away. So, I thought you should stay away. Luckily, you ignored me."

"I always ignore you, Sean. Except when you are offering me another drink."

"Ha, good man, you are."

Sean dropped me home, and I climbed the steps to my apartment wanting to sleep for the next week. My body ached. My head was pounding. My swollen lip and pinky throbbed. I had just taken a life. I needed sleep.

The door to my apartment was ajar. I pushed it open to see Don Johnson sitting on my couch, leafing through my copy of *Sports Illustrated*. I took a step forward, but before I could even speak, a giant fist crashed into the right side of my face. I crumpled.

"Oh, did that hurt?" the giant Canadian asked. "I have some wise advice for you, Seamus. Just let it be."

He grabbed me and tossed me into a chair across from Don. I rubbed my chin and looked up at him.

"Payback's a bitch, Seamus," he said, smiling. He wore a Lake Tahoe hoodie, heavyweight sweats, and retro Air Jordan's.

"I used to like you," I said.

"Busy day, huh, Seamus?" Don said. He seemed genuinely pleased to see me.

"It will not end," I said.

Don put the magazine down and picked up a glass of water.

"Hope you don't mind," he said, taking a drink. "Thought we'd make ourselves at home."

I jumped up out of the chair and tried to run for the door, but the giant grabbed me.

"No, no, Seamus. You are going to stay here with us," Don said. He took out a Beretta 9mm and placed it in front of him on the coffee table.

"Why, Don?" I asked.

"It's complicated, Shame. I met Richard Cory over a year ago. He seemed like a good guy. Philanthropist. Gentleman. He was charming and seemed to be genuinely interested in my work."

Don eyed his gun on the table. I could hear the giant breathing behind me.

"We partied together. He got me in some compromising positions. I was caught. He's a master manipulator. Set me up from the start. I was stuck doing his bidding or my life would be ruined."

"Seems like it's ruined now."

"Maybe." His eyes met mine. "I wish you would have stayed out of all this, Shame. I didn't know he was targeting PG. I didn't. And then you got involved. I begged him to let me get rid of you. I hoped you would trust me, listen to my reason. But sadly, you didn't. Showing up at his work was a big mistake. That sealed your fate."

"My fate's been okay so far."

He laughed.

"Yeah, I'll give you credit. Lily was a killer. Not sure how you outsmarted her."

"She underestimated me. Most people do."

"Well, Lenny and I here won't make that mistake."

"Lenny?"

"That's my name," the giant Canadian said.

I turned toward him.

"Lenny?" I nodded, "It fits."

"I'm named after my maternal grandfather," Lenny offered, without any prompting.

"Well, what now?" I asked, turning back toward Don.

"I think you know what," he said.

"I've already told them all about you, Don. It's over. Killing me won't do you any good. It will only make it worse." I was lying. In my quest to get PG free, I only mentioned Don to Sean Mannion. And I'm not sure he believed me. I was done for, and Don would walk free.

"I don't think so. With you gone, it's my word against yours. I might be damaged some, but I won't go to prison. I can't go to prison, Shame. You understand?"

"I get it. I've seen more of prison in the last week than I ever care to."

I scanned the room for weapons. The baseball bat was still by the front door. But Don and Lenny were both giants. They'd likely just take the bat from me and pound me with it. I'd maybe be able to make it to the kitchen and grab a knife. Two even, like some badass Samurai.

"I'm sorry, Shame. Your brother was a good man. I really liked him. Say hi to him for me, will you?"

I had a sudden thought of my mother, alone upstairs.

"Do me one favor?" I asked.

"Yeah?"

"You leave my mom alone. She hears a shot, she'll come running down here."

"Jesus, Seamus, what kind of guy do you think I am?"

I let the question pass.

Don picked up the gun from the table. He turned toward the couch and grabbed a throw pillow. He pointed both at my face. Too late for a kitchen run. Too late for anything. Would I have time to think about all that I had done? All that I had failed to do?

An image of my closed casket, on the altar of Our Lady of Angels, flashed in my mind's eye. No one would get a last look at me. Would Father Ryan forego his ruse to speak at my funeral? Doubted it. I took a deep breath and closed my eyes.

"I'm sorry, Shame."

Let it be.

CHAPTER FORTY-THREE

A SECOND AFTER I CLOSED MY EYES, my front door crashed open. There was an ear-piercing bang that reverberated and caused me to fall out of my chair. I heard heavy footsteps trampling through the apartment. I heard faint voices saying, "Go, go, go," and "Down, down. Get down on the ground!"

After a minute of sheer chaos, I felt a hand on my shoulder. I looked up to see Sean Mannion blinking back at me.

"You okay there, Seamus?"

"Not really. What the hell happened?"

"We paid a visit." I looked over to see Don Johnson and the Canadian giant lying face down on the floor. Their legs spread wide and their hands zip-tied.

"What was the bang?"

"Flash bang. Effective, huh? After I dropped you off, I saw Don Johnson's car parked around the corner. I almost missed it. I figured he'd come back to finish you off. I was going to just come back to your apartment, but I thought about how desperate Don might be. I wasn't going to play around. I called in for some back up. And here we are."

"My lucky day."

Rhodes came barreling through the door.

"You okay, Shea?"

"Yeah."

"Hell of a mess you uncovered," he said.

"I just wanted to help PG," I said.

"Mission accomplished," Rhodes said.

Two officers led Don and Lenny out of the apartment. Neither looked at me. I heard a scream and frantic yelling outside the apartment.

"Seamus, Seamus!"

My mother was being held back by a uniformed policeman. I walked toward her.

"It's okay, let her in."

She rushed me.

"Jesus, Mary, and Saint Joseph, what the hell happened? I heard a bang, and it nearly killed me with shock."

"Some bad guys were here, tied to the PG case. It's okay now. They've been arrested. PG will be free later today."

"Are you okay?"

"I am. It's been a long day, but I'm okay."

Rhodes came over to us.

"Mrs. Shea?"

"Yes."

"I'm Detective Rhodes. I'm very sorry for all this. Your son was very brave and helped us solve a complicated case. He's a hero. You should be proud of him."

She looked at the door for the first time; both hinges were off.

"Thank you, Detective."

"We'll need a statement, and we have to process the scene here," Rhodes said. "But the statement can wait. Maybe you could go upstairs and rest some? I know it's been a long day."

I wanted to kiss him, but that probably wouldn't go over well.

"Yes. Please. I need sleep."

I shook Rhodes's beefy hand and gave Sean a hug. My mother led me up the stairs to her spare bedroom, where I laid down and fell blissfully asleep.

CHAPTER FORTY-FOUR

AFTER A FEW HOURS OF SLEEP, I managed to shower and scarf down a turkey on sourdough. My forced drunkenness left me with a rather rude hangover. I made a mental note to call Bunny and get to a meeting soon.

Rev picked me up at 3:00 p.m., and we met Maria at the Hall of Justice. PG was scheduled for a hearing at 3:45 p.m.

The District Attorney of San Francisco held a rushed news conference Thursday afternoon announcing a break in the Monique Profit case. There had been more information uncovered in the tragic murder of this young girl.

"I've filed all the necessary paperwork," Maria said. "This should just be a formality. In a half hour, you guys should be walking your friend out the front door."

She led us into the small hearing room, a forty-by-forty-foot space with tan wood paneling all around and twenty rows of chairs stolen from a middle school auditorium. The room smelled like burnt leather. We squeezed into a couple of aisle seats and waited. I could see the top of PG's head. He sat in the second row, nervously looking from side to side.

Eventually the bailiff called his case. PG stood up, and Maria led him in front of the judge. Rev was loudly tapping his knee next to me. I reached out and stopped him. He nodded.

The judge looked ancient: thinning white hair, pale, wrinkled skin, and oversized reading glasses. He took his time looking over the documents in front of him. He glanced up at Pedro a couple of times and continued reading.

"Do you have a motion, Mr. Jones?" he asked the prosecuting attorney.

Rev dropped his head. I kept staring at the judge. The courtroom was silent, filled mostly with reporters. I looked for Jackie but didn't see her.

"We move to have the charges against Pedro Julio Gomez be dropped."

The judge removed his glasses and pointed at Pedro.

"Mr. Gomez?" he asked.

"Yes, your honor," Pedro replied.

"I am sorry that you were wrongly accused of this crime. As an educator, I can't imagine the horror you felt being forced to say you had killed your own student. I am pleased to release you from this court and wish you all the best in putting this sad chapter behind you. Case dismissed."

PG turned and hugged Maria. The room erupted. Rev and I hugged. We pushed our way through the crowd blocking the aisle and grabbed Pedro.

"I can't thank you enough, Shame. You saved my life."

I smiled. I had no idea what to say. Rev gave Maria a big hug and thanked her. PG's eyes were filled with tears.

"Quit your crying," I said.

"Tears of joy!"

We followed Maria out of the hearing room and into a lobby filled with reporters. We pushed through the swarm yelling Pedro's name and asking questions: "How does it feel to be out?" "What will you do next?" "Will you teach at the same school?"

I saw Jackie amid the crowd, smiling.

We made it outside to the stairs. Rev went on ahead to get his car. The sky was clear and bright. PG looked up and shielded his eyes. He took a deep breath.

A gaggle of reporters followed us. At least four TV crews, cameras in hand. PG turned and addressed them. I found Jackie and gave her a hug.

"I just want to say that I feel terrible for Monique Profit. She was a wonderful young woman. My heart breaks for her amazing mother. I will do everything I can to help people remember Monique and how special she was."

"How's it feel to be out?" Jackie yelled.

"It feels great to be free. I am very grateful to everyone who worked hard to clear my name—especially my amazing lawyer, Maria Luna. Thank you."

The reporters yelled more questions, but PG ignored them. He motioned to me to leave. I high-fived Jackie and led PG down the stairs. Rev pulled up just in time. I opened the front door of Rev's 4Runner and guided PG in. I turned and waved off the flock of reporters still yelling silly questions.

Maria stood off to the side and called them over, trying to give us cover. "It's been a long week for Mr. Gomez," she yelled. "He'll talk to you all after he gets some rest." The crowd did not move. They wanted PG and no one else.

Rev spun around after we entered and took off, dodging a few stray cameramen and reporters. He made his way up Bryant Street before turning onto Sixth Street, heading for 280. I had no idea where we were going, but I did not care.

"Woo-hoo!" Rev screamed.

"What the hell just happened?" PG asked.

"As near as I can tell," I began, "I have no idea."

"Jesus," PG said.

"Jesus is right," I said.

CHAPTER FORTY-FIVE

LATER THAT NIGHT, PG hosted a barbecue to celebrate his freedom. Every one of his thousand cousins seemed to be there, including Tito. They were spread out in Mr. Cohen's large backyard, unaffected by the cold. A Bluetooth player was blasting some Salvadoran music, the smell of tri-tip cooking on the barbecue, young kids dancing in the corner, men playing cards at an outdoor table—happiness all around.

Mamá beamed and rushed at me.

"Thank you, Seamus," she said, hugging me. "I knew you would help him. I knew you could get him free."

"I got lucky," I replied. "I'm just glad we got him out."

"I prayed. I prayed all day and night. I asked God to help him. To help you. I prayed and prayed and prayed."

"It worked," I said.

She walked me to the grill where Rev was turning three large tri-tips.

"Here, you help Rev. He's not much of a cook."

"That hurts, Mrs. G. That hurts."

She leaned in and hugged us both then walked away dabbing at her eyes.

"That's one happy lady," I said.

PG came over and put one of his cousins on the grill. He led me and Rev into his apartment. He told us to take a seat on his couch, while he went into his kitchen.

"My cousin gave me a nice little gift, and I want to share it with you two," he said. He walked out of the kitchen holding a bottle and three glasses.

"Macallan 18-year, boys."

"Damn," Rev said.

He filled the three glasses halfway and handed one to each of us. Eighteen-year-old Scotch. The smell was intoxicating.

I put my glass back on the table.

"I'm on the wagon, gents."

"What?" Rev asked, shocked.

"One of the signs of the apocalypse," PG laughed.

I took a deep breath.

"I mean it, guys, I'm on the wagon for a while."

Rev and PG looked at each other. PG nodded.

"More for us, Rev!"

I went and grabbed some tonic, and we toasted PG's release.

"Oh, that reminds me," Rev said. He reached into his pocket and pulled out his money clip. He unwrapped a one-hundred-dollar bill and handed it to me.

"What's that for?" PG asked.

"I bet him a hundred bucks he'd get you out," Rev said.

"And you bet against that?" PG asked, laughing.

"It didn't look good at the time," I said.

"Well-earned," Rev said.

"I'll take it. I need the money."

"Shame, I'll be honest, man. I thought you were done for," Rev said.

"Me too," I answered.

"I thought when I lost you at the church, I might have lost you permanently."

"You can't get rid of me that easy."

"I was worried. You are my one White friend, Shame," he said, laughing. "I wasn't ready to get a new one."

PG spit out some of his whiskey.

"I mean you are as White as they get. Not easy to find these days."

"Okay, okay. Why is this about me? He's the one that got thrown in jail," I said.

"I think you found your calling," PG said.

"What's that?" I asked.

"A shamus."

I looked at him, confused.

"Seamus Shea, the shamus. It's perfect, poetic even."

"Genius!" Rev said.

"A shamus is slang for a private detective," PG said.

"I know what a shamus is," I said.

"You should become a private detective."

I couldn't tell if PG was serious or messing with me.

"You want me to become a private investigator because of my name?" I asked.

"No. You solved this case in a few days," PG said.

"No need to be a columnist. Be a shamus. Seamus the shamus," Rev said. "Consider that one hundred dollars your first payment."

"I'll take it under advisement, gentlemen."

"Let's get the party boy outside," Rev said. "I'm sure people are looking for him."

We headed out to the backyard, and it was thick with people now. I could see Mr. Cohen up on his deck looking down at the melee. He nodded, and I raised my glass to him. I could hear the faint bark of Mister Mister, locked in the house.

About an hour later, I found PG in his apartment, half asleep on his couch. He was wasted.

"I love you, man," he said.

"I love you, too," I replied.

"You're like my Horatio, you know?"

I had no idea what he was talking about.

"Horatio. He's Hamlet's best friend."

"How come you get to be Hamlet?" I asked.

He started laughing.

"Fair enough. I'm your Horatio."

He soon launched into an impromptu lecture on Hamlet. I drank my tonic water and listened.

"Look at it from a Christian reading, the Trinity: Father, Son, and Holy Ghost. The father coming back as a Ghost. Hamlet as a Christ figure, meant to suffer the absurdity of this world. His father killed by his uncle who marries his mother. A few months after the death? Can there be anything more absurd?"

He was wasted.

"There are lessons throughout the play. Insights and wisdom. More in heaven or hell than are dreamt of in your philosophy."

He stood up and had to hold the arm of the couch to get his balance. He walked to the front window, the curtains were drawn, and he raised his hands to place his fingertips on the glass. He exhaled, fogging the space between his fingers. He turned back toward me.

"There is one passage I love. It's when Hamlet is told the king wants him to fight Laertes, and that he will wager on Hamlet. Hamlet thinks it's a death sentence. He tells Horatio, his buddy, that if he is to die, he will die now or if it's not now it will be eventually, he then tells him to let be."

"Let be?" I asked.

"Yeah, let be. He says he's okay with death. He says it again when he's actually dying. He's been poisoned. He tells those listening that he could tell some stories, but he lets it go and says, 'let be.' Twice, he says let be. This is the philosophy. The philosophy of the whole play. Live life and let be. Your father is killed? Let be. Your mother marries your uncle? Let be. The girl you love kills herself? Let be. That's Act I Hamlet versus Act V Hamlet."

He raised both arms up like a preacher calling up to God.

"Let be. Let be. Let be."

"Let it be," I said. "Paul McCartney and William Shakespeare, huh?"

PG looked at me with genuine surprise. He walked back and fell on the couch.

"I hadn't thought of that," he said. "Let be. Let it be. That's genius!"

He curled up on the side of the couch, clutching a throw pillow. I went into his bedroom and brought back his comforter. I covered him up and touched his forehead lightly. He was already asleep. I left him and headed back outside.

Most people had left, but I found Tito sitting by himself on a small bench deep in the backyard. He was wearing a white tank top and shorts. He seemed immune to the chill. His arms were impressive: thick and well-formed. He lit up a cigarette and offered me one.

"No, thanks," I said.

"Well done, Mr. Shea. I knew you had it in you." He blew a puff of smoke up in the air.

"Yeah, well, that makes one of us."

"No, I thought you were going to fuck it up. For reals. But I wasn't sure what else to do. But you did good. You did real good."

He continued to smoke, and we made small talk about PG, Mamá, and the Warriors. He was amiable and funny. We talked for a good half hour before he headed out.

I looked up at the starless sky. I thought of Danny. I had failed him. I didn't think I'd ever forgive myself for that. But today at least, I didn't fail PG. PG was free and safe and happy and drunk as hell. I wasn't quite finished though. I had one loose end to tie up.

It was late, but I knew she wouldn't care. I called Brenda Profit to ask a favor.

FRIDAY

CHAPTER FORTY-SIX

LATE THE NEXT MORNING, I stood at the rounded lookout of Twin Peaks, admiring the view. The Golden Gate Bridge alone on the left, the Marin Headlands looming behind it. Market Street running straight ahead, lining the way to the downtown skyscrapers and the Ferry Building. The Bay Bridge with its four slim brothers. The peaks to my right, Noe and Eureka, almost the highest points in a city of hills.

There were few clouds in the sky, but I could see a high bank of fog creeping in off the Pacific. Soon, the bridge, Alcatraz, and most of the bay would be covered in a blanket of white.

A handful of Japanese tourists were taking pictures and pointing at familiar sites. Two skateboarders sat nearby, getting ready to bomb down Twin Peaks Boulevard. I leaned against a weathered gray telescope, bracing myself against the wind, staring at the fog creeping toward the Golden Gate Bridge.

Detective Rhodes called me to say that the case on Monique Profit was closing. Lily was the killer. Lily knew Monique. They met at a scholarship club where Lily became her mentor. The story was she was obsessed with Monique, and it led to murder. Lily's obsession was well-documented. It was an elaborate and impressive effort to keep Richard Cory out of trouble. They had planned for everything. Rhodes did not mention Richard Cory, and of course, neither did I. For now, he was free.

"Hello, Mr. Shea."

I turned to see Richard Cory standing with his hands stuffed in a tweed overcoat.

"I told you we'd meet again," I said.

"You did, indeed."

"I didn't think you'd come," I said.

"I don't believe I had a choice. Do you have the file?"

I used Danny's file as leverage to get him to show up alone. There wasn't much in the file, but he didn't know that. I still didn't think it would work, but here he was with no one else around.

"I guess I do know a few things about you," I said.

"Are you wearing a wire, Mr. Shea? Is this the big Hollywood ending where you get me to confess on tape, and the cops come to take me away?"

"No wire. No recording. No cops." I opened my jacket and patted around my clothes. I even lifted up my shirt, displaying a pale, round belly. "I just want to talk."

"So, talk," he said.

"I want to make sure it's over. For me or PG or anyone else I know."

"It's over as far as I'm concerned," he said. "Lily cleaned things up nicely. I will miss her. And if anyone tries to involve me, there is—very intentionally, I assure you—little evidence to do that."

"Lily was effective," I said.

"Wasn't she? She served a purpose. Actress, Mossad agent, disillusioned and angry. And she liked money, and I have plenty of that."

"Of course."

"We met at an arms conference in South Dakota, of all places. Hit it off, you could say. And then I asked her to work for me."

I paused to check on the fog, which was nearly at the bridge now. It was high enough that it would soon envelop all of the Golden Gate. I thought about the drivers crossing the bridge and seeing this wave of white approaching. But then again, on the bridge, close to fog, you'd miss its immensity. Only from this distance, this perspective, could you see how tremendous the fog bank was. How overpowering it would be to the world-famous engineering marvel.

I turned back and asked the question I still could not answer.

"Why Monique?" I asked.

He pursed his lips.

"Her father was being somewhat unruly in his dealings with me, and I had to send him a message."

"That's it?"

"That's it."

"He didn't even know it was you," I said.

"He knew."

Kratos was a drug dealer, not a noble person, and it was a risky business, but his contact with Monique was limited. Richard Cory had to go out of his way to find out Kratos had a daughter and even more out of his way to take her life. Ruthless.

"But why send Kratos a message? Things were good. He was expanding, you were making more money. Why risk that?"

He brought his hands together and interlocked his fingers.

"Still playing detective, are we?"

"Humor me," I said.

"There isn't an easy answer to that question. I have always, in all my endeavors, been unpredictable. It keeps my competitors, suppliers, enemies, friends, on their toes. Things had been going quite well, but he was getting a little big for his britches, as the English say. He did a few things that were not advisable. Careless. I told him as much, and he wasn't very understanding. I felt I needed to remind him who was in charge."

"And Monique pays the price."

"Sadly, yes. I take no joy in it. I assure you."

His answer didn't quite convince me.

"Do you understand grief, Mr. Shea?" He asked.

"I think so."

"It can be devastating. Emotional pain destroys people, even more so than physical pain."

The wind had calmed some. I looked down at his wingtip Oxfords. He wore a royal blue suit and olive silk tie under his overcoat. Impeccable, as always.

"Why frame Pedro?"

"He was an easy mark, as Lily said. We knew about his mother. Knew he'd cave. We looked at a few teachers at that school and settled on him. He also had a strong relationship with her. We were going to make it love-gone-wrong, and then Lily found out a little late he was gay. Pity. Probably would have worked out better that way."

"How did she do it?"

"She met with both of them that morning. They were going to go over college applications. PG had no reason to suspect anything. At some point, Lily got him to get her paper towels from the bathroom. I think she faked having a bloody nose or something. The actress in her. PG went off. She killed Monique. He comes back, and she tells him he will take the fall, or his mother is dead. She gives him her address, details, etcetera. Quite remarkable, really. PG had no choice. He took the fall. The perfect plan."

It was the same story PG had told me, but I wanted to hear it from Richard Cory. I wanted to know how involved he was.

"But of course, we didn't count on you as his friend," he said.

He buttoned his jacket to help fight off the chill.

"I didn't stand by."

"Ah, no. That was unexpected."

"Sorry to disappoint."

"Yes, Seamus Shea, the private dick. Who would have thought?"

"I prefer private investigator."

"What?"

"I said that I prefer the term private investigator."

He looked at me, trying to determine if I was screwing with him or not.

"Maybe *I* should just kill you," I said.

"Hah! The boy scout takes a dark turn and kills his nemesis."

"I could do it. Just ask Lily."

"Well that was you or her. Survival. But me, now, no threat to you? Just pure revenge? That's not you Seamus. You are a good boy. A pleaser. No, Seamus, you won't kill me."

I grimaced when he said the words "good boy" and "pleaser."

"The police, then?" I said.

"I'm not too worried. I planned for this scenario. As you might imagine, I have good lawyers and a nice trail of evidence pointing to poor, poor Lily."

"Convenient."

The Japanese tourists and skateboarders had left. We were alone.

"My, that's impressive," he said.

I turned to see that the fog had covered most of the bridge now. None of the crimson color was visible.

"Monique Profit was a sweet girl with a very bright future," I said.

"Yes. I heard that about her."

"Monique did not deserve to die."

"Well, Mr. Shea, in the real world, there is a thing called collateral damage, and I'm afraid that's what Monique Profit was. She served a purpose. Lily, poor thing, was excellent at uncovering things. And she uncovered the fact that Monique was Kratos's daughter. And that they were close. She joined a scholarship club to connect with Monique. They talked quite a bit. I had an in, and I had to take it. Not personal; business, as they say."

"Yeah, they say a lot," I said.

He smiled.

"Yes, I suppose they do."

The wind whipped around us again, sharp and icy. You had to keep your feet planted firmly so as not to be knocked around.

"Do you know what they call those two peaks?" I asked, pointing over his shoulder.

He turned and looked up at Eureka.

"I do not," he said.

"One is called Noe, and one is called Eureka."

"A geography lesson? How wonderful. Pity PG isn't here to teach me some Shakespeare."

"Below us, the neighborhood to the right is Noe Valley. To the left is Eureka Valley. My father thought our neighborhood was blessed because he had a bible where Noah was spelled Noe. And we lived in Noe Valley."

"Charming."

"Do you know about Noah, Mr. Cory?"

"Religion, now? He's the one with the ark, right? All the animals, two by two? Missing a pair of unicorns, I believe."

"Correct. God thought Noah was a good man. He saved him."

The fog had almost reached Alcatraz. It was slowly taking over the entire bay. A few minutes from now there would be not much of a view of the bay, only a floor of white.

"Mr. Shea, let's not be so dramatic. Noah was a good man. I'm a good man. You're a good man. So be it."

"Nothing is either good or bad but thinking makes it so."

"I'm afraid you've lost me," he said, looking back toward his car.

"And so, I'm choosing to think this is a good thing. I've convinced myself this is a good thing."

He tilted his head sideways.

"I'm not following you, but that's hardly important at this point. Can I have the file, please?"

I reached behind my back and took out the file I had tucked in my waistband. I handed it to him.

"Good day, Seamus. I trust our paths won't cross again."

"I'm sure they won't," I said.

I raised my right hand up high in the air. He looked up and back down at my face before shaking his head.

"You are an odd one. Goodbye."

He turned to leave, but a large black Escalade pulled up and blocked his path. The side door swung open, and I could hear a muted scream as two familiar linemen pulled Richard Cory into the van. I gave a quick nod to Kratos in the passenger's seat before hearing the sound of the SUV's door slamming shut and it pulling away.

    I turned to look back at the view. The fog had completely covered the bay.

SATURDAY

CHAPTER FORTY-SEVEN

I WAS SOBER.

Two days.

Sean called me early. He sounded excited, almost happy.

"Some sad news, Shame," he said, in his country brogue. "They found Richard Cory, dead."

"Dead?" I said.

"Yeah, they found him up on Twin Peaks. It seems at some point last night he put a bullet through his head. Suicide."

"Jesus," I said. "Why would he do that?"

"Who knows. Money can't buy happiness, I guess. He knew the Feds were closing in on him. Pressure must have got to him. Anyway, thought I'd let you know. Gotta be a bit of a relief."

"Yeah, thanks."

"Anytime, Shame. I'm just glad it worked out for PG. Tell him sorry from me. I hope he understands folks were just doing their job."

"He does, Sean, but I'll tell him. You take care."

"You, too."

I dropped back on my bed and looked up at ceiling Jesus.

"Nothing is either good or bad, Jesus, but thinking makes it so," I said aloud.

I called PG and Rev and gave them the news. They were shocked; I did not tell them about the favor I asked Kratos for. That was between me, him, Brenda Profit, and ceiling Jesus.

I called Jackie.

"Wow, that's some news."

"He was Keyser Söze," I said. It mattered little now. Holly Woods had their man—dead, but still their man.

"Really?"

"Yeah. I'd like to make sure he doesn't end up a hero."

"No problem," Jackie said.

I filled her in on what I knew.

"You did good, Shea."

She was talking to me like a toddler, and I kind of liked it.

"Your friend okay?" she asked.

"He is. He's doing really well. We are all just glad it's over."

"What's next for you?" I knew what she was asking, and I did owe her, so I obliged her.

"Meetings. Meetings. Meetings. I met a guy I like. Think he's going to be my sponsor."

"Oh, Seamus, that's so great. So great."

I hung up, basking in the praise of Jackie. I looked up at ceiling Jesus, and even He seemed to be smiling.

I called Bunny.

"You helped me crack the case," I said.

"I did?" Man, I'm good."

"Knowing he worked at 555 California helped me narrow it down."

"Happy to help. All's well that ends well, huh?" he said.

"It worked out. Wasn't easy, but yeah, all's well."

"What about you?"

"Me?" I asked.

"You. You have your own issues."

"Yes. I have issues. I'm working on them."

"Damn right you are," he said.

"So, what do I do now?"

"Meetings. Read the Big Book. Meet with me. The usual."

"Meet with you?"

"Yeah, I'm your sponsor."

"Don't I get to pick my sponsor?"

"Typically. But sometimes your sponsor picks you."

"That's what happened to me?"

"You think walking into that church basement was some random act? Sitting next to me was random?" asked Bunny.

I was going to offer a smart-ass remark about his size or smell or food in his beard, but something stopped me. In the middle of trying to clear PG's name, why did I take time out to talk with a 300-pound, tattooed biker?

"Things are going to happen. You are in the pink elephant stage, right? You stopped drinking for a few days. You are feeling good. Those feelings pass, and it gets tough. For some, everyone's different. But don't think it's smooth sailing from here on out."

"I get that. I'm going to try," I said.

"That's all you can really do."

"But with all the stuff with PG, I haven't been alone with my thoughts much. That's when I get in trouble."

"Yep. That's why you gotta go to meetings. Get involved. Talk to me. Keep that mind busy on the right things."

"I also can't get over seeing that woman fall."

"That's gotta be tough," he said. "Especially with your brother. But it was you or her."

I thought that Bunny might not be real. That an obese biker with a modestly trimmed Rip Van Winkle beard did not exist. The guilt, the anger, the self-hatred had led me to create in my mind the antithesis of who I would want to help me. Bunny, from the comic name to his giant frame to the shady history and overbearing personality; Bunny represented everything I did not want AA to be. I must have created Bunny in my own damaged psyche. He could not be a real person. He just couldn't be. It would be too ironic, too absurd. But I had been talking to him on the phone. I had met him in person multiple times. I had promised to go to a meeting with him tomorrow. He was real. And I was in AA.

Eventually, I made my way upstairs to check on my mother.

"Would you like some tea?" she asked as I entered.

"Please."

"Black?" she asked.

"Yes, please."

She reached above her and took out two mugs and placed them next to the stove. She fumbled with her box of Lipton tea, took out two tea bags, and dropped one into each cup. She shuffled to the refrigerator and grabbed a small carton of half-and-half, giving one cup a good glug.

"How's PG?" she asked.

"Good. Relieved."

"I can imagine."

The murmur of boiling water grew on the stove. The silver kettle, a Mother's Day gift eight, maybe nine years ago, trembled on the burner. She turned off the stove and poured hot water into each mug. She tugged lightly on the string of each tea bag. She tiptoed toward me holding both cups, trying not to spill either.

"Here you go."

"Thanksgiving is this week," I said. "Is Mr. Banks joining us?"

"He is," she said, smiling.

"That's good," I said, and I meant it. I was quite anxious to meet Mr. Banks.

She sipped her tea and was quiet. The heater exhaled in the corner. There was a faint scent of eggs and blood pudding. She probably had a fry-up for breakfast.

"That will be the year anniversary," she finally said.

I leaned in. Did I hear her right?

"Yeah. One year," I said. "Went fast."

"I miss him, Seamus. Every day."

"Me, too."

"I don't know what I could have done. I didn't know he was in such pain."

"I didn't either. I think every day about what I could have done differently."

We sat quietly for a moment, swallowing our tea in faint light, facing off across her kitchen table. She sat motionless in her chair save the slight rise and fall of her body with each required breath. Her round Irish eyes stared curiously at the mouth of her cup, looking for insight in the tawny color of the tea.

Danny. That night we ate Thanksgiving dinner at this very table. Jenny was with me. Danny was alone. I got pretty drunk as I usually did at such uncomfortable family gatherings. What if I had clarity back then? Could I have stopped it? I didn't know. All that I did and all that I failed to do. I failed Danny. I knew that. I didn't know how to live without that regret. I broke down out of the blue sometimes thinking about him. I'd just say, "I'm so sorry, Danny. I'm so sorry." I didn't know what else to say. He was my brother. I loved him.

"Can I ask you about Dad?" I said.

"What about him?"

"Why don't you ever want to talk about him?"

She raised her cup to her mouth with both hands.

"What's there to talk about?"

"He died of a heart attack. It wasn't like he left us."

She scoffed.

"He did leave us, Seamus. He left you and Danny and me. Alone."

"But it wasn't his fault."

"No, it wasn't, but I was scared and all alone. I had you and Danny to raise. I had no idea how I would pay for things. It was a tremendous shock. I supposed I could have handled it better. I suppose I could have talked about it with you boys. But that's not what we did back then. My parents didn't talk about anything. Life would slap you in the face, and you would just keep on going. I bottled it up, yes. Was that good for you boys? Probably not. But I did the best I could. If you don't think so, well, tell it to your psychiatrist."

I could see the pain on her face. I had not thought of what a shock it would have been for her to lose her husband so young.

"Do you think he . . ." I began.

"Do I think he what?"

"Do you think he's in heaven?" I finally said.

She started laughing so hard she bumped the table and spilled her tea. I grabbed a dishcloth and handed it to her.

"That's a good one, Seamus. Oh, I needed that laugh."

She wiped up the spilt tea.

"I did, too," I said.

Let it be.

THE END

ACKNOWLEDGEMENTS

Thank you to Andrea Conroy, Assaf Tarnopolsky, and Richard Martin for their support and encouragement through the years. Thanks to Diane Glazman for her thoughtful early edits and feedback. Thank you to my early readers Bob Moser, Deborah Doyle, and John Kralik for your insightful comments on the manuscript. Thanks to the great team at Koehler Books, including John Koehler, Lauren Sheldon, Joe Coccaro, Adrienne Folkerts, and Nina Correa White. Thanks to all my family and friends who offered encouragement for my writing and have enthusiastically received this novel. Thanks to Mark for getting me in the rooms and Chris for keeping me there. Finally, thanks to my two amazing kids, Tatum and Ryan. I love you both very much.

www.ingramcontent.com/pod-product-compliance
Lightning Source LLC
LaVergne TN
LVHW041753060526
838201LV00046B/990